Katie Reus fell [...] [...] [...] [...] ooks she'd pilfered from her mom's stash. After changing majors too many times to count, she finally graduated with a degree in psychology. She now spends her days writing thrilling romantic suspense and dark paranormal romance. She currently lives near Biloxi, Mississippi, with her family. When she's not creating stories she can usually be found spending time with her family or one of the many eclectic animals they've adopted over the years. Find out more about Katie by visiting www.katiereus.com, connect with her on Facebook at www.facebook.com/katiereusauthor and Twitter @katiereus.

**Kati Reus's Deadly Ops series will blow you away. Here's why:**

'A f[...] aced, high-stakes romantic thriller . . . Strong characterization and [...] lily mounting tension are powerful weapons in this talented auth [...] rsenal' *Publishers Weekly*

'K [...] us has the amazing ability of pulling the reader onto the front li [...] e action and drama . . . A fast-paced, intelligent, and spirited [...] suspense, mystery, intrigue, and murder . . . It is a story of [...] k and grief; friendship and love; betrayal and revenge' *The [...] afe*

[...]d romantic suspense that will keep you on the edge of your [...] thia Eden, *New York Times* bestselling author

[...]otted, excellently delivered, emotional and sensual ride that [...]d and doesn't let go . . . delivers mystery, suspense, and a [...] nothing short of heart-pounding' *Night Owl Reviews*

[...] ense at its finest' Laura Wright, *New York Times* bestselling

[...] action, a solid plot, good pacing, and riveting suspense' [...] *Times*

[...]e danger, and enough sexual tension to set the pages on [...]bulous!' Alexandra Ivy, *New York Times* bestselling author

[...]omantic and suspenseful, a fast-paced, sexy book full of high-[...]ction' *Heroes and Heartbreakers*

By Katie Reus

# EDGE OF DANGER

# KATIE REUS

headline
ETERNAL

Copyright © 2015 Katie Reus
Excerpt from *A Covert Affair* copyright © 2016 Katie Reus

The right of Katie Reus to be identified as the Author of
the Work has been asserted by her in accordance with the
Copyright, Designs and Patents Act 1988.

Published by arrangement with NAL Signet,
a division of Penguin Group (USA) LLC.
A Penguin Random House Company.

First published in Great Britain in 2015
by HEADLINE ETERNAL
An imprint of HEADLINE PUBLISHING GROUP

1

Apart from any use permitted under UK copyright law, this publication may
only be reproduced, stored, or transmitted, in any form, or by any means,
with prior permission in writing of the publishers or, in the case of reprographic
production, in accordance with the terms of licences issued by the
Copyright Licensing Agency.

All characters in this publication are fictitious
and any resemblance to real persons, living or dead,
is purely coincidental.

Cataloguing in Publication Data is available from the British Library

ISBN 978 1 4722 3137 6

Offset in 11.7/13 pt Palatino LT Std by Jouve (UK)

Printed and bound in Great Britain by CPI Group (UK) Ltd, Croydon, CR0 4YY

MIX
Paper from
responsible sources
FSC® C104740

Headline's policy is to use papers that are natural, renewable and recyclable
products and made from wood grown in well-managed forests and other
controlled sources. The logging and manufacturing processes are expected
to conform to the environmental regulations of the country of origin.

HEADLINE PUBLISHING GROUP
An Hachette UK Company
Carmelite House
50 Victoria Embankment
London EC4Y 0DZ

www.headlineeternal.com
www.headline.co.uk
www.hachette.co.uk

*For the men and women who put their lives
on the line every day for complete strangers,
often without gratitude. Your sacrifices are
appreciated in ways words can never express.*

| FIFE COUNCIL LIBRARIES | |
| --- | --- |
| HJ438372 | |
| **Askews & Holts** | 06-Nov-2015 |
| AF | £8.99 |
| THR | IK |

# Chapter 1

Unmanned aerial vehicle (UAV): aka drone, an aircraft
without a human pilot physically aboard. Controlled by
computers or a pilot at another location.

Rayford Osborn strode down the brick sidewalk of
the quiet Georgetown neighborhood, trying to keep
his walk natural. Not easy when a wild energy hummed
through him. It was a little after ten and this area of the
city was relatively quiet. As a sedan drove by, he automatically pulled his hoodie down a fraction to hide his
face. A fucking hoodie.

His chosen adolescent attire grated against everything in him, but it was necessary for tonight's meeting. Things were about to change; he felt it deep in his
bones. His country needed to be on a different path,
and if that happened to make him richer, he wasn't going to complain. People who thought money was the
root of all evil were fools. He and his wife did well for
themselves, but more was always better. More money
meant more power. And power was everything.

As the car continued past him without slowing a

fraction, he let out a breath he wasn't aware he'd been holding. This cloak-and-dagger business wasn't for him. Since college and beyond he'd been so careful about his image, both in public and in private. No affairs, no drinking to excess, no drugs—nothing that could come back to bite him in the ass later on. So many of his peers had screwed that up in college, but not him.

Now what he was doing could get him sent to jail for the rest of his life, or more likely tried for treason and given the death penalty. Only if he and his like-minded allies got caught, of course.

Which they wouldn't. They were too good and had been flying under everyone's radar for too long. And now the time for talk was over. It was time to strike.

When he reached his destination, a high-priced townhome—they all were in Georgetown—the front door opened before he'd ascended the short set of stone stairs.

Thad Hillenbrand stood in the doorway, his icy blue eyes glinting as he frowned at him. "You're late," he growled as Rayford moved past him into the dimly lit foyer. "Everyone else is here."

Rayford shoved his hoodie back and loosened his plain black scarf from around his neck. "I walked from the Metro."

Hillenbrand's shoulders relaxed at that. "Which station?"

"Dupont Circle. And before you ask, I was careful of the cameras." The truth was, it was impossible to stay off all the CCTVs, but there was no connection between him and Hillenbrand. At least not an electronic or physical one. And Rayford already had a reason for being in the Georgetown area tonight if he was ever questioned. Once he'd left the Metro station, avoiding cameras had been a piece of cake. "I'm the last one here?" he asked, even though Hillenbrand had just stated he was.

The older man nodded once then gave a sharp jerk of his head that Rayford should follow. He'd only been in the townhome once before, for a covert meeting just like this one. He knew that Hillenbrand used the exclusive property to bring escorts to. It was the man's one vice and something Rayford had thought he could use against him at one point.

But Hillenbrand wasn't in politics—not directly—and made enough money on his own that he didn't need his wealthy wife's money if she decided to leave him. Not to mention the man treated his whores well so Rayford couldn't even blackmail him on allegations of abuse. It appeared he only brought his women here because it was convenient. Plus, his wife was cheating on him too, so she likely knew of his affairs.

Rayford might work with the man because they shared common goals, but he didn't like being involved with someone he had no dirt on. In his world, having leverage was king.

They only walked a few feet, bypassing the stairs, Hillenbrand instead opening the door that led to the basement.

Rayford went first on Hillenbrand's insistence. The man didn't like to have anyone at his back, and Rayford knew it was more or less a power play. But he didn't care. If things went well, soon he'd be the top aide to the most powerful man in the country.

A low hum of voices grew louder as he turned the corner at the end of the stairs and walked down the last three steps. Eight men in all were there, ten total including him and Hillenbrand. There was only one man Rayford didn't recognize. Something about the guy's face tickled his memory bank, but he couldn't place it. Blond hair, in shape, an almost forgettable appearance, but he knew he'd seen the man somewhere before.

Soon he'd find out, but he didn't bother asking Hillenbrand. The man was more cautious than any of them, and he wouldn't have allowed someone to come to this meeting he wasn't one hundred percent sure of.

"We need to fight a war we can win," Wagner, one of the men, said, stating something everyone in this room believed in. Mainly because he liked to hear his own voice.

So many of these men did. It annoyed Rayford, but he was used to the type. Hell, he worked for one. Men who couldn't stand not to be the center of attention. Rayford had no problem living in the background.

"But is *this* the way?" Padilla, a dark-haired man in his late forties, rubbed a hand down his face, his tension clear.

"If you have doubts, you're free to leave," Hillenbrand said, his edgy tone making the room go silent.

Because everyone knew his words were a lie. Padilla

could leave if he wanted, but if he did he'd be dead within twenty-four hours, likely less. They all knew what they'd signed up for when they began their cause, when Hillenbrand contacted them and brought them together. They all knew what was at stake and what the cost for backing out would be. It was like the mob. The only way out was in a body bag.

Padilla straightened against the brown Chesterfield where he sat next to Wagner, his gaze narrowing on Hillenbrand. "I don't have doubts, but I do have an opinion, which I'm free to voice, yes?"

Coming to stand next to Rayford, Hillenbrand crossed his arms over his chest as he faced down Padilla. "We're all welcome to our opinions, but in the end we know what has to be done, so these discussions are pointless and tiring. The current administration needs to be proven inept beyond a shadow of a doubt. We must pave the way for a new leader for the next election. Once we have our chosen man inside, we'll be even closer to our end goal. And we'll all be richer in the end."

There was a low murmur of agreement throughout the room. Rayford inwardly groaned. Just like the others in the room, Hillenbrand liked to speak simply to hear his own voice. Rayford hoped the man wasn't going to get long-winded on them now. He'd managed to break away from dinner at his wife's parents' house stating a work emergency, but he didn't have time to waste.

"The time for talking is over. Now's the time for action." Striding to the minibar, Hillenbrand picked up a small black remote. "If you will all direct your attention to the screen," he said, motioning toward the mini movie theater screen that took up one of the walls.

Hillenbrand used this as an entertainment room and occasionally let his college-aged boys use the place too. But he knew they weren't going to be watching a movie in it.

"About a month ago a U.S.–owned drone was stolen from a military base," Hillenbrand continued.

It wasn't public knowledge, but Rayford knew of the incident. His own boss was sitting on the information, waiting on the right time to release it for the best of their political gain.

"Now you all are going to see why." As Hillenbrand pressed a button on the remote, the lights in the room dimmed and a feed popped up on-screen that looked like an eagle eye from a plane.

"Is this live?" Rayford asked quietly, realizing it was a view from the drone.

Hillenbrand gave him a hard look and nodded before focusing on the screen once again. "Unfortunately I don't have audio, but we don't need it."

Though it was dark, the dash was clear enough with the night-vision capabilities. Not that it mattered because if this was a view from the drone, it would be controlled remotely and no one would actually be in the aerial device. Which raised the question—who was controlling it? This was the first Hillenbrand had told any of them about this.

"Go ahead," Hillenbrand murmured quietly, and Rayford realized he must have a small earpiece in.

Annoyance hummed through him at being left in the dark about who this other contact was, but he kept his emotions in check.

A long moment later a bright burst of light illuminated the screen, quickly followed by another. Those were *missiles*. Who was the target? This was a very dangerous weapon and he wasn't sure Hillenbrand was the right man to be in control of it. Rayford's anger and annoyance intensified as he watched a bright orange ball of flame light up the darker screen as the missiles detonated their target. The feed was in black and white, but the infrared showed the heat signature clearly, so he knew it was fire.

Before he could say anything, the ground shook just the slightest bit and his stomach lurched. Hillenbrand had attacked somewhere in Washington, D.C.

The screen went blank and the lights brightened as Hillenbrand smiled broadly. He'd just ordered the killing of Americans here in the capital and didn't give a damn. "There's no going back now for any of us. That was just the beginning. Unfortunately we'll have some hard choices to make in the coming weeks, but I have no doubt we're all up to the job. And I know you're wondering who the target was. The Nelson fund-raiser was just hit, eliminating our only real competition for the upcoming primaries."

Rayford's mouth filled with cotton as he struggled

to find his voice. They'd been talking and planning for so long, but he'd never imagined Hillenbrand would go after someone in their *own* political party. And never like this. He understood it, the need to eliminate everyone who posed a threat to the candidate they needed in office if change was ever going to take place, but . . . it seemed so violent. So unforgiveable.

Luckily he didn't have to talk because the room erupted in voices, everyone talking over one another. Some were excited; others were angry he'd made the decision without asking any of them. Now they were all trapped. No matter what happened, they'd all been part of this. Avoiding Hillenbrand's gaze, he made his way to the minibar and poured himself a scotch, his hand trembling ever so slightly. As he did, he realized where he'd seen the only man in the room he hadn't recognized when he'd entered. On the news.

The man worked for the DEA. Which meant Hillenbrand had brought him in because of who he worked for. Unless Hillenbrand had no idea who he was. If that was the case, they were going to have more blood on their hands because they couldn't allow anyone outside this room to know what they'd done.

# Chapter 2

Wet work: expression for murdering or assassinating someone (wet alluding to the spilling of blood).

*One week later*

Tucker Pankov ran a hand over his buzz cut, the dampness from his shower already drying. He'd be glad to grow his hair out again and spend at least a week at his place in solitude. He lived in a three-bedroom home in the Virginia countryside. He'd chosen to have acres and acres of space between him and his neighbors over a larger house in a suburb. He was rarely here and when he did get downtime, he craved the quiet.

For his last undercover job, as a psychopathic thug, he'd shaved his head, making himself look more the part of drug-peddling scum. He'd kept his same alias from the job he'd worked before that one with a true psychopath, Tasev, and it was a relief to shed that persona.

It was also a fucking relief that bastard was dead,

even if the DEA hadn't been the ones to officially bring him down. He was still surprised that his boss, Deputy Director Max Southers, hadn't been upset when the NSA brought down Tasev and his entire operation instead of his elite undercover DEA team, but in the end, Tucker didn't care who'd done it. He didn't care about the accolades, just the result.

As he stepped into his bedroom, he turned on the television. Headlines from last week's attack on a political fund-raiser dominated everything.

Tucker should probably have been surprised by the attack, but little could shock him anymore. The drone that had carried out the attack should never have been stolen in the first place. Heads were already rolling over that "oversight" in security, and while he cared about the massive loss of life, it had nothing to do with the DEA. At least not at the moment.

On the screen, Clarence Cochran, a politician who'd just announced his intention to seek the next presidential nomination for his party, was talking about the avoidable loss of life of a man who would have been running against him. Acting as if he cared.

Tucker rolled his eyes. For the most part politicians in Washington only cared about themselves. He actually belonged to the same political party as Cochran, but the guy was too much of an extremist. That was dangerous no matter what side of the political aisle a man stood on. For the next election he'd be voting against the party line if that moron made a play for the presidency. Tucker was reaching for the remote to turn it off when a breaking report flashed on the screen.

Max Southers, Deputy Director of the Drug Enforcement Administration, murdered in violent carjacking.

He blinked, ice invading his veins as he stared numbly at the screen, before he turned up the volume. Max was dead? No fucking way. He'd just talked to him a couple of hours ago. Someone would have alerted him.

*"You need a break, son, and I'm ordering it. Take a week off and just relax."* The corners of Max's dark blue eyes had crinkled in concern as he watched Tucker from across his desk.

Max called everyone in their team "son." It should have annoyed Tucker, since he had a father, but he loved the man. They all did. They'd all spent countless dinners at the man's house during their off time. Swallowing hard, he sat on the edge of his bed and listened as a somber-looking reporter talked about Max's murder, basically saying nothing at all. The police had no leads. They didn't know if this was random or related to one of his cases.

*Fuck.*

Standing, he grabbed his phone from his nightstand. He needed to call the rest of the team and Mary, Max's wife. Hell, he needed to verify that this was even true.

If they'd reported this without telling her first . . . hell no. He immediately rejected that. The DEA wouldn't have allowed that to happen. Unless the local PD had fucked it up and there'd been a leak. Because why had no one called the team first?

As he started to call Cole, his phone buzzed, his teammate's name appearing on-screen. Still numb, he answered, "You see the news?"

"Yeah." Cole's voice was grim. "Anyone contact you about it first?"

"No."

"I tried Mary and she's not answering."

Tucker's throat tightened as he stared blindly at the muted television. "You believe he's dead?"

"I . . . don't know. I can't imagine them running with the story unless they were positive."

"I'll call in a bit. We'll take care of her if it is." Mary and Max had been together thirty years. She'd been with Max since his Navy days, enduring long deployments and raising their two kids basically by herself for months on end. Max had been ready to retire in the next two years, to travel with his wife the way he deserved. Tucker's free hand curled into a fist. "And we're going to find out whoever did this."

"Fuck yeah." Cole's voice was raspy, the edge in the normally laid-back man's voice razor-sharp. "What the . . . are you watching the news still?"

"Yeah, hold on." He unmuted it, frowning as he listened to the reporter's words. Neither he nor Cole spoke for the next few minutes as he digested everything the man on the news was saying. The news station had received an anonymous tip that a Shi'a terrorist group was responsible for the murder of Max, that it wasn't a carjacking at all.

What. The. Hell.

"It doesn't seem possible," Tucker muttered. "Have you heard from the Leopard recently?" Leopard was their code word for Ali Nazari, an agent they had embedded in a high-profile Shi'a terrorist organization. Almost no one knew of his undercover role—just Max, Tucker, Cole, and two other teammates. It was too dangerous otherwise.

"No. We need to make sure the Leopard's files—"

"Max had a fail-safe in place in case something happened to him. I'll tell you about it, but not now." Never over the phone, even if their cells were encrypted. He'd drawn in a breath to continue when the power suddenly went off, his television and the steady hum of his heater going silent. Dawn was breaking, so he could see well enough without the lamp on his nightstand, but he didn't often lose power and there wasn't a storm raging. Maybe a breaker had flipped. "Let me call you back in a sec."

"All right."

As they disconnected, he pulled on a pair of jogging pants and grabbed his sidearm from his nightstand. Even though he knew it was loaded, he checked the magazine out of habit. Full. Exiting his room, he moved on silent feet down the hallway that led to the living room and kitchen. As he made his way, he passed the keypad for his alarm system, and a shot of adrenaline punched through him.

It was off.

The system was wireless and not linked to his power system, and it never went off-line. Not even when he lost power. He traveled most of the year and wanted his house secure even when he was gone, which was why he'd opted for this specific system. No way had it gone off without help. This was intentional.

His heart rate kicked up a fraction. Ducking into the closest room, his office, he quickly swept it. Empty. He moved to the window and had started to pull back the curtains when he heard a creak.

It was quiet, almost imperceptible, but he knew every sound his house made. It had been built in the forties and had real wood floors he'd had refurbished. And Tucker knew exactly where that creak had come from. A board at the beginning of the hallway, right where the kitchen opened up. It had a very distinctive sound.

Weapon in hand, he moved away from the window and crept to the doorway, giving himself enough room to have his pistol out and drawn without the worry of it being taken from him if someone attacked. If someone made a move, they wouldn't be able to make it to him before he fired a few rounds.

Whoever was in his home had to know Tucker was aware of his presence. Or at least guess. The house was too silent. Which took away a little of his advantage.

As he waited, everything around him sharpened, his

senses going into straight battle mode. Someone could be here to rob him, but his gut told him otherwise.

He lived far enough out that his place wasn't easy to find, and disabling his security system would have taken time and an expertise far beyond your average thief.

Another creak. This one closer.

Tucker tensed, his finger on the trigger. He wasn't just going to blindly shoot, but he was ready.

Another creak. That one next to the guest bathroom door.

Which meant the intruder would be in his path in three, two, *one*.

"Drop your weapon! Put your hands in the air!" Tucker shouted as the hooded man came into view, his own weapon—with a fucking suppressor—drawn. "Now, or I drop you where you stand." His voice was quieter now, his intent clear in each word. All it would take was a bullet to the head.

It was hard to read his facial expression because of the hood, but the man stood right around six feet, had a solid build. Wearing all black, including rubber-soled boots that made almost no sound, the intruder looked like a pro.

The silenced weapon clattered to the floor, the sound overpronounced in the quiet of his home, before the man put his hands in the air. When he moved, Tucker could see the bulky outline of a vest. If he had to take a killing shot, it would be to the head.

"Kick it away."

The man did as Tucker said.

"On your knees."

Silently the man started to kneel down but at the last second leaped forward.

Training kicked in automatically. Tucker fired, hitting the man in his calf as he tried to dive out of the way.

The hooded man cried out as Tucker swept into the hallway, conscious of his six as he trained his weapon on the guy.

He'd grabbed his fallen weapon.

*Shit.*

Tucker fired, two shots to the middle of the forehead. Normally he'd take a center mass shot, but there was no point with the guy wearing a vest.

The man stilled, dropping back with a thud as his weapon hand fell loudly against the wooden floor of the hallway. Tucker moved carefully, kicking it away before he checked the man's pulse and took off the hood. By the time he'd pulled it off, there was a slight blue tinge around his eyes, nose, and mouth.

Certain he was dead, Tucker checked his person for any identifiers and found none before he moved on to the rest of his house. Next he cleared his garage, then the shed. Before moving on he turned his power back on and reconnected the alarm. Resetting it so no one could infiltrate his house while he was gone, he swept his property. He found a four-door car with mud smeared on the license plate hidden off the side of the road about a mile away. Unfortunately there weren't any identifying papers inside. He memorized the plate, then raced back to his place.

Careful to avoid the blood pooling in the hallway, he grabbed his cell and found two missed calls. Both from Cole. As he pulled out his fingerprint kit, he called his friend back. He was going to call the police, but he was taking the guy's prints first. It wasn't that he didn't trust the locals, but the DEA had more resources and this was clearly personal.

Which meant the chances of this being linked to one of his cases was high. He had to know what and who he was dealing with, and he'd get answers faster than the local PD.

"Someone just tried to kill me," Cole said by way of greeting. "Can't identify him, but he was a professional."

*Well, hell.* "Me too. You called the cops yet?"

"No. Someone also went after Brooks. This isn't fucking random," he snarled.

"Anyone contacted Kane?" The last member of their elite group.

"Can't get ahold of him."

Tucker reined in a curse. "Get the prints of your guy. Then pack a bag. Can you dispose of the body?"

"Yeah."

"Do it. Then we rendezvous at location bravo." Their team had five backup places to meet if the shit ever hit the fan. They were all random and none had ties to any of them. Tucker picked the second location because it was the first that popped into his mind.

"You sure no cops?"

"You want to alert whoever sent these guys after us that they failed?" Because the moment they did that, they'd become sitting targets. No, they needed to ghost out while whoever was gunning for them thought they were dead or about to be. Then they'd regroup and figure this thing out.

"I know. Just feels like we're crossing a line."

Tucker snorted. He'd cross whatever line necessary to keep his men alive. "Bring all your weapons, ammo, passports—real and aliases—any burner phones and all your electronics if you're sure they're not traceable. We need to figure out who's after us."

"On it. I'll keep trying Kane."

"Me too." After they disconnected, Tucker packed everything he needed, then took care of the body and blood, storing the dead man in the trunk of the car he'd abandoned on the side of the road. It wasn't the first time he'd had to dispose of a body, not with the jobs he'd been assigned to, but it was the first time he'd removed one from his own home and wasn't telling anyone else about it. He cleaned up the blood the best he could, but if pros came in here with luminol they'd find the evidence.

But if anyone else came out here looking for him, he'd be long gone before they got here.

He needed to stay alive. Because whoever had come after his men had made the biggest mistake of his life.

# Chapter 3

Six: in military and law enforcement slang, "six" means "back." Phrases like "watch your six" or "I've got your six" mean to "watch your back" or "I've got your back." In warfare, your six is the most vulnerable position.

**"I** don't like this." Cole rubbed a hand over his newly cut blond hair. For the Tasev infiltration he'd kept it shaggy, playing the part of a mindless soldier. Now he looked like his usual deadly self.

"What the fuck else are we gonna do?" Kane demanded from the front passenger seat of the SUV he, Tucker, Cole, and Brooks were in.

Tucker shifted against his seat in the back. He didn't like this plan any more than Cole, but they had to do *something*. Their places were all under surveillance—by whom, they hadn't figured out yet—and they couldn't go into work because it was the first place their enemy would expect them. Plus, they didn't know if someone in the DEA had set them up. Their top-security clearances had been revoked in the system at work, which was a huge red flag. *None* of them could log in to anything past a basic level online. With such limited access, they were pretty much working blind. Could be a glitch, but likely not, since it had happened to all four of them.

It wasn't as if a replacement had been named for Max yet, so they had no one to turn to. No one they trusted anyway. Because of their undercover jobs, they were insulated from the majority of the people in the office for their safety and everyone else's. In short, they were fucked right now with no way to know if they'd been set up or even if they'd be arrested if they attempted to head into the office. "It's been two days since Max died," Tucker said quietly.

"And Ali guarantees it's not the Shi'as," Brooks said from the front, never looking back at them as he surveyed the quiet park.

It was before dawn and everything but the sidewalks was covered in a light dusting of snow. The street sweepers had been out about an hour ago to clear and salt everything. This was a well-used park in a nice part of Baltimore where crime was pretty much unheard-of.

Until now.

"Burkhart's not returning my e-mails." Tucker hated every bit of what they were about to do, but they needed an ally. Of course, what they were about to do was just as likely to make them enemies and put them on another hit list. They had nothing to lose at this point. "This will get his attention."

Cole snorted. "And it'll get us bullets in the head."

Maybe. Tucker shook his head. "Max trusted him."
Hell, Burkhart was part of Ali's fail-safe plan if the agent
ever got hung out to dry or Max died during the middle
of an op. He wasn't even with the DEA, but as the deputy director of the NSA and a lifelong friend of their
former boss, Burkhart was a man Max had clearly
thought had integrity.

Tucker hoped he was right.

"We're running out of time and we need help."
Kane's voice was determined, mirroring Tucker's feelings.

"I see a female runner," Brooks said from the front,
his voice grim. "Could be her."

"It's go time. Apparently," Cole tacked on, making
his agitation clear.

But in the end, they were a team and no matter what,
they'd act as one cohesive unit. They trusted one another in the field and they'd support one another in
this. Even though Cole was pissed, Tucker knew he'd
have his back no matter what.

He just hoped this plan didn't turn around and blow
their lives apart. Moving quietly with Cole, Tucker slid
out of the vehicle and made his way to a cluster of trees
that lined the park. He hated this plan, but forced his
doubts away because he didn't see any other option.
They had to do this.

Karen Stafford loosened her scarf around her neck as
her sneakers pounded against the pavement. Despite
the chilly January weather, she'd been jogging for thirty

minutes and had started to sweat a while ago under all her layers.

Inhaling the crisp air, she savored the quiet of the neighborhood as she made her way to her favorite park. This early she didn't run through the park, just around it where she was still visible along main roads. She also didn't run with an MP3 player because she liked the time to be alone with her own thoughts without any outside noise. She rarely got that with her high-pressure job at the NSA. Even if she didn't have the job she did, she still wouldn't run with noise pumping in her ears. She liked to be aware of her surroundings at all times.

She carried bear spray with her—because no mugger or would-be rapist was going to be able to withstand that kind of pain—and a switchblade. A gift from her brother, Clint, who'd died in Afghanistan seven years ago. Whenever he'd come home he always brought her gifts. Usually weapons because he'd been determined that she be able to protect herself since he couldn't be here. As if he could have watched out for her twenty-four/seven if he'd been here anyway, which was a ridiculous concept. But he'd always been so protective. He'd been more like a parent to her than their own useless father had ever been. Even though she missed Clint every day, she knew she was lucky that she'd had someone who cared about her, who would have done anything for her. Still, some days were harder than others and she wished she had someone in her life. Not just anyone, though, because she'd never settle. She'd seen friends do that and it was depressing.

Shaking those thoughts away, Karen increased her pace, enjoying the way her muscles burned and stretched. She ran every day no matter what. If it rained, she used the treadmill in her condo's gym, but she much preferred being outdoors, even in the cold.

When she came up to a four-way intersection, she slowed and jogged in place and looked both ways before crossing. There weren't *any* cars or people out this morning, which was a little creepy. Feeling paranoid, she unhooked her bear spray from her hip holster and held it loosely in her hand. Her friends made fun of her for the precautions she took, but she'd seen too much bloodshed in her job to take safety lightly.

As she reached the sidewalk that stretched along the park's small strip of a dozen parking spots, she slowed. A dark SUV with tinted windows sat in one of the spots, the engine running. The exhaust from the tailpipe was visible, and in the quiet she could hear the distinct hum of the engine. Glancing around, she didn't see anyone else.

Not caring if she was being paranoid, she slowed and turned back around to avoid going past the vehicle. She'd just take a different route today that didn't involve the park.

At the sound of an engine revving, she glanced over her shoulder. The SUV was pulling out of the spot and heading in her direction. Her heart rate kicked up. She knew she was probably acting crazy but didn't care. Veering off the sidewalk, she raced through the park where vehicles couldn't go. As she cleared a cluster of trees without the sound of running feet coming after her, she let out a shaky breath and kept up her pace.

Risking a glance over her shoulder, she nearly stumbled when she saw a man dressed in all black step out from the trees.

That face.

*Holy shit.* Recognition slammed into her with the intensity of a battering ram. Since he wore a scarf around his neck and a knit cap on his head, she couldn't spot one of the distinguishing features she'd seen in the file she had on him. But she knew he had a jagged scar around his neck and tended to favor shaving his head.

She knew it was him from his icy blue eyes.

Grisha. A murdering psychopath.

Fear took hold, its unforgiving grip squeezing around her chest like a vise, colder than the winter-morning air.

Though she wanted to run, she stopped and spun around on the sidewalk, raising her bear spray with a steady hand. No one could withstand this if she shot it in their face, and she just wanted the chance to get away. She certainly wasn't going to take the guy on in hand-to-hand combat. "Get back!" she shouted, her finger steady on the trigger. She was glad she wasn't outwardly shaking. She needed to paint a picture of calm even if she was trembling inside.

To her surprise, he held up his hands and almost looked apologetic as he watched her. "I don't want to hurt you, Karen."

Holy hell, he knew her name. So this definitely wasn't

random. Because why would this guy be in Baltimore of all places, in the same park she ran by almost every day? Did he know who she worked for? God, he probably wanted to torture her for information. She wasn't going to stand around and ask him a bunch of questions. The facts that he knew her name and was a violent criminal were enough for her to run for her life.

Whirling around, she raced down the sidewalk, her heart beating out of control, the sound of her blood rushing in her ears so loud she couldn't tell how close he was behind her.

She wanted to pull out her phone, but she'd strapped it around her ankle so it would be out of her way. She couldn't risk slowing down. If she could just get somewhere public, maybe she could flag someone for help.

As she moved deeper into the park, she cursed herself for coming this way, but he'd been blocking her exit. As she risked another glance over her shoulder, full-blown panic exploded inside her like fireworks. He was about twenty feet behind her and closing. He moved fast for such a big man, and she knew he wouldn't stop. The range on her spray was thirty feet, so she could take him. She'd only get one shot at this, so she had to do it right.

His expression was grim and he said something to her, but she couldn't hear anything above the blood rushing in her ears.

She could keep running, but he was going to reach her soon. And she knew without a doubt she'd lose against him in any sort of physical altercation. She'd seen pictures of what he'd done to someone who'd crossed him. This might be her only chance to get away or at least get help. Drawing in a deep breath, she let out a bloodcurdling scream, hoping someone would hear her as she stopped and turned to spray him.

Still screaming, she had started to press the trigger when a blur of motion out of the corner of her eye made her stumble backward.

A man in similar attire burst from the trees lining the sidewalk. There were two of them!

Pressing the trigger, she started spraying wildly as the newcomer tackled her. She flew back against the sidewalk, her head slamming against it as she lost her grip on the bear spray.

"Don't hurt her!" Grisha shouted.

But that couldn't be right. Unless he wanted to be the one to inflict pain. She tried to struggle, but the other man was on top of her and had her in a tight grip. She couldn't stop gasping, her chest terrifyingly tight. She couldn't breathe through the panic pressing in on her. Every horrible photo and crime scene she'd ever seen at work crashed in on her at once. She didn't want to be a fucking statistic! She blinked as everything around her became fuzzy. *Stay awake*, she ordered herself as the edges of her vision started to fade.

No, no, *no*. She couldn't be unconscious around these monsters. But she couldn't control her breathing. It was too fast, too panicked. Pins and needles erupted in her hands and feet. Her eyeballs felt as if they were bulging. The edges of her vision closed in. Her body refused to listen as darkness swept her under.

Wesley glanced at Selene as they neared their destination. The private plane was about ten minutes from its final descent, and he hated that the reason they were returning was that one of his oldest, closest friends had been murdered.

The whole situation didn't sit right with Wesley, and even though it wasn't the NSA's jurisdiction, he'd be looking at all the files to make sure the investigation was handled properly. He owed Max that much. Hell, he owed the man his life.

"You all right?" Selene asked softly from her seat next to the window. Her white blond hair was pulled back from the sharp planes of her face and braided tight against her head.

As if she were his own daughter, the computer genius rarely missed anything when it came to him. She was one of the few people who could read his moods. He could have said he was fine, but there was no reason to lie to her and she'd have known anyway. "No."

"We'll find out who killed him." Her expression turned fierce and determined.

His throat tight, all he could do was nod and stare blindly at his open laptop. Wesley had called Mary Southers before boarding the plane in Berlin and she'd sounded as if she was hanging in there. The woman was a rock, the type who could weather any storm. But losing Max . . . hell, it was just unfair.

Which was a stupid thing to say considering the shit he saw day in and day out. Wesley knew how fragile life was, how bad things happened to good people all the damn time. For some reason he'd just never thought he'd lose his oldest friend.

Max didn't even work in the field anymore. And that bullshit about a Shi'a terrorist group gunning for him was just that—bullshit—so putrid it stank. It didn't even make sense with the intel they'd gathered so far. Not to mention that the news stations had received that tip way too fast. Faster than the DEA, NSA, or CIA had. And *that* simply didn't happen. The DEA had done damage control and was currently denying those allegations, but the charges were out there for the public to dissect and conspiracy theorists to latch onto.

Now Wesley had to focus on the attack in the capital more than anything. He'd been in Germany working with their premier intelligence agency on something highly sensitive when a stolen, U.S.–owned drone unleashed hell on a political fund-raiser.

And no one could find the damn thing. Not even his best team of analysts. Whoever was manning it was good, because they'd covered their digital tracks well enough that they hadn't even left a bread-crumb trail.

Pulling up his e-mail, Wesley started scanning the most important ones first, trying to sift his way through the mess of them. Karen often went through his messages and alerted him of priorities if he was off-line for a job, but this was his most private e-mail account. No one had access to it but him.

When he saw one from an unknown address, he opened it and frowned. It was rare he got spam at this address.

Remember the tip you got on Tasev in Miami? It was from me. I made the call from a pay phone on Bayside Drive and I'm willing to bet you tried to track me even after Max told you the tip was anonymous. We need to talk about Max's murder. Contact me at this number.

Wesley quickly memorized the phone number. No name, but Wesley didn't need it.

There was only one man who would know all those details. One of Max's undercover agents. A man known only as Grisha, though Wesley knew it was just an alias. He actually had a file on the alleged criminal and all his supposed past exploits. He'd had Karen look into the man because he'd wanted to team up with Max on another case. That wouldn't be happening now.

Wesley checked the time stamp and cursed when he realized the message had been sent two damn days ago.

He pulled out his sat phone and called the number. Then cursed again when it went to an automated voice mail simply saying to leave a message. He tried it again with the same results. He shot off an e-mail to Karen asking her to get a trace on the number, then finished dealing with more correspondence that couldn't wait. Nothing in his damn job could ever seem to wait.

"What's that look?" Selene asked after he'd tried calling Grisha again.

"Remember the undercover agents from the Tasev case?"

Selene's pale blue eyes widened just the slightest fraction. "Yeah."

"I think one of them contacted me. Wants to talk about Max's murder."

"That's interesting."

He nodded. It was very interesting. The DEA and the local PD were handling the case, yet someone who'd worked with Max wanted to talk to him, an outsider.

And in his experience, that simply never happened.

# Chapter 4

Legend: an agent's alleged background and personal history, usually supported by documents and memorized details.

Karen tried to steady her breathing and gain her bearings. It was difficult when she was hooded, but she knew she was sitting in the back of a vehicle—not the original SUV, because they'd switched vehicles in a parking garage, though she'd feigned being passed out—and there were four men in the rows in front of her. She knew how many there were because of their distinctive voices. Unfortunately they were all speaking Russian. She didn't speak it, but she understood a handful of words and phrases. Her hands were flex-cuffed in front of her, which was better than behind her but still sucked. She couldn't stop her heart from racing out of control or her body's elevated temperature.

She was so not prepared for something like this. Sure, she'd taken some classes—in a well-lit classroom with trained instructors—but no in-the-field training for being kidnapped. She was just an analyst. She was good with computers and thinking outside the box, but she wasn't physically strong. Definitely not strong enough to fend off one of the men she'd seen, let alone four. And her imagination was going insane, thinking of all the things these monsters planned to do to her. Rape or torture. Probably both. Worse, she knew that most people cracked under torture.

One of the men she worked with, Ortiz, had told her just that during a conversation they'd had over morning coffee and bagels at the office. It had been in context with a case they'd been working on. He'd said that it was just a matter of time but it was simply human nature before pretty much everyone broke. If you couldn't channel the pain, whether psychological or physical, you cracked. And if for some reason you held out, one of two things happened. Death, or they found something else to use against you. Meaning someone who mattered to you. It was conceivable that even the bravest patriot would give up secrets because of a threat to a significant other or child.

That was human nature to its core.

"Burkhart . . . ," one of the men murmured in the midst of their conversation.

Oh hell. This was definitely about who she worked for. Which was a secret. None of her neighbors or friends knew. They all thought she was an analyst for a think tank, which wasn't that far off the mark. But no one knew she worked for the government or had one of the highest security clearances in the country. Right about now she wished she didn't. Or hell, if she was making wishes, she wished she'd stayed in bed this morning and skipped her run. They must want her for national secrets. She'd worked on so many cases over the years she couldn't begin to guess which one this was about. Maybe something to do with Tasev, a man whose operation the NSA had taken apart not too long ago. She knew Grisha had worked with the man, so that was a logical connection. Anyone who worked for Tasev had to be savage.

She swallowed hard as beads of sweat rolled down her spine.

After a while the conversation in the front trickled off, but there was a tension in the vehicle. Almost a palpable one that could be cut with a blade. She wondered if there was dissension in the group. If maybe she could use it against them to escape.

Because she was going to try as soon as she could. She knew it was better to let an attacker wound you instead of letting him force you into a vehicle at gun or knifepoint. She'd certainly failed that with her freaking panic attack at the park—though with four against one, she hadn't stood a chance. She still wasn't giving up hope.

Statistically speaking, she had the best chance of escaping immediately upon capture and before her attackers took her to their compound. Wherever that might be. She was all about statistics, and while she might not be physically strong, she was smart and held on to that shred of hope that this wasn't the end for her. She had to try to escape before they locked her down completely.

The vehicle slowed and turned. When it did, the road became bumpy as if they were on a dirt road or maybe gravel. They were going slow enough that they weren't on a highway or even a main road anymore. It was hard to know the exact amount of time that had passed since they took her, but she estimated a little over an hour. Which wasn't a help at all. She could be in D.C., Virginia, Delaware, or even Pennsylvania. Or they could have just driven around in circles so that they were still in Maryland. She didn't think so, or it hadn't felt like it, but she was too out of sorts to swear to anything.

"Karen, we're almost at our destination," the one named Grisha said without the slightest trace of an accent.

So they knew she was awake. She'd figured they had but had kept her head lolled to the side on the headrest. Now she didn't bother with the pretense. "What do you want with me?" Her voice was raspy and probably muffled to them.

"We're not going to hurt you. We just need to talk to you. We hooded you for your own safety. It's better you don't know how we got here, but I'm going to help you out of the SUV once we stop and take off your hood."

"What about my cuffs?" she asked calmly. Because she could play nice for a little bit, pretend she bought their lies about not hurting her. Maybe if she did they'd let their guards down. And the clock was ticking. Her window of escape narrowed each second that passed.

There was a short pause and she was under the impression the men were communicating. She heard slight movement and possibly whispers.

The man sighed. "We're going to take your cuffs off once we're inside. There are four of us and we're all highly trained. We don't want to hurt you and we will *not*, but if you try to escape we'll restrain you again. All we want is for you to hear us out."

She called complete and total bullshit, but nodded. "Okay." Oh yeah, she'd play along and act like the docile female until the time was right. Her heart pounded wildly against her chest at the anticipation of having her hood removed, of seeing where she was and gauging her escape.

The engine cut off as the vehicle suddenly stopped. Just as quickly, the hood was lifted and she found herself looking at Grisha and another man with blond hair sitting in the middle seat of the SUV. Instinctively she squinted. Even with the tinted windows, the sudden light affected her eyes.

She was in the third row, which she'd guessed, but now had confirmation. Two more men were in the front. One had black hair, green eyes, and a feral look to him that made her shiver in fear. The driver had dark brown hair and a beard that made him look as if he could be an extra on *Duck Dynasty*. And all of them were clearly fit and muscular. Just great.

She didn't say anything, just looked out the side

window and was surprised to see a normal-looking log-and-brick home. It was fairly large, probably twenty-five hundred to three thousand square feet if she had to guess. As she stared they started opening their doors, in one coordinated motion. All the men exited, and then Grisha pulled down one of the seats in the middle row and held out a hand for her.

She didn't want to touch him but gritted her teeth and let him help her out. She was going to play a role, and the more helpless she acted, the better. For now. An icy breeze kicked up and a shiver that was part fear and part cold swept through her.

Grisha and the blond both frowned, as if in concern. But no way was that right.

"Come on, it's warm inside." The blond held out a hand and motioned for the front door. He seemed to be avoiding touching her too.

That was fine with her. She noticed that Grisha and the two others weren't headed for the house but fanning out along the property, which seemed to stretch on forever. There was thick forest all around them and another building that looked like a barn about a hundred yards away. Even if she screamed she guessed no one was nearby to hear.

They'd gone to a lot of trouble to kidnap her and they weren't going to bring her somewhere where she could start screaming and alert someone to her presence. No, they would have gagged her if so.

The thought that no one was around to hear her scream made another shiver slide down her spine, this one pure terror. She tried to keep her teeth from chattering but couldn't help it. She was alone in the middle of nowhere with four scary-looking guys.

"I'm really sorry about this," the blond muttered as he motioned her up a short set of stone steps. "The others are checking the perimeter to make sure we're still secure. Then we're going to sit down and just talk. I'm really sorry we had to take you the way we did, but you'll understand once we lay everything out." The man actually sounded sincere as he opened the front door and stepped inside with her.

She resisted the urge to snort. *Liar, liar.* Instead of saying what she wanted to, she gave a half smile. "I really have to, uh . . . use the bathroom if that's okay." Despite the instinctive urge to attempt bolting right then and there, she reined it in. It would be foolish and she knew she wouldn't get far. She had to be smart.

"Oh, right. Ah . . ." He shut the door behind them and led her through a living room with a modern country feel to it. No personal items like photos anywhere.

He led her to a small room with two windows that was clearly used as an office. There was a futon in it with a blue-and-green-plaid quilt draped over it. There was also a masculine desk with a laptop set up on it and a few framed pictures of nature settings on the walls. No personal photos in this room either. Maybe it was a safe house of sorts. Or where they brought people to torture and kill. Ugh.

The blond started to open one door, which turned out to be a closet, then shook his head and opened another right next to it. The way he did it made her think he hadn't been here often. She filed that away. "This is the bathroom. I'll be right outside." He pulled out a switchblade and before she had a chance to reel back, he expertly cut her flex cuffs free before quickly closing the blade and putting the knife away.

The way he handled the thing made it clear he was comfortable with knives. Exceptionally so. He crossed his arms over his chest and leaned against the doorframe, watching her carefully.

She didn't say anything, just shut the door behind her and let out a ragged sigh. But she didn't waste time. As quietly as possible she pulled back the shower curtain just a bit. No window, not even a small one. Damn it. No wonder he was letting her in here alone. Since she actually had to pee, she quickly relieved herself, then scanned the medicine cabinet for a weapon. Nothing. Not even hair spray or something aerosol she could use.

That icy fear set in stronger now, slithering through her veins. This was truly happening. The only thing she could do was try to take on the blond guy. It was stupid, she knew, but one against one was better than one against four.

Taking a deep breath, she'd started to open the bathroom door when she heard the guy murmur something. Not to her, though. He continued talking and his voice grew fainter along with the sound of boots stepping away.

He was leaving his protective duty.

That stupid shred of hope bloomed inside her. She had a desperate, likely-to-fail plan, but she had to try. She refused to just give up.

Turning on the faucet, she let the water run and stepped out of the bathroom. He wasn't there. She wanted to peek out the doorway into the hallway but decided against it. Seconds would matter right now. Moving quickly to one of the windows by the futon, she slid the locks free and pushed it open just wide enough for her to climb through.

Instead of doing that, she moved back to the closet and ducked inside. Blood rushed in her ears as she heard boot steps nearby, then a vicious curse.

"I was only gone a second," the blond said.

"She went out the fucking window," one of the other guys snapped. "Call Tucker. I'm heading after her."

She didn't have time to contemplate who Tucker was, but she filed the name away. She heard muffled movement as someone climbed out the window. The bathroom door opened and someone turned off the faucet. More boot steps, then a door nearby slamming. Maybe the front door.

Though her hands shook, she knew she couldn't hide here forever. They'd figure out what she'd done eventually, and she needed to be gone before then. With a damp palm she opened the door and peeked out.

The curtains rippled in the breeze, but the room was empty. Heart pounding, she hurried out of the closet

and into the hallway. Her analytical side told her to
find a phone or weapon, but the most primal part of
her said she had to escape *now*. She had to get free, to
find help.

Instead of heading to the front door, she raced
down the hallway to what turned out to be a huge
bedroom.

After peeking out one of the windows and finding
the coast clear, she opened it and jumped out. Her
sneakers sank into the snow. Hating that she'd leave a
trail, there was no avoiding it, so she raced toward the
nearest line of trees. They'd see which direction she'd
gone, but she had a small head start. It was all she
could ask for at this point.

Her breath sawed in and out of her lungs as she
headed faster toward the woods, uncaring of the noise
she made. The next step was finding help. Maybe a
neighbor or a road where she could flag someone down.
Because she wasn't letting these bastards get her.

No way in hell.

"Fuck," Tucker muttered, racing over to the window
Karen had escaped from, Brooks with him. He'd yell at
Cole later for leaving her unguarded.

For now, they had the SUV keys and this place was
on fifty acres with the nearest neighbor even farther
away than that. He knew they'd find her, but he hated
the thought of her out in the cold too long, and that
she'd run because she was scared of them. Not that he

blamed her. They'd done a fucked-up thing by taking her, but their survival depended on her help. Because at this point they didn't know who to trust except Burkhart.

"No footprints," he muttered as he reached the side of the house. Brooks's footprints were there, huge and hard to miss, but no smaller prints from Karen.

"Fuck me," Brooks snarled, and dove back through the window.

Tucker raced along the side of the house, letting Brooks search inside. Cole and Kane had already spread out and had their phones on them in case they found her. It had been only a few minutes, so she couldn't have gone far.

As he rounded the side of the house, he saw another set of footprints leading from one of the other windows to the trees—and a flash of red disappearing into the forest.

Karen.

That auburn hair of hers was unmistakable. The woman was beautiful and clearly smart and right now had to be terrified. Giving chase, he pulled out his phone and called Cole. "Hold everyone else back. I'm bringing her in," he said tersely.

She was already terrified; she didn't need to be faced with all four of them, and while Tucker knew he was probably the scariest-looking of his team, he wanted to talk to her first, to at least give her the illusion of coming back with him without force. God, he hated that they'd resorted to kidnapping a woman. An *innocent* woman. Who was so fucking beautiful it stunned him. And he hated that he noticed that, but it was hard not to.

As he raced through the woods, he quickly caught sight of her. Her hair was in a ponytail, her bright hair like a flag waving behind her.

She looked back and, when she saw him, let out a startled scream before turning back around and racing even faster. He pushed himself into a burst of speed, wanting to get this over with. Thirty yards and closing.

Twenty.

Ten.

She suddenly stumbled, crying out as she tripped. A scream tore from her throat. One that made something protective inside him flare to life. He hated being the cause of her fear. Though he'd taken on the role of murdering criminal-for-hire for more than one undercover job, this was the real him.

He was on her in seconds, starting to crouch down to help when she rolled over onto her back, a short stick in her hand.

She lunged at him with it. Using moves he could do in his sleep, he disarmed her and tossed the stick away.

"Bastard!" she shouted, grabbing for another nearby stick.

"Damn it," he muttered, disarming her of that one too. Not wanting her to hurt herself or to drag this out longer than necessary, he flipped her onto her stomach and secured her hands behind her back as he straddled her hips. He didn't cuff her, though, just held her wrists together. She twisted beneath him. "Karen—"

She started crying. Not all-out sobs, but her body started shaking and he felt her pain and fear and knew what she must be thinking. *Fuck, fuck, fuck.*

So he did the only thing he could. "My name is Tucker Pankov. I work—worked—with Max Southers as part of an elite, undercover unit. Someone murdered him and set up me and my team to be killed too." Her struggles lessened a bit, so he knew she was listening. "Professional hits all at the same time. Now our clearances have been revoked and we don't know who the hell to trust. Wesley Burkhart is pretty much the only person Max trusted." Well, other than Tucker's team and of course Max's own family. "We've been trying to get hold of him for days and when we couldn't, we went after you. We're not going to hurt you. We need your help." He paused a second. "If I let you up are you going to attack me?"

She'd gone very still and it was clear that she was debating her answer. "Tucker Pankov is the dumbest, most made-up name I've ever heard," she finally said, her voice shaking with anger. Thankfully she wasn't crying anymore.

He couldn't help it, he laughed. Taking a risk that she might attack him again, he let her hands go. When he stood, she rolled over and shoved up to her feet. He noticed she winced when she put pressure on one foot, but she didn't make a move to grab another makeshift weapon or come at him again.

"Tucker Pankov is my real name." And he planned to show her his real jacket, not one of his many legends the DEA had for him.

Her lips pulled into a thin line.

She was going to read his file soon anyway, so he went for complete honesty. She deserved all the truth he could give her after what he'd done. "My father was a defector. He married a Southern woman and she refused to give me a Russian first name." His father was brilliant and, according to his mom, had been a pretentious asshole until he met and married her. Of course she didn't actually use the word *asshole*, but it was what she meant. The man had fallen for a true Southern belle and, to his own surprise, had taken to living in America quicker than he'd ever imagined. Not something that happened for all immigrants, especially ones who'd more or less been forced to flee their country, even if it was voluntary in the technical sense.

"You're just dropping all sorts of interesting information. Is this part of your plan? To convince me we're on the same side before the torture starts?" Her voice trembled and it was quick, but he saw the covert glance she made at one of the sticks. As if she wanted to lunge for it and attack him again.

"None of us have hurt you, something you'll realize if you think about it. We've gone out of our way not to, in fact." They weren't acting like normal kidnappers, and she had to see it. "I can tie you up and carry you back to the house. I don't want to, but I will." He injected steel into his voice. "So either walk with me or I carry you. Decide."

Gritting her teeth, she looked around the quiet woods and he knew the moment she decided to come with him. He knew it because he saw the defeat in her pretty, expressive green eyes.

She took a step forward and couldn't hide another wince.

"Are you hurt?"

For a moment it looked as if she'd say no, but then she nodded. "Twisted my ankle."

He moved closer to her, the snow crunching under his boots. When he made a move to pick her up, she flinched. Yeah, he was an asshole. "Listen, I can carry you."

"Are you ordering me?"

"No." Even though he wanted to.

"Then I'll walk."

Tucker rubbed a hand over the back of his neck, but it didn't ease any of the tension. "Fine." It would take a hell of a lot longer to get back to the house this way, and more important, she was clearly in pain, but he had to give her this bit of control.

He was so used to not giving a shit about the people he worked with in his undercover jobs because they were all criminals, all blights on society who preyed on the weak. This was different.

For a while he thought he'd lost the part of him that

cared about people, even innocent civilians, but as Karen Stafford held her head high, marching on through her pain back to what she assumed was probably torture or a death sentence, he realized he wasn't completely dead inside.

# Chapter 5

Tradecraft: the methods developed by intelligence operatives to conduct their operations.

"Karen still hasn't responded," Wesley murmured as he shot off another e-mail. He frowned at his laptop, then glanced at the time on his watch even though he already knew it was thirty minutes after the time she normally arrived at work. She hadn't e-mailed him or called and she was never, *ever* late.

Hell, the woman practically lived with her cell phone attached to her hip. Even when she went running she had it strapped to her ankle. More than an analyst, she'd recently moved into the role of his personal assistant and was invaluable. Well, *officially* moved into the role because she'd been doing more for him than her job required the last couple of years. In a few more years he thought she'd be ready to take on her own division, and he wanted to get her ready for it. That wasn't why he was worried. He cared deeply about Karen. She was part of the "family" within his group, and he looked out for his own people.

Selene glanced at him, her cell phone to her ear, and mouthed, *Hold on*. They were in the backseat of an armored SUV, being driven from the private airport to an off-the-books meeting in Baltimore. "She's still not at work," Selene finally said, ending her call. "No one's heard from her either. Ortiz has tried calling her and nothing." Her eyebrows pulled together, her normally neutral expression showing true worry.

Wesley tried to tamp down his own worry. Karen was a grown woman, but this wasn't like her. "I need you to go by her place," he ordered Selene before telling their driver to pull over at the next available rest stop. She was supposed to come with him to his first meeting of the day, but that wasn't happening now.

Selene nodded. "What kind of security does she have?"

"Standard but good. I've got the code to her condo, so it won't be an issue." He rattled off the six-digit code as they pulled to a stop. The other SUV tailing them stopped also.

"I'll call you when I get there." Selene was out of the vehicle and heading to their backup vehicle before he could respond.

Not that there was anything to say. He trusted Selene to do her job without having to micromanage. He had too many crises to deal with on a constant basis to have to follow up with his people. And while Selene was technically done with field assignments, she still did a lot of local, on-the-ground type of work for him when they were in D.C. or Maryland. Which, for her, wasn't as often, since she was now stationed in their Georgia office. But he'd needed her with him in Germany.

Even though he was close to the meeting point and Selene would likely be at Karen's place in less than ten minutes, he put in his Bluetooth and speed-dialed one of the analysts at the office. "Run all the CCTVs in a four-block radius of Karen Stafford's condo in the last two hours." He gave the address and the name of the park he knew she frequented. "And try to locate her phone." He wasn't sure if they'd be able to. She was careful about her privacy. They all were. Her phone was encrypted and he knew she'd taken extra lengths to ensure that she couldn't be tracked or located. But with their resources they should be able to find it.

"On it. Want to hold?" Elliott asked.

"Yeah." He scanned a file on his laptop as he waited, reviewing information on other vulnerable targets in D.C. and surrounding areas. After the attack on the Nelson fund-raiser, all the agencies were on high alert and pooling resources to find the missing drone and find who the hell was behind the attack. Even if Max hadn't been killed, Wesley would have been back in the country anyway because of the current security situation and the very important meeting he had in less than ten minutes.

"What am I looking for?"

"Her specifically. I want to see when she left to go running this morning and when she came back. And document any vehicles in that radius at the same time of her leaving the building. Expand the search for six blocks." It would likely be a lot of vehicles to sift through, but they had damn good resources to filter through unnecessary info. There was a chance she hadn't gone running at all, but the weather was clear, so he doubted it.

"All right . . . give me a few minutes."

Wesley continued reading the classified document on his laptop and included personal notes about places he viewed as being in imminent danger. He'd already started the process to increase the security level at three of them when Elliott spoke again.

"This is weird. I've got her leaving her place, dressed to run, but she never came back. She headed in the direction of the park, but then I lost her. There aren't any CCTVs in a few places around the park and it's like she just disappeared."

Wesley's heart rate kicked up a notch. Karen was smart and carried bear spray. More than that, she knew the dangers in the world and took precautions in most situations. It was one of the reasons he was grooming her for a new position. She looked at things with a critical, realistic eye because she knew how bad the world was—but she wasn't a cynic. All that didn't mean she couldn't have been hurt, though.

"Run the plates of the vehicles leaving the park or anywhere within a two-block radius of the park in the ten minutes directly after she disappears from your view."

"Running now," Elliott responded.

"What about her phone?"

"Nothing. Not even a ping that tells me the battery's out."

Unfortunately he was probably right. Even with the encryption they should have been able to get a hit on it. Wesley reined in a curse. "Stay on the line." He pressed MUTE on his earpiece, then pulled out another cell. There was a possibility he was being paranoid, but he didn't think so. If something had happened to Karen, their window of finding her narrowed with each second that passed.

He called a detective friend who worked for the local PD and requested assistance in a potential investigation. Off the books for now. He and Detective Portillo had worked together on more than one occasion and Wesley trusted the guy to be thorough. After he was sure the locals would canvass the park for any clues on Karen—including looking for her phone—he clicked back over to Elliott.

"What'd you find?"

"Eighty-six vehicles moving in and around that area at the time. Not including vehicles parked. I've run them all through the DMV database, and one of them doesn't exist."

Wesley straightened at that. "What?"

"Yeah. The license plate itself doesn't exist in any database. And it's wrong anyway. The combination of numbers and letters isn't right to be a real plate for this particular state."

Wesley knew that in addition to other specific state

identifiers, the majority of states used a three-letter, three-number combination for plates.

Now his blood chilled. If he had to guess, someone had simply put two license plates together. It was old-school tradecraft and very effective. Cut two license plates in half and then solder the separate pieces together, creating something virtually untraceable.

Elliott continued. "It's an SUV and the windows are too tinted, even the front, to get a view of anyone inside. Doesn't matter what angle I looked at it from. Might mean there's a reflective shield in place."

That wasn't a coincidence. "Focus on the SUV. Track them."

Though he tried to temper his worry, it was impossible as he waited for Elliott to give him something. Anything. Karen was sweet and while brilliant, she wasn't trained the way Selene was. If someone had truly taken Karen, she'd have to rely on her wits. Sometimes that wasn't enough when up against the monsters of the world. She'd worked on too many cases over the last year for him to narrow down what this could be about. But it had to be work related. The use of tradecraft indicated that.

"This isn't good, boss. . . . The SUV went into a parking garage downtown. I hacked into the internal server of their security system, and chunks of time have been completely stripped out. There's no way to see what happened once the SUV entered. And I don't know if the driver timed it, but a dozen vehicles left about ten minutes after the SUV entered. I'm fast-forwarding until now and that SUV still hasn't left."

"Run all the plates of the vehicles that left, forward pertinent info to my e-mail, and text me the address of the parking garage now," Wesley ordered before hanging up and taking an incoming call from Selene. "Yeah?"

"Her place shows no signs of a struggle. Coffeemaker is on. Looks like an automatic thing, so she was obviously planning on coming back. And her clothes for the day are hung up in her closet along with her shoes and coordinating jewelry. Bed's unmade. No sneakers in the closet."

Now Wesley's blood iced over. He quickly gave her the rundown of what Elliott had told him. "We're treating this as a missing person case as of now. Pull in who you want for a team and get to the parking garage now. I've already contacted Detective Portillo, but I'll let him know that you're going to coordinate with him. I'll hook up with you as soon as I'm out of this fucking meeting." He had a one-on-one with the director of the CIA and he couldn't miss it. Not when this was a matter of national security and the lives of hundreds of thousands of innocent civilians were at stake. There were some things they simply couldn't talk about over the phone or using any sort of technology. This was one of those times. Having Selene running this op eased some of his tension, but not by much. Not until they found out where Karen was.

"I want Ortiz and—"

"Whoever you want, Selene. Send the info to my phone along with any updates. I'll be dark for the duration of the meeting, but it shouldn't be long."

Once they disconnected he shut off his phone and other electronics as his driver steered up to the clandestine location of the meeting.

Rayford glanced in the rearview mirror as he pulled to a stop on Hillenbrand's block. Instead of taking the Metro and walking to the townhome, this time he'd borrowed a colleague's vehicle from work. Of course he'd been careful to drive around in circles and take an alternative route to even enter the neighborhood, but he was certain he wasn't being watched anyway.

At least not by law enforcement. There was always the chance that some reporter tailed him hoping to get a story, but at this point in his career it was unlikely. He had a proven track record and knew in certain circles he was mocked for being a straight arrow.

They could mock all they wanted, but with no skeletons in his closet, he never felt guilt or had to worry about past deeds coming back to haunt him. It was the reason his boss had chosen him, and why he was invaluable to the upcoming election efforts. The election his boss would win. Nothing was absolutely guaranteed, but now that their main opponent within the party was out of the way, they were even closer to victory.

As he approached Hillenbrand's townhome, a woman with blond hair and a polished look stepped out the front door, Hillenbrand with her. The man had his hand on her ass and was obscenely groping her breast as she giggled and gave him what was clearly a parting kiss.

Rayford gritted his teeth. Hillenbrand had asked him to come here and he couldn't risk being seen by one of the man's whores.

A woman who accepted money in exchange for sex would easily talk if she was pulled in by law enforcement. He couldn't have any viable connections to Hillenbrand. Bending down, he acted as if he was tying his shoe, even though he wore loafers. Today he was dressed in business casual, as it had been appropriate for the campaign work they'd been doing, but he'd snagged his colleague's hoodie from the backseat and kept it pulled over his head.

The woman's booted heels clicked along the sidewalk as she headed in the opposite direction. Once the sound was far enough away, he looked up. She was getting into a luxury sedan and oblivious of him, so he straightened.

Hillenbrand was waiting in the entryway, arms crossed over his chest and a pleased expression on his face.

Before he could speak, Rayford did. "You called me away from work for this. I don't expect to cross paths with one of your women again. Ever. This business we do is between us."

Hillenbrand's blue eyes went cold, but he nodded. "Fair enough. Now come on."

Silently he followed him back down to the entertainment room. He was surprised to see the DEA agent and another man there. Gary Harris, a skilled hacker with a lengthy criminal history. Hillenbrand used his services, but Rayford didn't trust the guy. Hell, he didn't trust anyone in this room but himself. But he was going to reach out to the DEA agent without going through Hillenbrand. Couldn't hurt to feel the man out, discover why he was involved with them.

He nodded at both men, though Harris barely glanced up from his laptop. The grungy-looking guy was stretched out on the Chesterfield, his sneakers kicked up on a table with no respect. He was a genius but disgusting.

"We've had a change of plans," Hillenbrand said. "The men I sent out to eliminate Southers's team have all gone radio silent."

"Isn't that normal?" This was out of his realm of expertise, but after the display with the drone the other night, Hillenbrand had introduced Rayford to the corrupt DEA agent. The man had briefly explained how the hit team would work. They'd all go dark while they killed Southers's guys, then confirm the deaths once they were in secure locations.

Hillenbrand shook his head. "No. It's been days. At least one of them would have checked in by now. And"—he nodded at the DEA agent—"we have a confirmation that the targets have tried to access their accounts at the DEA."

Rayford raised his eyebrows. "Recently?"

The blond-haired man nodded. "Yesterday." Which was the day after the hit team had been sent out. "I've revoked their access using someone else's system so it won't trace back to me. But we need them eliminated before they cause a problem."

Rayford's heart rate increased, but he forced himself to remain calm. Killing Southers's men was part of the plan. They needed scapegoats. "So, what happens now?"

"We're going to blow some shit up," Harris said, almost manic glee in his voice even though he still didn't glance up.

Rayford rolled his shoulders once, trying to ease his growing tension. He was uncomfortable associating with someone like Harris so closely. Unfortunately it was necessary. Rayford knew that in order to get his boss in the White House, he'd have to make some sacrifices. He also knew that while Hillenbrand was on the same side as he was, the other man was more in this for the money than politics. No matter what Hillenbrand said. Still, it didn't matter as long as their goal was the same. Once they started a war in the Middle East, they'd all get rich from the government contracts— Hillenbrand's number-one goal—and Rayford's boss would then take his place in history starting a war they could win. He'd go down in history as a great president and their political party would gain more power. A win-win. The fact that Rayford would also get rich from their plan was just a bonus.

Hillenbrand nodded at the screen and as if on cue, a video popped up. It showed two of their targets, Kane and Brooks, at a garden center of sorts. No, not just a garden center. The U.S. Botanic Garden. "What is this?"

"Footage of them scouting out the Botanic Garden as part of their 'terrorist plot' to bomb it," Hillenbrand said with that smug expression on his face.

Rayford frowned. He knew Kane and Brooks weren't actual terrorists, but the footage of them at the garden looked real. So did the way they were doing reconnaissance. Hillenbrand was obviously setting them up to look like terrorists, but Rayford wanted to know how they'd gotten the footage in the first place. "I don't understand."

"We had an issue there two weeks ago. Kane and Brooks were sent to search for a suspected criminal related to an ongoing investigation," the DEA agent said. "All off the books."

"Thanks to my unparalleled skill," Harris continued, obviously full of himself, "now it's going to look as if they planted bombs." The screen split, showing the men in various stages of sweeping the Garden, and in the second video it looked exactly as though they were indeed hiding explosives.

"Kids are there every day." Rayford didn't like the way this was going. He knew what he'd signed up for, but hurting children wasn't part of his plan. Hell, he'd taken his nephews there a few months ago. He didn't know if he could go through with this if they hurt kids.

Hillenbrand shot him an annoyed look. "No shit. We're not going to hurt anyone. Only one bomb will be set off." He glanced at Harris. "Do it."

A third frame appeared on the screen. It was a shot of the interior conservatory. He couldn't hide the automatic wince as a ball of flames burst free, sending glass and debris flying everywhere. It didn't look as if anyone had been injured, but he was only seeing one shot of the destruction and for all he knew, Hillenbrand was lying to him about no one getting hurt. "What about the other bombs?" Rayford was surprised his voice didn't shake.

"They're real, but unless the bomb techs are complete idiots, they'll find everything and be able to remove all the threats. It's not like we're going to set them off anyway."

"How does this help us?" Other than the obvious. Rayford figured they wanted to destroy the credibility of the four targets, but needed to know if there was more. This whole plan had been carefully set up and no one had thought to tell Rayford. He didn't like being in the dark and Hillenbrand seemed to thrive on keeping everything compartmentalized. It was making Rayford edgy. "And who actually set up the bombs?" he demanded, unable to keep his anger completely in check.

"To answer your first question," Hillenbrand said, heading for his minibar even though it wasn't even noon yet, "we're going to anonymously release the video footage we have to the media of Brooks and Kane setting the bombs. Then we're going to release their files—doctored files—showing their allegiance to the same Shi'a group believed to be behind their boss's death. Along with those, we'll include files on Tucker Pankov and Cole Erickson. We're ruining their credibility, giving them no place to run, and painting targets on their backs by every law enforcement agency in the country. If we can't kill them, we'll let the government do it for us."

Hillenbrand took a sip of his scotch, his eyes gleaming a little too madly for Rayford's comfort. "This is absolutely brilliant," he continued. "Everything is falling into place perfectly. We have four dirty DEA agents working with a terrorist group and killing Americans on American soil. The headlines are going to write themselves and we're going to get our candidate into the White House. When that happens, we'll get the war we want. The war we can *win*."

If not win, they'd have a president who started a war. That would help him get elected the second time. Voters wanted someone they perceived as strong. While there was no guarantee their guy would get elected, he had a strong military background compared to the only real opponent. If people were scared they'd turn to someone they knew would do whatever it took to keep terrorists off American soil.

And they'd all become very rich when that happened, Rayford thought, trying not to focus on that too much. It was hard not to be aware, though, especially since he'd been given an eight percent stake in one of Hillenbrand's companies. Not under his real name, of course, but the money would all be his.

It all sounded so simple, but Hillenbrand was correct. Everything did seem to be falling into place.

Still . . . "What about the video footage? Won't experts be able to tell it's been altered?"

Harris shrugged. "Eventually, but I'm very, *very* good."

"The news stations are going to run with the story," Hillenbrand continued. "By the time there's an official forensics video analysis, these guys will be listed as traitors and wanted by everyone in the damn country. They're fucked."

Plus, it would keep the authorities chasing their tails, which was a big part of this plan, he knew. No one could know the truth of what they were doing or they'd be the ones listed as traitors. And they'd all die for their crimes. Maybe not by the needle, depending upon where they were tried, but he wasn't stupid enough to think the government wouldn't covertly kill them for what they were doing.

# Chapter 6

Dry clean: certain actions or procedures agents might take to ascertain if they are under surveillance.

Karen fought the terror splintering through her as she and Tucker—if that was even his real name—entered the house through the kitchen door. Her ankle throbbed, but she was pretty certain it was only a mild sprain. It felt like a simple twist, something she'd done before. She wasn't concerned with her freaking ankle, though. Not when three more dangerous men were waiting in the kitchen for them.

She winced as she limped inside, then inwardly cursed. She didn't need to show any more weakness than necessary.

"What happened?" the blond one asked from where he leaned against a countertop. The other two were sitting at a round kitchen table, their expressions grim.

Karen had the irrational urge to move behind Tucker as cover, but she knew he wouldn't protect her from anything.

"She twisted her ankle," Tucker muttered.

The blond pushed up. "And you couldn't fucking carry her?" he snapped, a surprising amount of concern in his voice, before he turned to the other two. "Get up."

"I offered," Tucker said, but there was no heat in his voice as he moved to where the other two men had vacated. He pulled out a chair and motioned for her to sit.

Even though she wanted to be obstinate and stand, her ankle throbbed and there was no reason to remain standing and possibly injure herself more. As she lowered herself onto one of the chairs, Tucker pulled out another one. Without asking, he took her leg gently and propped it up on the chair.

While he moved, the blond one pulled out a first-aid kit from under the sink and the heavily bearded man went to the freezer. When he retrieved an ice pack, she realized they meant to help her.

Tucker moved so quickly, efficiently removing her sneaker and sock, it was a shock to her system when his big hands gently pushed up the bottom of her black running pants, rubbing over her skin. She hadn't expected any gentleness or warmth from him. She didn't want to believe that there'd been any truth to what he'd said out in the woods, but if there was . . .

"Can you roll it?" he asked, looking up to meet her gaze with those intense blue eyes.

Swallowing hard, she did a couple of times. "It's a little achy, but I don't think it's too bad." There was a tiny bit of swelling on the top, so she'd probably just pulled a ligament. Since she'd broken the ankle in the past, it was more sensitive. Something she was used to.

He looked over at the blond and held out a hand. Without pause the man gave him the first-aid kit. "I think it's a small sprain. Just to be on the safe side, I'm going to wrap it and put an ice pack on it. You'll just need to stay off it."

She nearly snorted. It wasn't as though they'd be letting her go anywhere. But she kept her mouth shut. No need to piss off the possibly violent men who were being inexplicably nice. At least temporarily.

"I told her my name," Tucker said, without looking up.

The blond nodded, clearly pleased. "Good. I'll get the files." He left the room while Tucker carefully but expertly wrapped her ankle with the ice pack. He made sure to put cloth between her skin and the pack.

She flicked a glance at the other two men to find them watching her. There was no hostility in either of their gazes.

"Escaping like that was smart," the bearded one said, a hint of something in his dark brown eyes she couldn't quite define.

She raised her eyebrows. It almost sounded like a compliment.

The other one chuckled, the small action making him a little less feral-looking. "We're never going to let Cole live that shit down."

"Fuck all you guys," the blond—Cole?—said as he entered the kitchen carrying a handful of legal-sized manila folders. The word CLASSIFIED was stamped on top of the one she could see.

"How's that feel?" Tucker murmured, drawing her attention back to him.

"It's good. Thank you, Tucker." She also decided to use his name. It was Psychology 101, but she was going to humanize herself as much as possible to her kidnappers. Maybe it was his real name, maybe not. But she remembered how one of the men in the office had said to "call Tucker" when he hadn't known she'd been hiding in the closet. He could be telling the truth at least about his name.

His eyes widened, probably at her use of his name. When his gaze dipped to her mouth, his expression going heated for a second, all her fears from earlier about being raped and tortured flared to the surface—until a faint red flush crept up his neck. Clearing his throat, he looked away seemingly in embarrassment and held out his hand to Cole.

As Cole gave him the files, she wondered at the flushing. It seemed so . . . real. Not something he was faking for her benefit. And a man who appeared almost embarrassed by checking her out didn't seem . . . she couldn't think of the right phrase. Because the man crouched in front of her wasn't harmless. He was clearly a trained killer.

A killer who'd just wrapped her ankle and was now looking at her with a tiny spark of hope in his eyes. Maybe he wasn't lying about needing her help. If his name was really Tucker and Grisha was an alias, she knew how legends were built in the clandestine world. Most of the intel would be fake to solidify a cover. Though some would be real. He'd have to be able to back up who his legend was.

He reached over and set the files on the table in front of her, still not moving. She wondered if he was intentionally staying crouched down so he wouldn't intimidate her with his size. She was average in height, but he was pretty huge. The other three were well built and muscular but not as tall as him.

"These are our real files from the DEA." He looked away then and nodded at Duck Dynasty. "That's Kane."

"Just Kane?"

The one supposedly named Kane cleared his throat. "My first name's Forest." He seemed almost embarrassed by that, but Tucker continued, indicating the one with black hair. "This is Paxton Brooks. And Cole Erickson is the one you outsmarted."

When she risked another glance at him he didn't seem annoyed or angry, just rolled his eyes. "You've given them years of mocking at my expense—if we survive this shit storm."

At the last part, the men seemed to sober. Tucker shifted slightly, drawing her attention back to him. "We know kidnapping you was fucked up and we'll pay for our crime, but we need Burkhart's help. He's the only one Max trusted. With Max dead, our roles at the DEA have been compromised and we don't know who to turn to. A team was sent out to eliminate all of us."

"Did you call the police?" God, why was she humoring them? And why did she ask such a naive-sounding question?

Tucker's lips pulled into a thin line. "No. We've hidden the bodies of the hitters."

"And some of our places are now under surveillance. It's subtle, but we spotted watchers at Brooks's and Kane's places," Cole said.

"You're sure?" she asked.

Cole nodded. "Yeah. We paid for random flower deliveries and the delivery guys got stopped by surveillance. Someone is watching for us."

"Did you at least get the fingerprints off the men who came after you?" Okay, she'd apparently lost her mind, but if they were going to tell her all this, she was going to ask questions. If they were telling the truth, she wanted to know everything.

Tucker nodded.

At least that was good. She didn't necessarily believe them, not by a long shot, but if what they were saying was true, having those prints was a good start for figuring out who'd hired the men who'd allegedly tried to kill the four of them. "Have you run the prints?"

"No. We've got contacts in other agencies, but running those prints could flag whoever sent the dead men. Since we don't know who's after us, we have no idea what their resources are, or if they're with another government agency. By now they've got to know they failed in trying to eliminate us, but we still don't want to flag ourselves."

"But you trust Wesley to help you?"

"Max trusted him."

Apparently it was as simple as that. "So what do you want from me?"

"Read our files and set up a meeting between me and Burkhart," Tucker said.

"He's going to know I'm gone by now." And knowing Wesley, he'd have already formed a team to find her. He'd be beyond angry too. Wesley considered his people family.

"We're well aware of that. He owes me and Cole so . . . we're going to throw ourselves at his mercy and hope that counts for something."

She raised an eyebrow. "He owes *you*?"

"Yep."

When it was clear Tucker wasn't going to continue, Karen looked at Cole.

The other man shrugged. "We helped one of his agents on a fairly recent op. Don't know her real name but she's tall, blond, sexy, and really fucking deadly."

That sounded like Selene, but it was such a general description. Maybe he meant on the Tasev op. It would make sense. Karen had run info given to them anonymously for that op. "So you think I'm just going to set up a meeting with Wesley for you?"

"We're hopeful," Tucker said.

"And if I don't?" For all she knew, the files were fake and they wanted to trap her boss. The reasons for ambushing him weren't important; he was the deputy director of the NSA. A prime target for all kinds of lunatics and extremists.

"We just need to talk to him. In person is preferred, but with you missing, he'll be answering all his calls now." Tucker pulled a badge from his pocket.

The others followed suit, flashing their IDs before putting them away. She'd seen her share of DEA, FBI, and CIA credentials to know when something was real. They were certainly worn enough in a way that told her it was doubtful they were bogus.

She rubbed a hand over her face. "I'll read your files." It wasn't going to matter much for these men, though. After she was done reading, she'd make the call to Wesley, but she knew he'd trace the call and soon these four men would be in handcuffs.

"Thank you," Tucker said, and after a quick nod, the other three men strode out of the kitchen.

She thought he'd leave too, but instead he pulled up a chair at the table. "You gonna watch me while I read?"

He snorted. "One of us is going to be watching you at all times."

Fair enough. After her brief escape they'd be stupid not to guard her twenty-four/seven. "Do you have anything to drink here?"

He seemed startled by the question as he stood. "Shit, yeah, sorry. We've got bottled water, sodas, some energy drinks, or I could make hot tea or coffee."

"Hot tea works. Thanks." At least her kidnapper

was polite. The whole situation was too surreal, but at this point a lot of her fear had subsided. Whether these guys were liars or not, she believed that *they* believed what they were telling her. Her father had been a manipulative alcoholic, so she'd gotten good at reading people over the years. It was one of the many reasons she was so effective at her job.

Another thing she'd noticed very belatedly when Tucker chased her down in the forest was that he wasn't armed with a gun. None of them were. There was a chance they had weapons strapped to their ankles, but the men she worked with, the agents and military types, were pretty standard about how they carried. Either shoulder or hip holsters.

"Do you have a gun on you?" she asked as he started filling a teapot with water.

He glanced over his shoulder, a kind of surprise on his hard face that told her she'd truly stunned him with the question. "No. None of us do."

"That's kind of weird for DEA agents." Alleged DEA agents, she thought.

"I didn't say we don't have weapons with us. I know you still don't believe us and that's fine, but we didn't need firearms to take you. That wasn't part of our plan. The last thing we want to do is hurt you. We couldn't take the chance you got hurt with one of our weapons." He turned away from her and moved to the stove.

Frowning, she picked up the top file and flipped it open. She didn't want to believe Tucker at all, but if trained killers had been sent after all four of them and they'd come to kidnap her unarmed, they'd left themselves vulnerable. She found that . . . interesting.

If it was even true at all.

Shoving those thoughts aside, she started reading the first page of Forest Kane's file and found herself half smiling at his first name.

An hour later, she'd made her way through all their files, and hated to admit it, but there was a ring of truth to a lot of what she read. So it was possible they were actual DEA agents. They'd shown her their badges too, and again, they all looked real, but that didn't mean anything. They could be fakes or they could be real and the men corrupt agents.

Something in one of the files intrigued her, though. "That op you mentioned, where you helped an agent of Wesley's, where was it?" she asked, looking up from Tucker's file.

He was at one of the counters making her a sandwich. He'd shed his jacket, and the long-sleeved black shirt fit him as if it had been custom-made for his big frame. She hated that she noticed how built he was.

"Miami," he said without turning around.

*Well, hell.* "Tell me more about it." There had been a brief mention of an op in Miami in the allegedly official, classified file she'd just read on him and Cole. Most of the info had been redacted, but it had been around the same time Wesley ran an op there and it had ended at the same time the NSA brought down a vicious criminal named Tasev.

Now he paused but finally turned and brought the

ham and swiss cheese sandwich over to her before sitting across from her once again. "Cole and I were undercover working for a man named Tasev." Tucker watched her carefully for a moment, as if waiting for a response. When she didn't say anything, he continued. "My alias was Grisha, something I think you already know, considering your reaction when you first saw me. We'd infiltrated his organization when it came to light he was planning a large-scale attack on the United States. You already know those details, so I won't bother with them. Tasev captured one of your agents—though we didn't know she was NSA until Max told us later—and we worked together. Cole and I split before your guys infiltrated so we could maintain our aliases for possible future use."

From the file she had on "Grisha," she knew the man had worked with Tasev. Wesley had given her Grisha's file and asked her to run the info they had on him and compile a list of his past jobs. It had been almost impossible to pull info on him, which was interesting all by itself. Just as interesting as what he'd just told her.

"I gave him a tip about the water plant. Well, not him directly, but Max did."

Karen straightened at that. That information wasn't even in the NSA's file on the operation. She didn't respond, though, wanting to see what else he had to say.

"I called Max from a pay phone on Bayside Drive. And I know you guys tried to track me. Burkhart would have been stupid not to try."

"You were very good at avoiding CCTVs," she muttered. She'd been the one who'd tried to track whoever had given Max that tip, and the guy had been skilled at evading. Way too good not to have been trained. She'd never gotten a clear shot of his face. Had it been Tucker?

He had started to respond when Cole strode into the room, his expression dark. "You need to see this now," he said to both of them.

Before she could get up, Tucker was there helping her stand. Belatedly she realized she should have protested, but he held her elbow as they followed Cole into the living room, his fingers callused and once again incredibly gentle. Her ankle was just sore now, confirming that she hadn't done any real damage to it.

Brooks and Kane didn't even look up as they entered. She sat on one of the buttercream-colored couches with Tucker sitting on the armrest directly next to her.

"The conservatory and the Capitol building have all been evacuated. . . ." A female reporter was animatedly talking, though her expression was serious as she motioned behind her to an image of the Botanic Garden in D.C. The woman was stating that a small terrorist group had bombed it, but luckily no lives were lost. And right now the FBI's bomb squad was in the process of clearing the place.

"Turn it up," Tucker said.

As Kane increased the volume, pictures of the four of them filled the screen. "The suspects in the botched bombing are all disgraced DEA agents with suspected ties to a Shi'a terrorist group operating . . ."

Karen's eyes widened as she watched and listened

as the reporter continued, showing a video of Kane and Brooks at the conservatory. It looked as if they were planting bombs. Karen knew that videos could be faked, but from the way the men were moving in and out of the conservatory, she doubted someone had faked them actually being there.

"Motherfucker," Kane growled.

Brooks was silent, but his expression was murderous.

"We were there two weeks ago," Kane said, drawing everyone's attention. All his focus was on Tucker, though. "That footage of us is real. We were there, but that shit with us planting the bombs is fucking fake." The man was practically vibrating with each word, the rage in him vivid.

"I know it's fake." Tucker's voice was quiet but seemed to have an effect on the other man, who calmed a fraction. "Why were you there?"

"Anonymous tip that some shit was going down and they wanted us to get eyes on the place. We used our credentials to bypass security. All standard. I'll give you the rundown later."

"They're saying we planted those bombs a couple hours ago," Brooks finally said, his eyes glued to the screen.

"Security sweeps the Garden every night. They're very thorough," Karen said. She knew because of a couple of security issues they'd had in the past. She went to reach for her cell phone but remembered they'd taken it from her. She glanced up at Tucker. "What time is it?"

"Little after ten," he said without looking at his watch.

They'd kidnapped her in the early-morning hours, so unless they'd planted bombs at the conservatory directly before that and . . . "Did they say what kind of detonator was used?"

"No."

"No, of course they wouldn't," she murmured, itching to call her people and get more details. More than anything, she wanted her computer. Then she could start running the information they'd given her and fact-check. She felt naked without her laptop. But she figured that was impossible for now.

Without knowing what kind of detonator was used and the range for the remote, she couldn't be sure the four men with her were innocent of this crime, but as she analyzed the morning's events she started thinking that it was very possible they were being set up.

Especially after that conversation she'd just had with Tucker about Tasev. He knew way too many details about that op; details that hadn't been in the official file. Which he wouldn't have had access to, so it stood to reason he'd been there. On top of that, they'd kidnapped her with a very specific purpose: to talk to Wesley. Tucker had made it clear that he wanted to see him in person but would settle for a phone call. And Tucker had to know Burkhart would send in a team as soon as he found out Tucker had kidnapped Karen. So the men were taking a big risk by kidnapping her simply to talk to her boss. They'd given her files that, in her experience, looked real. She wouldn't know more without being able to cross-reference some of the information, and she couldn't do that without her computer.

"That bombing just happened?" she asked, and realized they were all staring at her. Gah, she sometimes forgot her surroundings when she was thinking.

They all nodded.

It stood to reason they could have an accomplice or accomplices helping them. Someone else who'd set off the bomb even if they hadn't. But that didn't sit right either. Not with the time frame when the bombs had been planted. Tucker seemed way too hands-on to let someone else take over something like that. "It's odd that the news stations have that footage so soon."

Again, they all nodded. "I thought the same thing about Max's murder," she continued. "All that intel the stations had about the Shi'a ties. We didn't even have that intel." So there was no way a news outlet got the drop on them. No, someone was feeding the media bullshit.

With the drone bombing at the Nelson fund-raiser, her team with the NSA had been so focused on security the last two days that she hadn't thought much about the circumstances of Max's murder since then, but it bothered her. She looked at Tucker again. "You guys are definitely being set up and they've got to have government ties. If what you've told me is true and your clearances have been revoked, it's someone in the DEA. But this is bigger than one person. Planting bombs, sending out intel like this to news stations, sending a team of hit men after you guys . . ." She shook her head, trailing off.

She wasn't certain she believed them, but . . . her gut told her they were telling the truth.

# Chapter 7

Salad bar: an informal reference to the service ribbons
found on a military uniform.

"Who at the DEA has the access to revoke your
clearances before all this happened?" Karen
asked, her green eyes focused and intense.

Tucker glanced at the others before looking back at
her. It sounded as if she might believe them, but he
wouldn't bet on it just yet. "We've come up with a list
of names."

She nodded and he could practically see the gears
turning in her head. It shouldn't be so sexy, but she did
this thing where she bit her bottom lip and concen-
trated so hard it was clear that no one else existed while
she was deep in thought. She'd done it multiple times
over the past hour when she was reading their files. He
wondered what it would be like to gently sink his own
teeth into that full lower lip. "That's good. They'll also
have to have the sort of clearance to know who your
team is. From what you've said, not many people have
that kind of clearance, right?"

He nodded and the others murmured in agreement.

"Setting you guys up for treason is a huge undertaking, so whatever the reason behind all this is, there will be a personal thread. I'm guessing you guys were picked for a reason. That reason could be Max, so have you added anyone who might have a grudge against you or Max personally? Maybe one or all of you . . . I don't know the complete scope of your job, but someone who got passed up for a promotion, someone who didn't make your team, whatever. If not against you guys, then definitely Max. Wanted his job or maybe not something so obvious, but . . ." She made a frustrated sound. "There's a reason you four were picked, and once I have all the names, we can run financials. Because something like this is always about money." She snorted, the sound so irreverent it made him smile. "I might be wrong, but even when people try to dress up things under the guise of revenge or religion or whatever, the bottom line tends to be about money."

"You believe us, then?" Cole asked before Tucker could.

She scrunched her nose, the action far too adorable and something he shouldn't be noticing. But it was hard not to be aware of this woman on the most basic level. She'd been kidnapped but had remained cool under pressure. She'd been afraid but hadn't let the reaction rule her. She'd been smart enough to escape, though only temporarily. And okay, yeah, she was gorgeous. Since they'd taken her when she was out jogging, she didn't have a scrap of makeup on and she was stunning without any enhancements. Big green eyes dominated her face, and over the past hour while she'd been reading their files he hadn't been able to take his eyes off her. Or stop fantasizing about what it would be like to run his hands through her long auburn hair—

"I'm not sure yet," she said, her words cutting off his train of thought, which was just as well. "I mean, if you guys were terrorists I don't know why you'd be sticking around the country or trying to get a phone conference with my boss. Well, there are reasons I could think of, but . . ." She shrugged. "From what the news has said so far, there was no loss of life at the Botanic Garden and something tells me that if you guys had set that place up to blow, there would be massive casualties."

"That's a fucked-up compliment," Tucker said.

To his surprise the ghost of a smile teased her lips. "You know what I mean."

Yeah, he did. "So you'll call Burkhart for us?"

She nodded.

"After we talk to him we'll let you go," he said, the promise out before he could stop himself. "You can take all our information and run with it."

The room went silent, Karen's eyes widening and his team just watching him. He gave his men a hard look. "We took her to get Burkhart's attention. He'll answer when we call this time." And if they set up a meeting with Burkhart, the guy would think it was a trap. Which meant there was a chance Karen might get hurt. That wasn't acceptable.

"Works for me," Kane said first with the others quickly agreeing. None of them had wanted to go this route in the first place, but they'd been backed into a corner.

Karen watched him as if she wasn't sure she believed him but nodded. "So, what happens now?"

"We're going to call Burkhart with your phone." Her eyes widened but she didn't respond. Probably because she was thinking the NSA would be able to trace them in seconds. Under normal circumstances they would, but not today. "I'm going to lay out everything that's happened to us and ask for his help. We've got the fingerprints of the men who came after us and a list of potential corrupt DEA agents and employees. We haven't been able to look at their financials, but that should be child's play for the NSA. And all this should be enough for him to help us figure out who's behind whatever this mess is."

There was a trace of fear in Karen's eyes that tore at him, but he ignored it. She was probably wondering if they planned to call Burkhart and hurt her with him listening in exchange for whatever demands she imagined they had.

When she didn't respond, Tucker stood and headed for the back bedroom. They'd stored their electronics and unloaded weapons in the room, including a heavily encrypted laptop and her cell phone. He knew the second they put her battery back in they ran the risk of being tracked. Unlike on television where it took two minutes or some set amount of time to track a number as long as someone was on the line, that was bullshit.

If a phone had its battery in, the FBI or NSA or whoever could remotely route in to it and use it as a microphone. Theoretically, of course, since that was illegal as hell. As far as tracking her phone went, the NSA would be able to triangulate its location using nearby cell towers, since she'd turned off the internal locator—and he'd checked.

So they had to make that task, if not impossible, really difficult for the NSA. At least long enough to make the call and get the hell out of here undetected. His team was all former military and skilled when it came to infiltrating corrupt organizations and blending in to whatever surroundings they needed to. They wouldn't have been part of Max's team otherwise. And they were all more than competent when it came to technology, but none of them were hackers. Thankfully they'd learned enough over the years to block calls when they needed to.

He quickly turned on the computer, then activated the program necessary before plugging her phone into it with a USB cable. Finally he put the battery in and turned it on.

Back in the living room Karen was watching the news with the others. She stiffened when she saw him, her body pulling taut with apprehension as he set the computer and phone on the coffee table.

"Tuck," Cole said, a wealth of meaning in that one word.

Tucker looked at his friend and shrugged. They'd worked together for well over a decade, long before they'd joined the DEA together. They'd gone through boot camp in the Corps together. They practically read each other's minds. Right now they were taking a huge risk. Too many things could go wrong. The encryption on the phone might not work or Karen could sell them out. She might not know exactly where they were, but she'd know how long they'd traveled and for all they knew she'd figured out the location. That last part was doubtful, but this call was still a risk. She could blurt out enough information to be dangerous. But not making the contact with Burkhart was a bigger risk. "We've gotta do this."

He made the call and wasn't surprised when Burkhart picked up on the first ring. "Karen?" His tone was cautious.

"I'm here," she said, her eyes on Tucker. "I'm sitting with Tucker Pankov, Cole Erickson, Paxton Brooks, and Forest Kane."

There was a beat of silence. "Are you hurt?" he asked, unable to hide the tremble of rage in his voice.

"No, I'm fine. They . . . approached me this morning about an issue concerning Max's death. I just saw the news and, Wesley, I think there's a possibility they're being set up."

"Whoever's in charge, talk." A sharp, deadly order from a man used to being in complete control.

Burkhart had to hate that he wasn't in control at the moment and Tucker hated that he was the one who'd taken it away. It sure as hell wasn't going to make the guy easier to work with. "This is Tucker Pankov. I sent you a message a couple days ago about Max's murder."

"Grisha."

"Yeah."

"You want to meet with me."

"Yes. Or we can send you what we've got via messenger. Someone in the DEA is setting us up and we don't know why. The day Max was killed, hitters were sent to each of our residences. Our very *private* residences." Their real homes weren't even listed with HR. Not that it would be difficult for someone in the agency to find if they tried hard enough. Clearly. "We don't know why, but we have the fingerprints of the hitters." He wasn't going to come out and say the men were dead, but Burkhart must know what he meant. "Then our clearances were revoked. We don't know by who, but our homes are being watched. After the shit on the news this morning, it's clear someone wants to discredit us. Max trusted you, and at this point you're our only resource." And if he wouldn't help they'd go deep into hiding, completely off the grid. But only as a last resort. Men like them didn't run. Tucker wasn't going to let some strangers steal his life.

"You think kidnapping one of my people is going to ingratiate you?"

"They didn't kidnap me," Karen said before he could respond.

All four of them looked at her in surprise. Wesley ignored her as he continued. "The four of you will meet with me and bring Karen. Unharmed. Bring all the documentation you have and we'll try to help you. If she's hurt in any way, you'll regret being born." A sincere promise.

"Wesley—" Karen started.

"Understood," Tucker said, knowing that Burkhart wouldn't believe anything she said right now. He would think she was under duress and he couldn't blame the guy. "We can meet you in two hours." He named a location that was public enough but difficult to set up an ambush at.

Burkhart snorted and named another location. An abandoned warehouse. Tucker knew he'd be walking into a trap but didn't see another choice. He wasn't going to play hardball with the only man who could help them. "We'll come unarmed and send Karen in first. And you fucking owe me for Tasev. You owe me twice for him." Because of the tip that stopped the poisoning of a water supply that could have killed tens of thousands and because of his help with the female agent. "And you know as well as I do that Max wasn't murdered by some Shi'a group. Whatever the fuck you do to us, we want justice for his death. I know you do too."

Burkhart was silent for a long moment. "Be there in two hours. Karen's unharmed or you're all dead."

The line disconnected and he nodded at his guys. They were already packed and ready to go, so he didn't need to order them to gear up. "The three of you will relocate to destination delta. Stay there until you receive orders from me."

"Fuck that," Cole snapped. "We're not leaving you to—"

"You are and you will. In case things don't play out the right way, there's no sense in all of us going down.

You three will go to ground until I check in. That's an order," he said quietly, looking at all of them.

Their expressions were mutinous, especially Cole's, but in the end they all nodded and filed out of the room.

He glanced at Karen as he started packing up the computer. They needed to get going. "Why'd you lie for us?"

Her expression softened and she lifted her shoulder a fraction. "Maybe I'm stupid, but I believe you guys. You're clearly walking into a trap and you're going anyway. After the news it would make more sense for all of you to disappear. Or if you had some other nefarious plan, it would have made more sense to use me as a bargaining chip. I analyze bad situations every single day, and this whole thing just feels wrong."

"Nefarious plan?" he asked, hiding a smile.

She rolled her eyes. "Whatever."

"You're not stupid, and I'm letting you go before I meet Burkhart." He didn't doubt the NSA would be careful in apprehending him, but things went wrong sometimes and he wouldn't risk it with Karen. He'd give her enough time to contact Burkhart so the NSA knew she was safe and unharmed before they met with him.

Standing, she blinked in surprise. "You're serious."

"Yep." Now that he had Burkhart's attention, he was sending all the info they'd compiled to the man's e-mail.

"So if I wanted to walk out the front door, I could."

He shrugged. "You wouldn't get far on that ankle,

and I'm not letting you contact him before my team is long gone from this house, but yeah, you're free. I'm going to bring you into D.C. and let you go, okay?"

Her lips curved up a fraction. "Okay."

He wasn't certain anything would ever be okay again, but he was going to do his best to find Max's killer and clear his and his teammates' names. If he couldn't clear their names, he at least wanted his teammates out of the way and safe. They didn't deserve to go to prison.

Wesley buzzed Elliott on his phone. "My office, now." They hadn't been able to run a trace on the call from Karen's phone, which frustrated but didn't surprise him.

Selene watched him from her seat across his desk, curiosity in her pale gaze. "You're not calling the DEA about this?"

He was still undecided. He'd read Pankov's real file and the guy was a patriot. Had a freaking salad bar of military medals and awards listed on his jacket. The other three were the same as Pankov. And Max had loved those four men. That held weight with Wesley. "We tell no one about this yet."

"She sounded okay," Selene said, clearly trying to make him feel better.

"She could have been under duress." God, Wesley couldn't even think about Karen being hurt. After the bombing at the Botanic Garden, all the intelligence agencies had been sent files on the four men. The four men apparently holding his analyst captive. Everyone was coordinating to get a lead on the men, to find their location. As of now he knew that the DEA and FBI were officially tearing apart the men's houses.

"True." She didn't say more, but he guessed Selene was thinking about how Tucker Pankov, aka Grisha, had helped her during an important op. "What about that e-mail he sent you?"

Before he could respond, there was a knock on his office door. "Enter," he said.

Elliott stepped inside, the tall, lanky man shoving his hands in his pockets. He nodded once at Selene as he hovered near the door.

"You can shut the door," Wesley said quietly.

"Uh, sure. Am I in trouble? I'm still trying to triangulate that call—"

"You're not in trouble. What else are you working on right now?"

He perched on the edge of the chair next to Selene. "I've still got programs running info on the documented vehicles from the parking garage this morning, but I'm working on a—"

Wesley held up a hand, not needing a rambling explanation, and he knew that was where this was headed. "Hand it off to someone else. I need you to run the financials of Tucker Pankov, Cole Erickson, Paxton Brooks, and Forest Kane."

"The bombers from this morning?"

Wesley glanced at Selene, then back at the analyst. "I don't know that they're what the media are saying. I need all the info you can gather on them. More than the stuff in their files." He cleared his throat. "I also need you to run the information on five other names. All DEA employees, and I need you to do it covertly. They can't know we're looking into them. If they have an offshore account, if they're having an affair, I want to know about it. Any cases they worked on with Max Southers, flag for me. No detail is too small."

Elliott nodded slowly. "I might have to break some privacy laws."

"Do what you have to. I'll take the heat if it comes down to it, but you know how to cover your tracks." None of this would be on the record. Wesley just needed info so he could start unraveling this mess.

At that Elliott relaxed and ran a hand over the zigzag pattern of tight, short braids on his head. A Princeton graduate, he was a little eccentric and fit right in with the team Wesley ran. "Am I doing this alone?"

"You want a partner?"

"Depends on how fast you want the info and which group you want me to focus on more."

That was another thing Wesley liked about the guy. He admitted when he needed assistance. For Elliott it was about getting the job done, not about accolades.

Both groups were important, but Wesley needed the info on the four men who'd taken Karen—and he sure as hell didn't believe she hadn't been kidnapped despite what she'd said. "Pull in a partner. Your choice but let me know who and make sure they know this stays between us. You focus on the first four. Time is critical on this. You've got one hour to give me a detailed report."

Elliott was gone in seconds. Before the door had clicked shut behind him, Wesley was calling Ortiz. He had to set up a team long before Pankov and his guys showed up at that warehouse.

"Should I tell Detective Portillo about this?" Selene asked as the phone rang in Wesley's hand.

Wesley paused, then shook his head. "No. The local PD has Karen's picture. If someone sees her they'll contact you. I don't want to publicly announce she's with them." Because if Pankov was telling the truth and he and his guys had been set up by dirty DEA agents, he didn't want Karen becoming collateral damage.

# Chapter 8

Redacted: text that has been removed or obscured from a file before public viewing. Often seen in classified texts.

"Here," Tucker said, handing Karen the switchblade he'd taken from her that morning.

Surprised, she took it and slid it into her jacket pocket. They were in yet another vehicle, this time a ten-year-old truck with tinted windows. There had been multiple hidden vehicles at that property. "You trust me not to stab you?"

He snorted and shot her a sideways glance. "You could try." It wasn't exactly arrogance in his tone, but a certainty of his abilities.

A part of her she didn't want to acknowledge thought that certainty was sexy. But being aware of Tucker like that seemed insane, even if she knew it was just biological. Still, it was hard to deny he was a very compelling man. "If I hadn't seen you in action, I might think you were crazy to give me this."

He was silent a moment, glancing in the rearview

mirror as they neared an exit. They'd been driving mostly in silence for the last hour and she could sense the tension rolling off him. "Who's Clint?" he asked, surprising her.

At the mention of her brother's name, she stiffened. "How do you know that name?"

"It's on the blade."

Of course he would have noticed; she wasn't thinking. She immediately settled back against the seat. Her brother had had the handle engraved. "Right. Ah, my brother. He died in Afghanistan."

At that, Tucker looked at her again, this time with compassion in those blue eyes. She was starting to be able to read his expressions, however subtle. While he'd first scared the hell out of her, now that she knew who he really was, it was easier to relax around him.

He was still intense and his big size was a little intimidating, but she wasn't scared of him anymore. Maybe that made her naive, but he'd gone out of his way to make her feel at ease. And there was that part of her she was trying so hard not to be aware of that was . . . very curious about Tucker in a purely feminine sense.

"I lost a lot of friends over there. I'm sorry," he said quietly.

She nodded, not sure what else to say. Clint had been the only family she had—the only family that mattered anyway—so when she talked about him it tugged open old wounds. Right now she was grateful she had "family" looking for her even if Tucker would be letting her go. With her degree she could have taken any number of jobs, but she'd chosen to work for Wesley because, like her brother, she believed in protecting her country. Today she knew without a doubt that she'd made the best decision because Wesley and her friends were truly more than just coworkers.

"What branch were you in?" It hadn't been in the file he'd given her. Or maybe it had, but some information had been redacted.

He shot her another one of those sideways glances that told her the answer without him saying a word.

"Marines?"

He was half grinning, the action completely softening his face in a way she hadn't expected. "You know it."

"Freaking Marines," she murmured. She worked with a lot of former military types and she could usually tell which branch they'd been. "Cole was too?"

He nodded. "Yeah. We were in boot camp together."

"You guys seem close." She wasn't ashamed to admit that she was information gathering. After this mess she'd be going through multiple debriefings, so learning as much as she could about these men would be important. But even as she had the thought, she knew she wasn't just fishing for information. She wanted to know more about Tucker—and she refused to dig deeper on the why.

"He's like a brother to me."

"A little like a younger brother, I imagine," she said.

Tucker steered toward the next exit. She tried not to

watch how the muscles in his forearms flexed, but he'd shoved his sleeves up and it was difficult not to notice how very male he was. "Why do you say that?"

"The way they all listened to you." The other three men in that cabin were clearly just as trained and intimidating, but when Tucker had given an order, they did what he said.

"You shouldn't jog by yourself so early in the morning," he said suddenly, clearly deciding to ignore her last statement.

The abrupt change in topic jolted her. "So says my kidnapper."

"Exactly. The bear spray and knife are good, but it was too damn early for you to be out by yourself." His frown deepened and he sounded almost protective. "Maybe you should use the gym in your condo instead."

The protective tone made something feminine in her flare to life, but it also annoyed her. "I live in a safe neighborhood and I've never had a problem before. And if it hadn't been a team of trained professionals, I wouldn't have been taken. I could have taken on just you with the bear spray." She didn't need or want advice from anyone. Not when she'd been taking care of herself for a long damn time. No one without training could have gotten away from him and his team this morning.

He made a derisive sound, as if annoyed with her. As if he had a right to be. "We need gas and after this I'm dropping you somewhere very public."

"What?" She knew what he'd told her, but it just seemed so soon. She turned in her seat as he pulled into a nearly deserted gas station. She noticed he'd picked one right before they got into the actual downtown area. Less crowded.

Avoiding her gaze, he nodded. "After I drop you off I assume you'll call Burkhart. I'm going to do the same and just let him pick me up instead of going through a whole clandestine meet at a warehouse."

She bit her bottom lip, feeling irrationally worried about the man who'd kidnapped her that morning. "You shouldn't wait somewhere public, not with the recent broadcast." As she said that, she looked around the gas station, suddenly worried about him being spotted. People were usually so involved in their own lives that they didn't notice others, but Tucker had a distinguished face. Everything about him was hard and intense. The kind of man you wouldn't want to go up against in a fight. The kind of man who was hard to ignore.

"Now I feel even shittier for taking you," he muttered.

She turned back to look at him as he stopped in front of a pump and turned off the engine. "Why? I mean, yeah, you *should* feel bad for kidnapping me, but why do you feel worse?"

Instead of answering, he just gave her a long, hard look that *might* have had a hint of desire in it before he grabbed a ball cap and got out of the truck. She wasn't exactly sure what was behind that look, but it warmed her from the inside out. Frowning, she sat back against the seat and did what she always did: she started analyzing her strange reaction. She couldn't be affected by her kidnapper . . . could she?

Almost against her will, she watched him head inside the store. Probably to pay in cash. With a ball cap, sunglasses, and the thick scarf around his neck, he was hiding most of his face. He certainly was trusting her not to run off. If she was going to flee, now was the time. She was starting to trust him and that made her feel she was being incredibly stupid. The same kind of stupid woman her mother had been. So what if he'd been in the Marines like her brother? And so what if he'd been a nice kidnapper? He was still her freaking kidnapper.

God, it was as if she already had Stockholm syndrome. She didn't actually believe he'd kill her instead of dropping her somewhere, but she couldn't risk staying. With shaking hands, she unstrapped her seat belt and slid across to the driver's side. Her side faced the big window front of the store and she wanted all the cover she could get. He'd taken the keys, of course, and since she had no idea how to hot-wire a vehicle, she kept moving, just barely opening the door and easing out. She wasn't familiar with this neighborhood, but it couldn't be that hard to find a pay phone or borrow someone's cell phone.

With her heart racing, she watched Tucker inside the store. He wasn't even looking outside. Which seemed weird. It was as if he was intentionally turning his back to her. That couldn't be right, though, unless he wanted her to run.

Taking a deep breath, she popped up from her position hiding behind the truck and moved quickly to the side of the store. From there, she could see the rest of the street. A strip of stores lined either side of the street. There was even a Starbucks.

Without looking back she started running. Her legs strained, her breath sawing in and out as she pushed forward full speed. Her ankle twinged each time her foot hit the pavement, but she ignored the pain. A quick glance over her shoulder showed that no one was following her. Still, she didn't allow a fraction of relief to slide through her. Not yet. Not until she was completely free.

The cold air burned her lungs, icy and cutting. As she neared the Starbucks and saw multiple people inside, some on their laptops, others on their tablets, and even some just drinking coffee and chatting with friends, her surroundings felt almost surreal. She slowed her pace so she didn't look quite as manic.

She'd been kidnapped this morning, yet here she was, running up to a coffee shop as if she didn't have a care in the world. Shoving her trembling hands into her pockets, she crossed the parking lot. As she reached the entrance, she nearly jumped out of her skin at the sound of her name.

"Karen?" a man called out.

Fearing that it was Tucker, she turned to find a policeman getting out of an unmarked Explorer. He was in full uniform, though, clearly a patrolman. How did this guy know her name? Before the thought had formed, she realized Wesley must have filed a missing person report. It would certainly make sense.

He had a cell phone in his hand and looked at the screen, then her. Yep, he was looking at her picture. "Karen Stafford?"

Throat tight, she nodded and stepped back from the glass door. Clearing her throat, she nodded. "I'm Karen."

"Have you been injured?"

"I'm okay." Nervously she glanced around, expecting Tucker to jump out of nowhere. But deep down she figured he'd let her go. There was no way he'd have just let her escape like that. He was too trained and too smart. And he'd let her have her knife back. It had almost felt like a peace offering. Or maybe that was wishful thinking.

Watching her carefully, the man nodded. "Do you know who Selene Marks is?"

Marks was one of Selene's aliases, so Karen nodded. "Yes, we work together."

"Good. Can you please come stand by my car? I have instructions to call her." His tone was kind, but he wasn't asking, he was definitely ordering.

Nodding, Karen did as he said. He pulled out his radio and made a call to his station, calling for backup.

She listened as he finished the call and quickly made another one. Closing her eyes, she leaned against the side of the Explorer and massaged her temple. Too many conflicting emotions hummed through her.

Her eyes snapped open at a very familiar voice. "Drop the phone or I put a bullet in you."

She pushed up from the vehicle.

Tucker stood behind the cop, a gun trained on the back of the man's head. The cop's jaw was clenched tight, but he let the phone fall from his fingers. It clattered against the sidewalk. Moving with a lethal efficiency, Tucker removed the guy's radio, gun, pepper spray, and even his backup weapon in a matter of seconds.

She barely had time to think, he moved so fast.

"Karen, open the driver's door," he ordered without looking at her.

His face was a mask of hard, intimidating lines. "Don't hurt him," she rasped out.

"I'm not going to. Open the damn door."

With shaking hands, she did.

"Get in," he said softly to the patrolman.

It was clear the other man had to fight his instincts. "Don't be stupid. No one's been hurt. Just let the woman go."

Tucker ignored him and gave the guy his own cuffs. "Secure yourself to the steering wheel. *Now*," he ordered when the guy paused a fraction too long.

As soon as he did it, Tucker slammed the door shut and reached for her. She flinched away from him, not wanting his hands on her. She was so stupid for thinking he'd let her go, that he'd just *let* her run away. No, he'd been planning to kill her or worse all along.

Iciness slid down her spine, making it difficult to breathe, to think.

"Damn it, Karen, the gun's not fucking loaded," he snapped, frustration more than anything in his voice as he holstered his weapon out of sight.

His words shook her out of her near panic. "What?"

He grabbed her arm and shot a look over at the Starbucks. "We need to get the hell out of here. We're going to have more company than just cops soon. Shit," he muttered, practically dragging her with him until they reached the truck on the opposite side of the parking lot. He opened the passenger door and, not waiting to see if she got in, raced around to the other side.

She contemplated running again, but a glance over her shoulder showed a Starbucks full of people staring out the window at them in horror. Most of them were on their phones, probably calling the police. What if she ran and they got caught in the cross fire? Tucker might have said the gun wasn't loaded, but he was a kidnapper. He could easily be lying.

She jumped in as he started the engine.

"I'm sorry, Karen. I was letting you go but saw that fucking cop. I doubt he's dirty, but if someone with the DEA is monitoring their transmissions, they might overhear I took you." He made another snarl of frustration as he peeled out of the parking lot. "You can't trust anyone but your own people at this point, not even the local PD. If someone other than the NSA gets wind that I took you, you could be a target. That's why I wanted to drop you off somewhere," he said, turning into a nearby parking lot to a hardware store. It was a couple of blocks over and well out of sight of the Starbucks.

He parked near the parking lot exit, but left the truck running. "I wasn't lying—the gun's not loaded." He slid it across to her as he pulled a magazine out of his jacket pocket, which he also handed to her. Next came a cell phone—her cell phone. Then her battery. "I figured you'd find someone to help you and borrow a phone, but I had to be sure. I'm sorry about back there, but I need you safe. Take the pistol, your phone, and this truck and start driving. You'll need to put the battery in and call, but your people will pick you up soon, no doubt."

Holy hell, she hadn't been wrong about him. He was letting her go. She should be elated, but . . . "What are you going to do?"

He shrugged and glanced out in the parking lot, his hand already on the door handle. "Find another vehicle and get in touch with Burkhart. With the locals now involved, I definitely don't want you near me."

She'd started to respond when sirens blared in the distance. They were close already. That seemed so fast. Fear for his safety clawed at her. "Tucker, you just pulled a gun on a cop, you're apparently wanted for kidnapping me, and all law enforcement agencies think you're a terrorist. You can't . . . you can't head out on foot here." Karen knew how things worked. The local PD wouldn't be opposed to using lethal force against someone who'd just pulled a gun on one of their own and who had allegedly bombed the Botanic Garden, a place where kids frequented daily. Tucker might be skilled, but he wasn't freaking bulletproof. "You have a better chance of staying alive if you have me with you. They're not going to open fire on you when you have a hostage. Just drive and we'll call Wesley from a secure place so he can pick us both up." When he started to argue, she shook her head. "I'm not leaving you out here to get shot by the fucking cops! I . . . all the evidence suggests you're being set up and I'm going to help."

His jaw was clenched tight, but he kicked the truck into reverse anyway.

"And I'm keeping this gun." She moved it into her lap, the heavy weight giving her comfort. She might be just an analyst, but everyone at the agency put in hours of weapons training. "You were really letting me go, huh?"

He snorted and pulled out what was definitely a burner phone. "Cole might be distracted by a beautiful face, but I'm not," he murmured, dialing a number. "I figured you'd run at the gas station, so I gave you a window." Before she could respond, he said, "Hey, Mom. I . . . I know, I know." His voice was softer than she'd ever heard it. "Listen, whatever you see on the news, it's all lies. Yeah, I know you believe me. You and Dad need to go stay somewhere safe. . . . You know where. I'll explain more. . . ."

Hating that she was overhearing such a private conversation, Karen turned and looked out the window. As she heard Tucker reassure his mom that everything would be okay, she decided then and there that her gut instinct about this man had been spot-on. He might have kidnapped her, but his motives were justified and he'd oddly been looking out for her when he dragged her away from the police officer.

She might be making a huge mistake by staying with him, but it didn't feel that way.

Sweat trickled down his spine as his fingers flew across the keyboard, the clacking overpronounced in the quiet office. He'd infiltrated an unused room at the DEA for his own purposes, using the credentials of an agent on maternity leave. Since he was familiar with the layout of the building it had been easy enough to avoid security cameras so that no one could trace this back to him. Well, maybe not easy, but doable. All systems had flaws and he had no problem capitalizing on a vulnerability. The DEA deserved this for being too cheap and lazy to run a diagnostic of their safety measures this year.

He was taking a huge risk, but the payoff would be worth it. He'd spent years slaving away for an organization that didn't appreciate him. Had never appreciated all his hard work. After that asshole Max Southers had passed him up for yet another promotion, he was done kissing ass and playing politics.

It didn't matter if he did. He never got ahead anyway. Just because he didn't have military experience didn't mean he wasn't qualified, but for some reason it was like an invisible black mark on his record. Keeping him out of certain social circles. He'd graduated summa cum laude from a top university with a bachelor's in criminal justice, had gone on to get his master's, and had an incredible success rate with closing his cases.

But Max Southers hadn't cared about any of that. The guy had had it out for him for some reason. Arrogant fucker. Now he was dead and his precious fucking team were all going to die too. Because there was no way the DEA or any other law enforcement agency would let their "treasonous" actions go unpunished. It was sweet, ironic justice that men like Pankov would be accused of treason when they were such obnoxious patriots. They all thought they were better than him.

They were wrong.

When Hillenbrand had originally approached him, he was suspicious that it had been a trap. That maybe someone at the DEA had suspected his discontentment or even knew about some of his backdoor dealings. So he'd been careful, but Hillenbrand wanted change in this country, just as he did. Maybe he wasn't as extremist as Hillenbrand or his cronies, but he liked the money he was getting paid. And from what he could tell, Hillenbrand was more in this for the money than the men he worked with too.

And if everything went according to plan, there'd be a lot more. So if he had to take some risks at work, it was worth it for the payoff. As he linked an offshore bank account to one of Cole Erickson's accounts, he smiled to himself. He was making sure there was a clear trail incriminating all four men, but it couldn't be too obvious.

When his phone buzzed in his pocket, he jumped, then cursed himself. He glanced at the screen, and a shot of adrenaline slammed through him as he read the alert. Tucker Pankov's parents had just received a phone call from a number with a D.C. area code. He stopped what he was doing and called Hillenbrand.

"Yeah?" he answered on the first ring.

"I might have a hit on one of the targets."

"That's good because one of them was just spotted in fucking D.C.," the man snarled. "Pankov took down a cop."

"He killed someone?" That didn't sound right.

"No, but he's got a woman with him. Sounds as if he's kidnapped her. I'm not sure what's going on." His tone made it clear that was why he was so angry. Hillenbrand liked to be in control of everything.

"Someone just called Pankov's parents. The number's got a D.C. area code. I don't recognize it. Possibly a burner. I can try to get someone here to trace it, but there will be a record of—"

"My guy will do it," Hillenbrand snapped.

He rattled off the number and let out a huff of annoyance when Hillenbrand just hung up. If rudeness was all he had to deal with for such a high payday, then he could deal with it. At this point he could deal with anything because very soon he'd be quitting his job and retiring somewhere warm.

# Chapter 9

Gun: term for a mortar or artillery piece. Military or
former military personnel don't use it to describe a
pistol or rifle. Instead they often use the term "weapon."

Rayford took a sip of his scotch, not caring that it
was early afternoon. He was ready to drink half of
Hillenbrand's bottle as he watched that grungy hacker,
Gary, work on triangulating a cell phone number.

"If the local police are involved, shouldn't we just
give them the info? Anonymously or something?" Rayford asked, glad his voice didn't shake. This was a little
too hands-on for him.

Hillenbrand shot him a derisive look before turning
back to watch Gary work. "It's better if we kill Pankov
outright. If he gets brought in for questioning, who
knows what he'll say? And we don't know who that
woman is either."

"Didn't your contact say she'd been kidnapped?"
Who cared who she was? Hillenbrand seemed to have
contacts everywhere, including someone in administration he'd paid off at the D.C. Police Department.

"Yes, and she was flagged as a priority even though she'd only been missing for a few hours. My contact knows literally nothing else about her. That's not good. Since it's doubtful Pankov and his men randomly kidnapped a woman, she must be important to them somehow. Unfortunately her name is common enough it's been hard to find out who she is."

"You think Pankov's men are with him?"

Hillenbrand's jaw clenched, but he didn't spare him another glance. "How the fuck do I know? They weren't reported as being seen."

"What if . . ." Rayford cleared his throat, wondering if he'd been a fool to get involved in all this. Everything had seemed so clear at the outset. Even after the bombing of the Nelson fund-raiser, he'd still been sure of his decision. Now it felt as if he was getting his hands too dirty. For a man who'd spent his life avoiding scandal of any kind, this was making him edgy. Not to mention that they'd pissed off four very trained and deadly men—men who'd killed or done something to the hitters Hillenbrand had sent after them. "What if he does get brought in alive? Him or the others? What if they're able to prove they weren't involved with the bombing at the Garden? Or what if—"

"Enough," Hillenbrand gritted out. "If that happens I have a backup plan."

Rayford blinked. "Backup plan?"

Hillenbrand let out an exasperated sigh, then jerked his head in the direction of the door. They were still in the entertainment room of his townhome. Rayford followed him, stopping when Hillenbrand did. Hillenbrand glanced over at Gary, who was still typing away like a man possessed. Rayford doubted the guy was even aware of them at this point, but he guessed Hillenbrand didn't want to disturb the hacker.

"Our DEA contact is our fall guy if things go south, so stop worrying. I picked him for a reason."

"Seriously?" He couldn't even hide his surprise.

Hillenbrand gave a sharp nod, as if annoyed at being questioned. "He's disgruntled and I have proof that he's taken kickbacks before. He was such an easy mark. That's how I knew to approach him in the first place. He's already gotten his hands dirty before and he had issues with Southers. Not exactly public knowledge, but his beef with Southers was known enough within the right circles at the DEA. He's the perfect scapegoat if we need one."

Some of Rayford's fear eased, but if the DEA agent took the fall for setting up the others, it would screw up their ultimate plan of blaming the Shi'a terrorist group and starting another war in the Middle East. Now that the goal was finally within reach, he wanted it too bad. Wanted all the money he'd make with Hillenbrand's contracts and the power his own boss would gain. Eventually he planned to tell his boss what he'd done, but Rayford needed to give him deniability for now. "What about our end game?"

"We"—he nodded in Gary's direction—"have already linked him to the same group we linked the others to. It'll look like he wanted to implicate four innocent men he worked with but still make sure his terrorist organization took the credit. So we still get what we want in the end."

The Iran-based Shi'as would be blamed and Hillenbrand and Rayford's candidate for president could start a war—as soon as he took office, of course. Rayford nodded, breathing easier. It bothered him that Hillenbrand was just telling him this now. If the other man could set up his own contact, who was to say he wouldn't try to set up Rayford? But that wouldn't make sense, not when Rayford was linked to the next potential president. And not when Rayford was indirectly linked to Hillenbrand's own company.

Even so, Rayford realized he needed to pay attention to everything now, to have a backup plan of his own. Damn it, he needed dirt on Hillenbrand. Dirt completely unconnected to the drone theft and subsequent bombing. Something not connected to him; something he could use against the guy if he ever got backed against a wall. Shelving those thoughts for now, he had started to respond when Gary called out.

"Got him!" His tone was smug as he linked the screen from his laptop to the screen on the wall. "I'm not sure how long he'll have that phone, but that's where he is at this moment."

Hillenbrand was already on one of his own burner phones, calling someone. The tone of the conversation made it clear the man on the other end was a hired mercenary. Rayford knew the guy had men like that on his payroll—clearly, since he'd sent a team after Pankov and his men—but it still made him uncomfortable knowing Hillenbrand had resources like that at his disposal.

When Hillenbrand hung up, his grin was like the Cheshire Cat's. That hint of madness was back, just a glint in his eyes that made Rayford want to finish the rest of the scotch bottle in one sitting. He kept his emotions locked down, though. Hillenbrand couldn't even have a hint that Rayford was uncomfortable around him. He just needed to remain calm and ride this thing out. In the end they'd all get what they wanted: money and power.

"So?" he asked, eyebrows raised when his partner didn't say anything.

Hillenbrand's eyes gleamed just a bit brighter as he said, "I've got guys stationed all over the city and someone on Pankov and the woman now. My contact's only a block away from them. Going to kill the woman too just in case."

Tucker handed the phone he'd been using to Karen. "Go ahead and call Burkhart now. He'll have heard from the locals that you've been spotted. If your people are as good as I think, they'll have tagged our location by now anyway."

Her lips pulled up a fraction and he wished he could see her smile for real. She was already so beautiful, he knew she'd be even more stunning when she smiled. Not that he should be noticing that anyway. There was no way in hell he'd ever have a chance with her, especially not after he'd kidnapped her by way of meeting. "If they haven't yet, they will soon. There are just too many ways to track us now that we're in D.C. I promise Wesley will give you a fair shot. He'll be annoyed it's just you and not your team, but— What's that guy doing?"

Tucker was pulling through a four-way stop when an SUV's engine suddenly gunned before barreling at them. Cursing, he pressed on the accelerator, trying to get out of the way. He zoomed through the intersection, but the SUV clipped the back bumper of the truck.

Karen let out a short yelp as the truck did a three-sixty. Heart in his throat, Tucker held the steering wheel firmly as the vehicle spun on the icy roads. He eased his foot off the gas, not wanting the brakes to lock up. He'd taken enough defensive driving classes to—

Metal crunched as the SUV rammed into the driver's side, sending them skidding across the intersection and slamming into a stop sign. He'd disabled the airbags, as he always did on an op, so at least they didn't deploy. He couldn't risk one slamming him in the face and stunning him or making it impossible to get to his weapon if he was being attacked. Tensing at the impact, he unstrapped his seat belt and jumped across into Karen's side of the vehicle. His adrenaline was pumping so hard now he barely felt a thing.

Her eyes were wide with fear, but at least she wasn't panicking and she didn't look injured. He'd worry about that later. First, he had to eliminate this threat.

Tucker grabbed the pistol from her and slid the magazine in as a barrage of bullets hit the driver's-side door and window. The old truck had bullet-resistant windows and was armored, but he didn't know what kind of firepower their attacker—or attackers—had. He shoved her onto the floorboards, using his body to cover her.

"Stay put, Karen. This truck is armored. You'll be safe for now. And call Burkhart." He tried to look through the driver's-side window, but the glass was spidering out from the impact of the bullets and probably the crash. Same with the windshield.

He needed to get a visual on their attacker. Which meant getting out of the fucking vehicle. He hated leaving her, but he had to keep Karen safe. He'd dragged her into this mess and he'd be damned if she got injured or worse because of him. He knew one thing: this wasn't the cops and it wasn't the NSA. Neither would open fire on them like this, not with Karen in the truck with him. This was a brazen attack in broad daylight. Had to be the same asshole—or more likely assholes—who'd set up his team.

She was shaking and her ivory skin had gone a grayish color, but she nodded. "I'll make the call."

The firing had stopped, probably because the shooter realized the truck was armored. Which gave Tucker a small window to get outside and go on the offensive.

There was no one waiting to ambush him on the passenger side, so he opened the door and dropped down, his boots thudding faintly against the sidewalk. They were on a quiet street in a residential area, which pissed him off even more about this attack. He'd just seen a traffic sign for a school zone. It hadn't been flashing and he was certain it was too early for kids to be getting out of school, but coming after him and Karen in a school zone made him want to rip apart whoever was after them even more than he already did.

It was still silent, so he ducked down and looked under the truck. He spotted only one set of feet. Men's boots. The guy was cautiously moving toward Tucker's truck. Bold, to do it without cover. Maybe the shooter thought he and Karen had been knocked out during the accident. He was about to find out how very wrong he was.

Closer, closer, closer— He fired at the man's ankles, hitting first the left, then the right. Hitting the bone like that would hurt like a motherfucker and prevent him from being able to walk.

The man screamed at the unexpected sharp pain. His bones had probably splintered, the damage vicious. Tucker felt a perverse pleasure at the sound of the guy's agony.

The man lay on the ground on his side, a MAC-10 in one of his hands as he tried to push up. Whoever had trained this guy had done a piss-poor job. This attack was bold, yes, but it was weak.

In a situation like this it was doubtful the shooter

knew who'd hired him, but since there was a possibility he did, Tucker wanted him alive. He had started to move, planning to approach him from the rear of the truck, when the guy suddenly shifted positions, rolling onto his side, weapon clutched tightly in his hand.

The second the man's gaze locked on Tucker's under the truck, Tucker fired, hitting him twice center mass, then once in the head in case he was wearing body armor. Tucker bit back a curse as he stood and scanned his surroundings. There was a vehicle approaching from one of the side streets. *Shit, shit, shit.*

It was either a civilian or law enforcement—or backup for this guy. None of those options were good. The only thing on Tucker's side was the damn cold weather. No one was out walking their dog or pushing a stroller in this temperature.

Moving quickly, he rounded the back of the truck and slowly approached the sprawled man. Blood spread under him, the crimson mushrooming out under his body in a macabre pool.

Tucker still had his weapon trained on him, but kept his peripheral on the approaching car. It reversed quickly, the tires squealing as it swiveled in the opposite direction—probably because the driver saw Tucker's weapon. A civilian, then. Just as well, and better than a freaking cop.

He tapped the guy once in the eye with his boot even though he'd taken a head shot. No movement. It was impossible to fake being dead or unconscious if someone jabbed you in the eye. The body's reaction was too reflexive. Something he'd learned in the Corps.

He kicked the MAC-10 away, then did a quick check of the man's body. No ID. He had started to move to the guy's SUV when he heard a shuffling behind him. Weapon raised, he swiveled but immediately lowered it.

Karen stepped out from the back of the truck, her ponytail rumpled, her eyes wide, and his laptop bag in hand. "The closest any of my people are is twenty-five minutes out." Even as she spoke, multiple sirens blared in the distance.

He didn't know that they were intended for him, but he figured they were. Now that he'd been spotted in public, soon there would be a citywide manhunt out for him—if there wasn't already.

Tucker didn't like leaving Karen, not when this guy had been coming for both of them. Tucker might have been the target, but it was clear the killer hadn't cared if she was killed in the cross fire. "Give me your phone."

She seemed startled but handed it over. He snapped a few pictures of the dead guy, then turned her phone off and took out the battery. "I've gotta go. Twenty-five minutes is too long. You can stay or come with me. I don't like leaving you to the locals, because I don't know who to trust. My parents' phone must have been under surveillance. They must have tracked us using my burner." Something he'd considered before making the call to them, but he'd also tossed the cell out the window immediately after placing the call. No one should have been able to tail them. So if someone tracked his throwaway phone, they'd have had to have someone in the direct vicinity of Tucker. Which was a lucky—or unlucky for the dead guy—break for the people after Tucker. He sure as hell wouldn't make a mistake like that again.

Karen looked at the bullet-riddled, destroyed truck, then at the dead guy. She swallowed. "That guy wanted both of us dead."

It was certainly possible. When she met his gaze again, he knew she was coming with him. Even though she'd probably be safer away from him, a fierce protectiveness jumped in Tucker's chest at the thought of taking care of her. He'd gotten her into this mess and damn it, he wanted to be the one to keep her safe, to stop this threat once and for all. And he couldn't get past how someone had tracked them so damn fast. He could easily guess how they'd done it, but it had been too fast. It could have been the DEA, but it could have been another agency. What if whoever was behind this had the cops on their payroll too? There were too many unknown variables.

"I know a place we can go, off the grid. Safe for at least a few hours," Karen said, limping toward him. "I'm not meeting anyone but Wesley at this point. We had a mole in the NSA not that long ago. I don't think it was my people, but . . ." She looked at the truck again and gave a slight shake of her head. "I'm not staying here like a sitting duck." There was determination in her voice as she spoke.

He knew he should tell her to stay put, to wait for her people, but . . . he needed to keep her safe. The desire to do so ran deeper than he'd imagined. He nodded at the driver's SUV. "Come on." He just needed to get them away from this intersection before stealing another vehicle. He hated that he might be dragging her into the line of fire again, but at the moment neither of them had a choice.

# Chapter 10

Bravo sierra: slang for the word *bullshit*.

Selene barely reined in her temper as she exited the armored van with Ortiz keeping pace. Yellow tape sectioned off an entire intersection and she counted a dozen black-and-whites in addition to some unmarked police vehicles. There was also a fire truck and a county morgue van. Someone was gonna be pissed at her, but she wasn't letting anyone else take the dead body. She was going to find out who the asshole was who'd tried to kill Tucker and Karen.

"Karen was in there," Ortiz said, more a growl of anger than a question, his gaze on the bullet-riddled truck—which was thankfully armored or they would likely have been removing her body. Whoever had come after her was clearly not a pro.

"According to her and a scared soccer-mom witness, yeah." Selene had gotten a call from Karen and had seen the visual of the vehicle on their satellite feed, but the sight of the truck this up close and personal pissed her off.

Karen was an intrinsic member of their team and on top of that, she was a sweet person. She was often that voice on the other end of the comm when they were running ops, keeping everyone sane. Everyone loved her, and Selene knew Wesley was grooming her for a promotion in the next year or so. The woman remained calm under the direst circumstances.

"You sure she's not under duress?" Ortiz kept his voice low as they moved through a growing crowd of onlookers.

Why the hell hadn't the locals gotten these civilians out of the way? Selene frowned at the sight, then quickly dismissed it. Not her problem.

Ortiz continued, his expression dark. "I remember Grisha—uh, Tucker—and that guy is seriously trained."

He'd have to be to go undercover with a monster like Tasev and survive. But Selene didn't comment on that. "As sure as I can be. Karen's smart, and if she was under threat she'd have slipped in her code word. I'm going with my gut on this."

"Your gut tell you he's not involved in the bombings?" he murmured, his voice even lower as they approached the crime scene tape.

"Pretty much." From their analysis and other evidence, it didn't make sense.

"Yeah. Same here." Ortiz had read the files too.

Selene flipped her badge out to a young female cop. "NSA. We need to speak to Detective Portillo."

Before the woman could respond, a man with black hair peppered with gray nodded at them. "Let them through." He had on black slacks, a thick black coat, and a scarf and knit cap in the same color. His nose was red and his eyes puffy. He clearly had a bad cold but had come in to work anyway. The only thing that gave away that he was a cop was the badge slung around his neck on a silver chain. That and his world-weary expression.

"Agent Marks?"

Selene nodded at the use of one of her cover names and held out a hand. "Detective Portillo, this is Agent Garcia." For now they were both using aliases, even with the locals.

The detective nodded, his expression grim. "You feel like telling me what the fuck is going on?" he asked after they shook hands. "Some asshole opens fire on an armored truck two blocks from an elementary school—one my niece goes to. And my witness said there was a woman matching the description of your missing girl, with a guy with a gun."

So they didn't know it was Tucker Pankov yet. "As of right now I'm not sure what's going on myself," Selene said. "First, Karen isn't a missing person anymore. She's fine and being debriefed with us as we speak." A tiny lie Selene didn't feel bad telling. "I need you to send out a bulletin to your people asap. And second, we've gotta take the body." When Portillo opened his mouth to protest, Selene reached into her jacket pocket and pulled out a folded piece of paper.

"Look," she said, handing it to him. "This is just a jurisdictional thing. I'm not trying to step on your toes, but it's about national security. You did us a solid today and we're not going to forget it. I don't have a choice in taking this body, so before you get pissed at me, remember I'm simply the messenger." She kept her voice soft and hoped her young appearance would help her. It usually did and she took full advantage of it.

There could be serious animosity between federal and state agencies and she'd always thought the tension was bullshit. In her opinion, they were all on the same side in the end and she didn't give a crap who closed a case. "You know this isn't about getting our faces in the paper. We're not the FBI." She murmured the last part, not surprised when it earned her the ghost of a smile. His jaw was set as he finished reading the warrant, so she continued. "No one's gonna know we were here except you." Meaning it would never leak to the media.

It was clear he wanted to argue, but in the end it would be pointless, and she was glad he realized that because she didn't have time for that kind of crap today.

"This connected to the bombing today?" he asked as he handed the paper back to her.

Surprised that he'd made the connection, she nodded. "We think so. And we're just trying to make sure this doesn't happen again. If there's anything I can tell you, I will." As her weapons mentor, a former USMC sniper instructor, would have said: *bravo sierra*. Complete bullshit, because she couldn't even tell this guy her real last name, but she was all about keeping the peace between her people and his.

"Boss, there are two tow trucks here, both drivers saying they're supposed to take the truck," a fresh-faced man who looked as if he'd just graduated from the academy said as he approached them.

Portillo sighed, his jaw tightening again. Yeah, they'd be taking the truck too.

"Excuse me, I need to take this," Selene murmured, pulling her buzzing cell phone out of her pocket.

She nodded at Ortiz as she did, silently telling him to start the process of loading the body. They'd come with a team of people but hadn't wanted to intrude on the scene with everyone until after she'd talked to Portillo. He deserved that respect.

"Done," Ortiz said quietly, pulling out his own cell as she answered hers.

It was Elliott. "Yeah."

"I lost them." More than frustration, there was a note of surprise in his voice.

Selene wasn't surprised, though. Tucker was trained, and when it came to avoiding being tracked, Karen would know more than anyone how to stay off the grid. The two of them working together could disappear if they wanted to. "Don't sweat it. I'm pulling the missing person report on her. Finding her isn't our focus now." Because Karen had made it clear she'd come in when she was ready. "We're bringing the dead body in, but I'll scan the prints and send them to you. Anyone get a hit off his face yet?" Karen had texted them a picture of the dead guy before she went dark again.

"Not yet."

"Run it against the group of guys from earlier. See if there's a link. You might get a faster hit on him. And we need his ID," she stressed even though Elliott knew how important this was. Once they disconnected she looked up to find Ortiz helping to bag the body. They weren't going to worry about an autopsy. Not when they knew how he'd died. Nope, they needed to find out who he was and who'd hired him.

And why.

Karen forced herself not to duck and hide as a car drove down the street, passing her and Tucker. She was definitely not cut out for the cloak-and-dagger business, despite what she did for a living. They were walking down a quiet Baltimore street lined with brownstones. She'd wrapped her hair in a scarf from Tucker's duffel bag and he'd changed into different clothes he'd had in it.

Other than more weapons and ammo, there hadn't been anything else in the SUV they'd left behind. After ditching that SUV, Tucker had stolen a Toyota Corolla, then a minivan, then a Jeep. They'd switched vehicles so many times, but it had been a smart move. Especially when it was clear that whoever was after Tucker and his men didn't care about a little collateral damage—like her. Considering that his pursuers had set off a bomb at the Botanic Garden, she shouldn't have been surprised.

Part of her knew she should have let Tucker go and just waited for the police and someone from her own team, but she hadn't wanted Tucker going off by himself. By now she was convinced he was being set up and the man needed all the help he could get. She found herself feeling oddly protective of him. After a quick text to Selene with the pictures of the dead guy and letting her know that she was going to ground with Tucker, Karen had taken the battery out of her phone once again. Wesley might give her grief later for the choice she'd made to go into temporary hiding, but she didn't regret it.

"You sure this place is safe?" Tucker asked, wrapping his arm around her shoulders.

She knew it was for show. After ditching the last vehicle a few neighborhoods over, they'd been walking casually to their final destination as if they were two friends, or maybe more than friends, for the last ten minutes. She liked the feel of his strong arm around her, though, and leaned into him. Everything about him was solid, and though she probably shouldn't be noticing, she loved how masculine he smelled. She had the irrational urge to turn her face into his chest and burrow closer against him. "Should be. She's out of the country for two weeks. She doesn't have a boyfriend or a pet and no security system." Right now she was glad for that lapse in security. Her friend had told Karen about her trip in person over drinks one night, so there wasn't a paper trail about it out in cyberspace.

"What does she do?" he asked.

"Oh, just marketing stuff. She works for a big international firm, has no idea who I really work for. If we're lucky she'll have pizza in the freezer." Because after everything that had happened, Karen had gotten a massive adrenaline dump and was in a free fall now. She was shaky and cold and needed food. And a shower, but she'd settle for something hot to eat. "Can I use your laptop once we get there?"

He paused, the crunching of their shoes over the icy sidewalk and cars slowly cruising down the street the only sounds. "Yeah."

"Good. I guarantee Wesley's already running the financials for the men on that list you sent him, but I'm going to do some digging of my own."

"You don't want to call Burkhart once we get there?" He looked down at her. He was wearing a ball cap and sunglasses, but she could tell he was frowning at her.

"Not really. I need time to regroup and think." As soon as she called Wesley they'd be brought in for a debriefing, and Karen was exhausted. She'd been kidnapped, shot at, and had gone on the run with a man she found frustratingly sexy. There was nothing more she could provide to the NSA at this point and she needed to decompress.

Which meant sleep.

If her going in would have changed something, she'd have sucked it up, but after an insane day she was shelving her guilt.

Putting Wesley off for a couple of hours wasn't going to hurt them. And she'd made it clear to Selene that this was her choice, so the NSA wouldn't be hunting for her anymore and wasting resources. Or they shouldn't be.

"Is that okay with you?" she asked.

He nodded. "Yeah. Lying low for a few hours won't hurt anything," he said, mirroring her thoughts. "I texted Cole with one of my burners a while ago and told him to send the fingerprints of the dead guy to Burkhart, so they've got everything we have. My presence won't change a thing. And the more hours I stay out of hand-cuffs and probably jail, the better."

She was glad they were on the same wavelength. And she planned to help make sure he didn't go to jail. "This is it," she said, nodding to the brownstone with a blue-and-white wreath on the door.

"Do you know if she has a key outside anywhere?" he asked quietly, covertly scanning the street.

It wasn't late enough for most young professionals—the typical age group who lived in this area of the city—to be home yet. So if they were going to break in, it was a decent time to do it. "No. I figured you had some B-and-E skills, though."

He let out a low chuckle, his grip around her shoulders tightening for a moment. Why did she like the feel of him holding her so much? Warmth flared inside her and she really wanted to experience more than just a light half hug from him.

"You figured right," he murmured. They strode up the short walk, and without glancing around or look-ing as though he was up to something, Tucker bent down and pulled a small black kit out of his sock.

Seriously? The guy had a lock pick kit in his freaking sock. "You're like a criminal Boy Scout type. Always pre-pared," she muttered as he made quick work of the lock.

Laughing, he opened the door and ushered them inside. It was chilly in the foyer, probably because her friend hadn't planned to be here and hadn't turned the heat up as high as usual.

"I'm going to sweep the place just to be safe. Don't turn on any lights," he murmured, already moving through the home, heading up the stairs first.

She slipped off her sneakers and walked down the hallway to the kitchen, only stopping to turn the heat up a little. There was just enough outside light streaming through the closed blinds that she wasn't working blind. A peek in the freezer had her smiling in relief.

"Pizza," she murmured to herself.

"I won't say no to that," Tucker said from behind her.

Karen nearly jumped at the sound of his voice. She looked over her shoulder to find him only a few feet behind her. The small duffel he'd shoved all their stuff into was in his hand, and he set the laptop bag on the kitchen table.

"Will you set up your computer while I pop the pizza in?" she asked.

He paused the same way he had when she asked to use it, but nodded. "I've got serious encryption on this thing, but if you link directly to your systems with your credentials, you run the risk of Burkhart tracking us. I'm turning myself in to him anyway, but I don't love the thought of an assault team kicking in your friend's door and—"

She shook her head, cutting him off. "I'm not going

to be using official work resources." She pulled out the extra-large pizza and smiled. *Food.* She felt she could eat the whole thing herself. "You're not the only one who has illegal skills," she added.

His responding chuckle made another burst of warmth spread through her.

After she preheated the oven, put the pizza in and set the timer, Tucker had the laptop up and running for her.

"Who's your top choice for who set you guys up?" she asked as she remoted into one of her favorite programs. She didn't have to download any software and could use it anonymously. In addition to running their financials, she wanted to do a search on these men to see if they were linked to any shady organizations. Looking for keywords in certain forums and other areas on the Net was her first order of business.

When he didn't answer, she glanced up to find him leaning against one of the counters, arms crossed over his massive chest. He was like a big, really sexy statue. She should be uncomfortable with him, but instead, the longer they spent together, the more she found herself attracted to him. At first she thought he wouldn't answer but then she realized he was thinking.

"My gut choice is Daniel Vane. He's an asshole and hated Max. But I think that's more of an emotional reaction. Raul Widom is the more realistic choice. With Max dead he's in a position to move up the ladder faster and the guy is seriously power hungry. One of those people you hate working with because he doesn't seem to care about anything but himself. It's all about closing cases and getting the media spotlight for him, not doing the job right. A born fucking politician," he muttered in disgust.

"That's good." Karen moved the two men to the top of her list, but all five men had to be viable to even be on it in the first place. She hadn't realized how much time had passed until the timer on the stove beeped. She started to get up, but Tucker waved her back.

"Do your thing. I'll set this up. What do you want to drink? She doesn't have much, but there are water bottles, coconut water"—he made a disgusted sound, making Karen smile—"and Red Bull."

"Will you check her pantry?" she asked without looking up from the screen. "I think she's got a bottle of red wine." Karen was going to replace everything they were using, and while she felt a twinge of guilt for invading her friend's space, it was such a huge relief to be sitting safely somewhere that it outweighed most of it. Plus, she knew her friend wouldn't actually mind if she knew Karen was here. Carline was one of those people who would do anything for a friend.

"She's got two bottles. Same brand," he said, pulling one out. He didn't say anything else, just searched around until he found a bottle opener.

When he placed a plate on the table in front of her, she didn't bother moving the laptop out of the way as she grabbed a slice. Right now she didn't care about manners.

"If I talk to you, will it mess up your concentration?" Tucker asked.

She glanced up at him and shook her head. The man looked like a caged animal, all tense energy thrumming off him. It was clear he didn't like sitting still. No, he was definitely used to being a man of action. It was undeniably sexy. "Not really. I'm just running some programs to start basic profiles on these guys. Actually you can start telling me about each of them. Overall thoughts, family life, relationships at work, anything that has to do with their personalities. Often we'll have a psychologist read files of certain individuals to help round out our information. Especially when we have a wider suspect pool. Start with Daniel Vane."

Tucker started talking, the steady cadence of his voice soothing. Not too fast, not too slow, just right. Gah, what was wrong with her? She didn't need to be noticing anything else about this man. It was so damn hard not to, though, when he had such an incredible presence. Sitting so close to him, she seemed to have perpetual butterflies in her stomach.

He continued peppering her with information as dusk fell outside, and while she created yet another file for one of the suspects, he turned on a dim light in the kitchen so they wouldn't be in complete darkness. It was more than enough for her to work in.

Hours later she was pleased with what they'd come up with as she scanned the file. This information was gold, the type of stuff that wasn't easily searchable online. When they were done, she looked up at him once again.

Now he was leaning against one of the counters, water bottle in hand, instead of sitting across from her. "What is it?" he asked, suddenly straightening, as if he read her mind.

She wasn't sure how she felt about him reading her so easily. Not because she felt in danger with him. After everything that had happened, that wasn't even a concern anymore. He was way too protective for her to worry about that. The protective edge to him made her wonder if he felt something for her.

Pushing back from her seat, she stretched her legs out in front of her. Thankfully her ankle wasn't bothering her more than a dull ache she'd been ignoring the past couple of hours. "I want to send all this in to the office." Because she wanted Elliott and whoever else Wesley had on this task force to combine their information. And it would show her team that she'd been working behind the scenes—and prove that Tucker hadn't hurt her.

Tucker nodded. "Okay. Do it. I'm willing to go in now."

"You're sure?" She shouldn't even be asking, because it was time, but she surprised herself with the question.

He nodded. "I've done nothing wrong and I want to clear the names of my men."

His men. Tucker didn't say anything about himself. Yeah, that was why his team had listened to him even when it was clear they'd wanted to buck his orders about not coming to D.C. Now more than ever, she was determined to help him.

She pulled her cell phone out of her pocket and called Wesley once she'd put the battery back in.

Selene picked up on the first ring, surprising Karen. "Hey. You okay?"

"Yeah, I'm fine. Is Wesley with you?"

"No, in a meeting. He's gone dark, so I can't reach him. All his calls are being forwarded to my number. He's pissed about what you did." There was no censure in Selene's voice, which made Karen breathe easier.

"He'll get over it," Karen said dryly.

That earned her a chuckle from Selene. "That's exactly what I said."

"Listen, I've spent the last couple hours with Tucker going over the men on that list he sent you guys. I've compiled a decent file for each of them." Her questions wouldn't be as good as a full-scale interview or interrogation, but Karen had been at her job for four years. She knew the right things to ask in a situation like this. "I'm assuming Elliott's working on this, but I wanted to make sure before I send him everything." And Karen planned to utilize more of her resources once she had access to her work computer.

"Yep, he's on it. Send away. . . . You sure you're okay?"

They had a code word that Karen could work into the conversation if she was under duress. They all had one. "Yes, I swear. And by now you've tracked my cell phone and have someone en route to get us. Tucker and I are at a friend's brownstone. She's out of town, has no clue I'm here. No one does, so we're safe. And you don't need to breach the freaking place. I'll answer the door."

"It's just you and Pankov?" Selene asked, ignoring most of what Karen said.

"Yeah."

"Put me on speaker."

"Hold on." After doing so, she laid the phone on the table in front of her. "You're on."

"Tucker Pankov, this is Selene Marks." Karen didn't negate Selene's use of an alias. Of course the woman would use one; she always did. "We met in Miami last year. I don't know that I properly got to thank you for your help."

Moving like a predator, Tucker sank into the seat across from Karen, his entire body pulled taut. "Max said you guys wrapped everything up tight with that op. Nice to hear your voice again."

"So . . . you've got yourself stuck in a pile of shit, huh?"

To Karen's surprise, Tucker laughed, a real one. The action smoothed out the hard planes of his face, giving him a softer look. She wanted to be the one to make him laugh like that again. "Guess you could say that."

"We ran those prints you sent us. . . ." Selene let out a low whistle. "They appear to be pricey hitters. Former jobs have them listed as contractors, but looking at the way they've been paid, I say they're hired guns, not just personal security. And those guys are linked to the dead guy we found at the crash site of your truck earlier. He's former Army, just like the first four sets of prints, but not a hired gun like the others. At least not well-known enough to be on any databases, and his financials don't indicate hired mercenary. All of them were in the same division, which tells us a lot about them and whoever hired them."

"You found out who hired them?" Tucker sat up straighter, his gaze intense.

"No, but we're working on finding a common thread. Trying to see if we can link one or all of them to someone on that list of DEA agents."

Tucker shifted a fraction against the seat, hope flickering across his expression for a moment before it was gone and his stoic mask was back in place. "Your boss believes me and my guys?"

Selene made a noncommittal grunt. "Something's not right here and your alleged crimes don't match up with the profiles of you and your men. Sometimes people go off the tracks for whatever reason—money, religion, revenge—but none of that fits the profile here. The more we dig, the clearer it becomes this is a setup. A very thorough one. And just my personal opinion, from all accounts you've gone out of your way not to hurt Karen. Even that cop you held up at gunpoint, you could've just shot him but you didn't. Doesn't sound like a cold-blooded killer who tried to blow up the Botanic Garden."

Tucker rubbed a hand over his face, seeming to relax for the first time since Karen had met him. "Just let me know how you want this to go down. I can come out first and your people can bring me in or Karen can leave the place first and I'll come out next. I'll keep my hands visible and strip off enough so you can see I'm unarmed."

Selene was silent for a long moment, then said, "Take me off speaker, Karen."

Without pause Karen took the phone off speaker and put it to her ear. "What's up?"

"While Wesley's dark, I've got some operational latitude. That said, after I got your call and we picked up that dead guy from the locals, I wanted to be sure we knew how you guys were tracked. Elliott came up with it, so I can't take credit for it, but we started looking at all the immediate family members of Pankov, Brooks, Kane, and Erickson. There's a new wiretap warrant for any family the four of them might reach out to, which makes sense after the bombing. But Elliott discovered that a few of their family members had already been under surveillance for the past *month*. The order originated from the DEA, but he's not sure who from and the paperwork is sketchy. We're going to find out, though."

"Tucker called his parents from a burner phone when we were driving. He tossed it right after making the call, though." Still, it wouldn't have been the hardest thing to track them for someone with the right equipment. It just meant that someone had access to satellites and had been lucky enough to have someone in the area to hunt them down.

"He didn't toss it soon enough," Selene said. "Someone with a lot of resources is out for blood. That attempted hit in the middle of the day . . . I saw pictures of the truck you were in. So, answer me honestly, how would you feel about sitting tight with Pankov for another couple hours?"

Karen met his gaze again and couldn't fight the shiver of awareness that streaked through her. "Okay."

"I figure you can use a few hours of sleep and you're sure as hell not going to get it if we bring you in now. But be real with me."

"It's fine, Selene, I swear." Though she was unsure why Selene would be asking. At this point she was running on fumes and could do with some rest. Being with Tucker made her feel surprisingly safe.

"Ortiz and Freeman have their hands full with an assignment, but when they're done I'm sending them over to get you. Only Elliott and I are aware of this place, so absolutely no one will know where you are. I know you and Ortiz are friends and he's one of the only guys I trust implicitly with your life. I just need to make sure you're okay staying with Pankov. I'd pick you up myself, but—"

"Okay." Karen didn't need to hear any more. Wesley had left Selene in charge for a reason and if Selene wanted to wait for two men she trusted to pick them up, that was more than fine with Karen. "I could use a shower now anyway." At her words, Tucker's eyes flickered with surprise before his gaze went molten. He'd obviously figured out that Selene wasn't sending someone to get them right away.

Feeling her cheeks heat up, she glanced away and wrapped up with Selene, telling her where they'd ditched the dead guy's SUV. Of course Elliott already knew where it was, as he'd tracked them right up until they'd stolen the Jeep. Then he'd apparently lost her and Tucker. Once they'd disconnected she relayed everything to Tucker.

He was surprised Selene was waiting but didn't seem to mind. "If you want to grab a shower I'll clean up down here. Then I'll take one after you," Tucker said.

"We could both take one." As soon as she'd said the words she realized how it sounded and cursed her fair skin. Her cheeks heated up as she hurried on. "I just meant there are two bathrooms upstairs, so you don't have to wait or anything."

His expression barely changed as he watched her and she wished she knew what he was thinking. "I'll wait."

Okay, then. After e-mailing Elliott the files, she hurried upstairs and tried not to think of what it would be like to actually share a shower with someone as sexy as Tucker. She'd only seen bits of his exposed skin, namely those delicious forearms, but it was impossible to hide that built body under his clothes. She couldn't help wondering what the rest of him looked like.

As she thought it, she was also very aware of the fact that there was only one bed in her friend's place. The other room was used as an office. She planned on crashing after her shower and wondered if Tucker did too. Nerves fluttered in her stomach at the thought of sharing a bed with him. The thought of kissing him—or more—got her a lot more flustered than she'd thought possible. He probably wasn't even thinking along those same lines. But if he was . . . she wouldn't mind sharing more than just a bed with him.

# Chapter 11

Going dark: when an operative cuts all communication
for a certain period of time.

Tucker ran a towel over his damp hair as he stepped
out of the guest bathroom. As he moved into the
hallway, he tensed at a humming sound until he realized
it was a blow-dryer coming from the other bathroom.

Despite what he'd told Karen, he'd snagged a quick
shower while she was taking hers. He didn't like that
this place lacked a security system, but he was armed
and this was a fairly safe area as far as homes went.

After another quick check of the place, he tossed his
clothes and the ones Karen had left on the floor of her
friend's room into the washing machine. They wouldn't
be here that much longer, but he wasn't sure when
Karen would get clean clothes again. Then he put on a
pair of sweatpants he kept in his duffel bag. He and his
team were always prepared with extra clothes, and in
this case he had clothes and ammo. He'd given his
money and fake passports to Cole before they left the
house.

By the time he was heading back up the stairs, the sound of the hair dryer had stopped and he could hear Karen moving around in her friend's room. Though he wanted to stay up until the team from the NSA arrived, he knew he needed to catch a few hours of sleep. At this point he had no idea what the future held and he was running on fumes. Since he'd be meeting with Burkhart soon, that wasn't acceptable. He had to be in top form when he talked to the head of the NSA.

The bedroom door was half-open, but he knocked on it anyway as he stepped into the entryway. She was wearing plaid pink-and-black pajamas she must have borrowed from her friend. They were a little long on her, so she'd rolled the sleeves up at the wrists. Still, they didn't do anything to hide the outline of her full breasts. What he wouldn't give to cup them, to tease them with his tongue—nope. Not going there again. He'd already had to take a cold shower to cool down, not that it had helped. Jacking off had, though. Or he'd thought it had until he saw her standing there looking refreshed and so fucking gorgeous he experienced another one of those jolts to his system he'd only ever had around her.

Her green eyes widened when she saw him, her gaze trailing over his bare chest. Shit, maybe he should have put on a shirt, but he'd known they'd be sleeping soon. At first he thought it was just shock, but then he got a hint of something else. As though maybe she liked what she saw.

Still, he didn't want to make her uncomfortable. "I'll

put on a shirt," he murmured, moving for the duffel bag he'd left at the foot of the queen-size bed. "And I'll be bunking on the floor. Is that okay?" Mostly for security reasons, but he wasn't letting her out of his sight for reasons he didn't want to examine too closely.

"No," she said quickly.

He paused with his hand on the bag. He hadn't thought she'd care about him sleeping on the floor. It bothered him that she did. "Uh, I think it would be better if we stay in the same room. We need to stay close. We can sleep on the couches downstairs instead, though." If he had to he'd just sleep in the hallway if she was that nervous. Because he wasn't leaving her unprotected.

"Oh no, I mean, you don't have to put on a shirt. And we can share the bed." Her cheeks flushed pink and, fuck him, his dick went hard—okay, harder than he already was.

He stood and picked up his bag, holding it low and hoping he looked casual and not as if he was trying to cover up his annoying erection. He'd always been in control of his dick. *Always*. Until, apparently, Karen. "I've had worse sleeping conditions than this. With a blanket and pillow, I'll be good to go."

She shook her head and stuck her chin out. It was slight, but he'd noticed that she did it when she was being stubborn about something. Like when she'd told him she wasn't leaving him to get shot by the cops. She'd been so fierce and determined he'd known that arguing with her would have been pointless. And okay, he hadn't wanted to leave her anyway. "That's stupid. Our first meeting was you kidnapping me." He winced at her words, but she half smiled as if it didn't bother her before continuing. "I'm just saying I think we're way past any sense of formality or whatever. I'm freaking exhausted and I know you have to be. I bet you and your team were up super early planning to grab me. And while you might be used to crazy days like today, you need to sleep too. If you try to sleep on the floor I'll just get down there with you. Which will make you feel guilty and then you'll end up in the bed anyway. So just give in now and save yourself—and me—a headache."

He blinked in surprise, an unexpected grin curving his mouth. The woman was an absolute force of nature. "Fine, the bed it is." God help him, he really hoped it led to more than just sleep. Which was a stupid thought considering the circumstances, but the thought of being able to hold her, kiss her . . . He shut that thought down.

She gave him a real smile and for a moment he forgot to fucking breathe. Actually forgot to draw in a breath. It was like a punch to his solar plexus. The woman was stunning.

"I knew you'd see it my way," she murmured, still smiling as she turned from him and pulled the covers down.

Her friend had some kind of Arabian Nights theme happening with the striped red, gold, and purple comforter and a billion pillows—which Karen shoved onto the floor.

EDGE OF DANGER    143

"I don't know why she needs all these pillows," she muttered, shaking her head.

There wasn't much light in the room, since they'd opted to use them only when necessary, just a night-light in the attached bathroom and one in the bedroom. It was more than enough for him to see all her curves as she moved, getting the bed ready.

That was when he realized he was still standing there like a moron.

Moving into action, he shut the door and locked it, then pulled his weapon from the back of his waistband. "This is loaded," he said, laying it on one of the dressers next to the head of the bed. "I've got another couple weapons in my bag and extra ammo if we need it." He hated the spark of fear in her gaze, but he had to say it. "I doubt we will, but just in case. And . . . I just need to get this out. If shit goes haywire and something does happen, I need you to run. Okay?" She had to be safe. Not just because he was the one who'd dragged her into this mess, but because some intrinsic part of him couldn't deal with it if she wasn't.

"Okay." She said it a little too quickly and there was no conviction in her voice.

"Karen—"

"Tucker, I'm so tired my eyeballs actually hurt," she said, sliding into the bed and pulling the covers up to her waist.

"Me too," he murmured, sliding in next to her, prop-ping a hand under his head. He knew how big he was and tried to keep to his side of the bed so she'd have more space. If it had been a king-size bed, it would have been easier, but even with a queen, his feet were pretty much hanging off the thing and his shoulder touching hers.

She lay on her back too, but looked stiff, so he half rolled onto his side. "If you want you can curl up against me. I know I take up a lot of space."

To his complete and utter surprise, she did just that. Hell, he hadn't exactly expected her to; had been thinking she might tell him to take the floor after all. And it made that insane protective urge swell up again.

Tucking her head against his chest, she curled right into him and gently laid her hand on his side. There was nothing sexual about her touch, even if he wanted there to be. Then she let out a contented sigh, her breath fanning over his skin. She might be lean, but there was an incredible softness to her. He wasn't sure if it was the circumstances or her, or probably a combination, but he couldn't ever remember feeling so drawn to a woman before. She brought out too many damn feelings in him. He didn't hate it.

Compared to his experiences with women in his past, this was definitely different. He'd had one-night stands, though not many because of the nature of his work. The one woman he'd been in an actual relationship with had betrayed him in the worst way possible. But he shoved that thought out of his mind, not wanting to dwell on her or his past when he had a woman like Karen in his arms. She was like no one he'd ever met before. He'd actually kidnapped her, yet here she was, helping to clear his name.

"You're so warm," she murmured drowsily.

Ah, she was about to pass out. Explained why she was so willing to use him as a human pillow. Fine with him. Holding her like this was foreign in his experience, but perfect. She must have used some kind of vanilla shampoo. Or maybe that was just her. Whatever it was, she smelled amazing; something he tried not to pay attention to. It was difficult not to, though, when she was pressed up against him, all soft, gorgeous woman.

At least her entire body wasn't flush with his or she'd feel his very-hard-to-hide reaction to her. Not that it would have mattered, as she fell into a deep sleep within five minutes.

As soon as she was under, he wrapped his arm just a little more snugly around her and let himself drift too. He couldn't help thinking that if things between them were just a little different, if a woman like Karen gave herself to him, he'd never let her go. But he figured he'd fucked things up completely as far as that was concerned. She might be willing to help him, but considering that he'd kidnapped her, he doubted she'd ever want more from him.

Relaxing as much as he'd allow himself, he pushed out a long breath. He wouldn't go into a deep sleep—he was too primed right now, but a quick rest was exactly what he needed.

Karen jerked awake with a start only to have Tucker's heavy arm tighten around her.

"You're okay," he murmured, his hand smoothing up and down her spine in a gentle motion.

Though her heart rate had kicked up a couple of notches, she immediately settled at the feel of him next to her. Her internal clock told her not too much time had passed since she dozed, and it was still dark outside. "What time is it?" she murmured, her cheek pressed against his chest. His very bare chest. He had a smattering of dark hair, but he wasn't smooth. Her fingers were splayed across his taut abdomen and it took all her self-control not to stroke up and down all his cut muscles. She knew he'd just been comforting her earlier when he offered to let her sleep on him. She couldn't read anything more into it.

"A little after eleven." His voice was quiet, without a hint of tiredness.

He was like a machine. Or just very, very trained to live in certain conditions. Not her; she needed her sleep to function like any sort of normal human being. "Hey, whatever happened to my clothes?" she asked suddenly. They hadn't been on the floor when she got out of the bathroom earlier, but she'd been so exhausted she hadn't thought about it.

"I threw them in the wash with mine. Got up an hour ago and put most of them in the dryer. Hung up the pants, since they're those dri-fit material. Hope that's all right."

The thought of him touching her underwear made her blush, but whatever, she was past caring about something like that. It was really thoughtful that he'd even done that. "Thank you."

He grunted a noncommittal sound that could have meant anything. "How're you feeling?"

"Amazing. You're like a furnace," she said, savoring his warmth and wishing she was doing more than just lying in his arms. The last guy she'd been intimate with was her last boyfriend about two years ago. He hadn't been able to handle her crazy work schedule and deep down, she figured he'd known she was holding back part of herself. She had to when she couldn't even tell him what she did for a living. If she'd foreseen things getting serious, she would have been truthful with him, but if he hadn't been able to deal with her work schedule she had little faith he'd have been able to deal with anything else.

With Tucker, it was so freeing that she could be real with him. Of course, the circumstances were different, since he'd kidnapped her, but she didn't care. It was so damn liberating that he knew what she did for a living, that she didn't have to hold back with him. With his arms around her, it was hard to ignore what being held like this—by Tucker—did to her body.

He chuckled low, his breath warm over the top of her head. "Try to get some more sleep. We've got a couple hours till they pick us up. Might as well take advantage."

He was right, she knew. But she also knew that once they got picked up, things would start moving at warp speed. She might not ever see Tucker again. For some reason that thought set off a twinge in her chest. "Why'd you decide to join the DEA?" she asked. This wasn't the kind of thing outlined in his official file and she was genuinely curious.

Tucker was silent for a long moment, his breathing steady in the quiet room. She wasn't sure he'd even answer, but he did. "Max approached Cole and me. I'd never planned to stay in the Corps forever and it seemed like a good career change."

"Do you like it?"

"The undercover work can be difficult."

She knew he was thirty-four from his file and that he'd been with the DEA for six years. Yeah, that kind of work could wear on someone. "You plan on staying with them?"

His chest rumbled as he let out a low laugh. "If we don't get arrested and thrown in prison for treason, I honestly don't know. After the Tasev job . . . I've been thinking about a change."

"I don't blame you." She had no idea what he'd done or seen over the last six years, but she knew what a monster Tasev was. Working for that guy, even for a couple of months, had to have been difficult.

His hand continued to stroke up and down her spine, the gesture so soothing. Her nipples automatically tightened at the feel of him. "What about you? How'd you end up with the NSA?"

"They recruited me while I was still in college."

Given her test scores, her major, and her analytical mind, it wasn't really a surprise they'd approached her.

"And?" he pushed, when she didn't continue. "You didn't have to say yes. Why'd you go with them?"

"I . . ." She thought about lying but decided to just be honest, especially after everything they'd been through the past day. "I was just finishing up with my master's when my brother died over there." Since Tucker already knew her brother had died in Afghanistan, she didn't spell it out. "He was the only family I had and I know it sounds cheesy, but I wanted to make a difference for our country. I think it's part of the reason they approached me, but I could be wrong. And at the risk of sounding even cheesier, when I was growing up my brother protected me and I think it helped instill this need in me to help those who can't help themselves. I don't care that pretty much everything I do is behind the scenes, I sleep better at night knowing I have a part in keeping our country safe." Keeping the very real monsters at bay. Though it wasn't all just out of the goodness of her heart, she knew. Some of it was about pure control. She needed to feel in control and she didn't need a psychology degree to know it was because of her lack of control as a kid.

"You two were close?"

"Yeah." She realized she'd started drawing little circles on his stomach, but he didn't seem to mind. Even so, she stilled her fingers. "I'm about to overshare, so if you don't want to hear all this, tell me to stop."

"I want to hear."

"My father was an alcoholic and Clint basically raised me. He joined the Marines when I was seventeen. I think he wanted to hold off another year, but by then I was pretty self-sufficient and had already landed a bunch of scholarships. We grew up pretty poor." She'd been considered white trash but didn't tell Tucker that because it still shamed her. Intellectually she knew that was stupid, but some things ran deep. Being from a small town where everyone knew everyone else's business made it hard to escape the scorn or, worse, pity of others. She could deal with scorn, but people feeling sorry for her was somehow worse. It was why she'd been so determined to get out of the town she'd grown up in and put miles and miles between her and everyone in her past. "My dad was a dick, but he wasn't abusive. Just a freaking waste of space."

She waited a moment, to see if he'd judge her, but he kept rubbing her back. She hadn't even realized she'd tensed up. When he didn't respond she relaxed and continued. "When girls my age were going on dates and excited about the prom or whatever school function, I was studying my ass off." And she'd worked two jobs but didn't say that. "Nothing was more important to me than getting out of that town. Clint saved what money he could for me. Said he didn't need it while he was deployed anyway. All that combat and hazard-duty pay added up." Her throat tightened and it took a moment for her to gather herself.

She wasn't even sure why she was telling Tucker all this. For some reason she wanted him to know something real about her.

"Anyway, thanks to scholarships and my brother's help I was able to get a good education. He wasn't that much older than me, but he was always more like a father to me. I didn't think about it until I was older, but a kid that age shouldn't have had so much responsibility thrust onto him. He did and never complained about it, never made me feel guilty or like a burden." Her throat tightened again and despite her best effort, a few tears escaped.

"Shit, don't cry, honey," Tucker murmured, swiping at her cheek with one of his thumbs.

She didn't look up at him, though. If she did she was afraid she'd kiss him or do something else equally stupid. She let out a watery laugh. "I'm fine, I swear. I just don't talk about him much."

"I'm sorry you lost him," he murmured, his grip tightening just a fraction.

"Thanks." He'd been in the Corps, so it was easier telling him this.

They were silent for a few minutes, but it didn't feel awkward. The rumble of his voice actually surprised her when he spoke again. "About four years ago I almost died on an op. I can't give specifics, but you might have seen a note about it in my file."

She'd read his file thoroughly, and though good portions had been redacted she'd been able to glean enough information. "In California, right?" The file hadn't said anything about him almost getting killed, though, just that someone else had died. A female agent.

"Yeah. I'd been on the op for about six months with my . . . partner, I guess you could say." There was an odd note in his voice. Almost like muted anger. "We were more than just that, though. At first it'd been part of our cover, being lovers, but eventually it became real. For me anyway. I ignored things I shouldn't have ignored, didn't want to see that she was dirty." He let out a sigh, the sound resigned, as he continued. "She betrayed me, thought she'd gotten me killed. It's how I got this." He tapped the scar on his throat. "We let her believe it because it was easier for me to extract myself from the op that way."

"What happened to her?"

"Got killed a week later. Her own fault too, got greedy." He let out a bitter laugh, the tension in him mounting.

Karen could feel his muscles pull tight under her fingertips. Against her better judgment, she smoothed a hand down his stomach. She wasn't quite brave enough to wrap her arm around him. "Why'd you tell me?"

He shuddered under her touch but didn't seem to mind. "You told me something personal and . . . I wanted you to know something personal about me. Something you couldn't get from a file. Just so you know, I'm not fucking sorry she's dead either." There was a bite to his words.

"I don't blame you." From his tone she felt as if he expected that admission to revolt her or something.

He stilled for a moment. "Really?"

"Why would I? She betrayed you and her country. And for what? Fuck her. If it hadn't been you, it would have been someone else she stabbed in the back." That kind of betrayal was the worst. When you worked in certain fields, the men and women literally depended on you to have their back, to keep them *alive*. To turn on people you worked with day in and day out was so many kinds of wrong.

"I'm not a good man, Karen. I . . . I know you've read my Grisha file. Not all of it's fake." The words came out almost stilted. As if he didn't want to tell her but was doing it anyway.

"I figured." Did he think she wouldn't understand that he'd done violent things to create his cover? It took a moment for it to register why he was telling her. Did he want to warn her off . . . him?

Silence descended on the room again, but this time it wasn't calm. It wasn't awkward either, but there was a palpable tension lingering in the air. It could be her imagination, but she didn't think so.

Even with the faint light from the night-light and a few streams of illumination from the streetlights outside peeking through the windows, she couldn't tell if he was aroused. The covers were bunched too much by his waist and she wasn't completely draped over him.

She wished she was, though. Which was probably insane, considering the circumstances, but this man affected her in a way she didn't completely understand.

Taking a chance, she shifted her body, moving her

leg and hip so that she was cuddled closer to him. The second her leg brushed against his erection, he let out a quiet hiss.

"Sorry," he muttered.

"You shouldn't be," she whispered, then cringed at herself. She risked a look at him. Being so close to him was wreaking havoc with all her good sense. Her nipples were already hard and she couldn't help wondering what it would feel like to have those callused hands and hot mouth on her. She wondered if he'd be gentle or rough and realized it didn't matter. Both options were arousing.

When she looked up into his eyes, only inches separated them. Despite the dimness, it was easy to make out the harsh planes of his face. It was clear he was turned on even without the physical indicator.

She shifted against him, moving up, ready to kiss him, but froze when he pulled back, his message clear. Oh God, she'd read the situation entirely wrong. Her face heated up and she was thankful for the dark as she pulled away and rolled over. How absolutely embarrassing.

"Karen, I . . ." His fingers skated over her spine. "You've been through a lot the past twenty-four hours. I don't want you to do anything you'll regret later. I . . . can't take advantage of you," he muttered. His voice was tight and raspy and he let out a low curse before she felt the bed dip as he got up.

Surprised, she turned over to find him striding from the room in quick, hurried movements.

She told herself to go back to sleep, to forget what had just happened. Of course that was impossible now. Flopping onto her back, she let out a groan. Why had she done that?

When she heard the shower in the guest bathroom start, she cringed again—until his words registered. Words that had been in direct contrast to the signals she'd read in his face and body. He didn't want to take advantage of her? Fine, she'd take advantage of him.

# Chapter 12

Safe house: a house in a secret location, used by spies or criminals in hiding.

Tucker let the steaming water rush over him and inwardly cursed himself. What the hell was wrong with him?

*The sexiest, smartest woman I've ever met makes a move to kiss me, and I pull back like a fucking pussy?* He should seriously be committed. He had more important shit to worry about right now, but thoughts of Karen consumed him. When she'd been practically draped across him, all he wanted to do was devour her mouth, to taste and tease every inch of her. His cock ached as he thought of her.

Groaning, he scrubbed a hand over his face, then paused at a slight shuffling sound. He'd brought his weapon with him, but it was on the back of the toilet tank. The shower curtain had some kind of Parisian theme on it and was too opaque to see through. Moving quietly, he started to reach for it but stopped at Karen's voice.

"It's just me." She sounded nervous, unsure of herself.

That was his fault and he hated it. He stood there under the pulsing water, wondering what the hell to say. If she touched him now, there was no way he could turn away a second time.

"I . . . could be embarrassing myself here, but when you said you didn't want to take advantage of me, did that mean you don't want me?"

"No!" The denial came out harsher than he'd intended. Which earned him a sigh of relief from her. His fingers itched to pull the shower curtain back, to drag her in here with him, but he resisted. Barely. "It's just been a crazy day. We shouldn't make any decisions that you'll regret in a couple of hours." She'd been through so much and he'd kidnapped her. It was one of the things holding him back. Sure, he'd given her the chance to leave, but it was impossible to forget what he'd done.

"*Me?*" She sounded incredulous.

He let out a harsh laugh. "Yeah. Trust me—you'll regret it." Why would a woman like Karen want him? He'd fucking kidnapped her, held her against her will. Under normal circumstances she probably wouldn't have looked at him twice. Not with his scar. They were in an intense situation and emotions were high. People made stupid decisions when they were out of their element.

"How about you don't make decisions for me?" she snapped.

Before he could respond, he heard her practically stomping from the bathroom.

*Damn it.* He turned off the shower and grabbed a towel. He'd only come in here to find some damn relief and get some space from her. Just being near her messed with his head. Quickly drying off, he tugged on his pants and picked up his weapon before hurrying after her. He shouldn't have run off like a coward, but he'd known what would happen if he stayed.

In the bedroom, she was sitting on the edge of the bed, her body bowstring tight. She looked at him once, then glanced away, the annoyance in her expression clear.

"Karen—"

"Please, don't. I'm just . . . I don't want to talk," she muttered, before lying on the bed, curled on her side, facing away from him.

He told himself to walk away, to head downstairs and get his clothes out of the dryer, or get a midnight snack. Hell, just sleep on the floor. *Anything* other than what he desperately wanted to do. Instead he stalked to the bed, and made the likely stupid decision to ignore the voice in his head telling him to walk away from her.

She rolled onto her back, staring at him as he crawled over her. Surprise was in her gaze, but she wasn't pushing him away. It would be so much easier if she did. Because if she said stop, they would. Instead she was looking up at him as though she wanted him as much as he wanted her. His hands were propped on either side of her head as he looked down at her, his body caging her in. There was no fear in her eyes, just a raw, simmering heat.

It floored him that she felt the same attraction. She'd seen his file, she knew what kind of man he was, and she still wanted him. His cock was heavy between his legs and all he could think about was being buried inside her, hearing her say his name as she climaxed.

As he looked down at her, all his previous reasons for keeping his distance seemed pathetic. Maybe in a few hours he'd regret this, but no, he knew he wouldn't. He could never regret being with this woman. The only thing he hoped was that she didn't regret being with him.

"Tell me if you want to stop," he murmured, watching her eyes as he spoke. He wasn't strong enough to walk away from her. And he knew he wasn't going to want to stop, so whenever she put the brakes on, he'd stop.

Her lips pulled up into a sensual smile. "You sure? I don't want to pressure you into anything." The teasing note in her voice made him laugh.

This woman seriously made him come undone and she wasn't even trying. As he bent his head, she met him halfway, her lips brushing over his at first, sweet and teasing. He tried to keep it light, but one taste of her and he was consumed with the need to taste all of her.

Fisting a hand in her hair, he held on to the back of her head as he stroked his tongue against hers.

Arching her body into his, she wrapped her legs around his waist and slid her arms down his back, trailing her fingers over his bare skin. He loved the feel of her hands on his body. Her touch was so damn gentle, but he could feel how much she needed him, and that she was holding back. He didn't want her to ever do that.

Since he knew this might be the only chance he ever got with Karen, the only chance to run his lips and fingers over every inch of her body, this had to be perfect for her. He wanted her to remember this, to burn for him whenever she thought about him. He wasn't good with words, but he could show her exactly how amazing she was without them.

Reaching between their bodies, he started unbuttoning her pajama top, moving at a frantic speed he knew was probably pathetic, but the need to see her bared to him eclipsed everything else.

He wished he could turn on the lights or see her in the bright daylight, but as he peeled the top open, his mouth watered at the sight of her breasts. Full with hard-tipped nipples. She was definitely more than a handful. For such a lean woman, she had some serious curves and he planned to kiss and stroke every inch of her.

Feeling possessed, he helped her strip it completely off, then tugged her pants down her legs. She was completely bare, a surprise, and it was fucking hot. Though he felt almost desperate with the need to taste her, he gently ran his finger along her wet slit. Her thighs immediately fell open wider, the sight of her spread open for him almost enough to make him lose control.

"I want to taste you," he managed to get out, his words hoarse.

Her fingers slid through his hair and she arched her hips up in a silent invitation. It was quite possibly the sexiest thing he'd ever seen. He told himself to work up to it, to tease and lick, but he needed to taste all of her so badly he shook with it. There was no way he could reject what she was offering.

Inhaling her sweet scent, he flicked his tongue along the length of her wet slit. She jerked against his face, an erotic moan tearing from her lips as she rolled her hips in that insanely sensual way.

He stroked again and again, avoiding her clit and just using his tongue.

"Tucker," she moaned, and he knew how much he was teasing her. From the slickness he tasted, he had no doubt how turned on she was, but he wanted more. Wanted her trembling with the need to climax. Some primal part of him wanted to imprint himself in her mind so that she'd never forget him or this night.

Unable to hold out any longer, he slid a finger down her slit as he continued stroking. When he pressed it inside her she nearly vaulted off the bed, her fingers digging into his head as she groaned again. She was so damn tight and all he could think about was how she'd feel around his cock.

"Lick my clit," she half begged, half ordered.

The demand was the hottest part of it. His erection

pressed insistently against his pants, but he ignored the ache. Now all that mattered was Karen.

The sharpest sense of protectiveness and possessiveness welled up inside him as she made herself completely vulnerable with him. He sure as hell didn't deserve it, but the fact that she'd given herself over to him like this, after everything he'd put her through, floored him.

Narrowing in on her clit, he wrapped his lips around it and sucked on the small bud.

"Tucker . . ." His name came out as a strangled moan, her fingers digging into his head, then moving to his shoulders. Her short fingernails pressed into his skin as he flicked his tongue over her sensitive bundle of nerves.

When she started to close her legs around his head, he pressed against her inner thigh with his other hand.

With each flick, she rolled her hips against his face. He slid another finger into her and groaned as he felt more proof of how turned on she was. Her inner walls clamped around his fingers impossibly tight.

He began stroking them in and out as he teased her clit. The faster he moved, the more erratic her breathing grew. She made little gasping, moaning sounds, clearly beyond words at this point. Her body was strung taut, every part of her tense.

He increased the pressure of his tongue, taking cues from her responsiveness. When she let go of his shoulders and clutched the sheets beneath her, he knew how close she was.

As soon as he had the thought, she surged into orgasm, her climax coating his fingers as her body trembled and she continued rolling her hips against his face. She moaned his name over and over, the sound of her pleasure ricocheting through him.

Knowing he was the one who'd made her come, that it was his name she was crying out, he felt a sharp sense of triumph surge through him.

The unabashed way she just let go had his dick pushing even harder against his pants. He couldn't ever remember being this turned on. Hell, over the last four years he'd only had a couple of one-night stands. After being betrayed he hadn't wanted to be with anyone else, not emotionally anyway. So a couple of quick fucks had held him over when he needed release. He'd been on so many undercover jobs he hadn't been able to fuck anyway.

Karen wasn't just an easy lay and she was anything but a one-night stand. It was stupid to think they could have something real, but he didn't want to let this thing between them go. Didn't want to settle for only tonight.

But if it was all they could have, he was going to make damn sure she remembered it.

As her breathing steadied and her legs loosened around his head, he slowly withdrew his fingers from her. Watching her while he did, he took pleasure in the way her eyes widened when he slid his fingers into his mouth.

It was impossible to tell in the dimness, but he would bet her cheeks had turned red if her surprised expression was anything to go by. He loved seeing her blush.

Shifting slightly, he dropped a kiss on top of her mound, then moved up to her lower abdomen.

"That was amazing," she murmured. She sounded almost lethargic as he continued a path to one of her breasts.

"We're not even close to done," he whispered, feathering kisses around one of her hardened nipples, but not quite touching it yet.

Her fingers slid over his head, her touch gentle. "There are condoms in the nightstand. I looked," she said in a rush.

It took a moment for her words to register. He looked up to find her watching him, that simmering lust in her gaze. Sliding a hand up her smooth hip and over her ribs, he stopped only when he reached her other breast. Gently he cupped it, surprised by how heavy it was. He loved the feel of her skin and the way her eyes went heavy-lidded at his touch.

"We don't have to go that far." God, was that actually him talking? The words scraped out against his throat. He desperately wanted to sink into her, to feel her tight body clenching around his hard length, but he didn't want her to feel any kind of pressure.

"I want to." She dug her fingers into his head, her gaze going hot. "I feel like I'll regret it if we don't." There was a hint of something in her tone he couldn't quite define.

Whatever it was, he agreed with her. He felt as if

he'd regret it for the rest of his damn life if he didn't completely claim this sensual woman. "Me too. I . . . for the record, I've been with two women in the last four years, no one in the last nine months, and I've been tested." Anyone who went on undercover jobs was tested regularly. "I'm clean." He needed her to know, especially since she was aware of the undercover jobs he'd been part of.

Her eyebrows lifted, clear surprise in her gaze. "She really did a number on you," she said quietly, stroking her fingers down to his neck, then upper back.

Her insight made him glad he'd opened up to her. Keeping that shit bottled up for so long had worn on him. Nodding, he said, "I didn't love her, but I thought we stood for the same thing." That had been the hardest part to deal with, that someone he'd thought he knew, trusted with his life, had completely betrayed not only him, but everyone attached to the op. Looking back, he knew the signs had been there; he just hadn't wanted to piece them all together, to see the truth. Maybe he'd been undercover for too long at that point—who knew?

What he knew now without a doubt was that Karen was someone he could trust with his life. To be with her, someone the complete opposite of the woman who'd betrayed him, someone who'd put her own ass on the line for him when she had no reason to, seriously humbled him. She had every reason to hate him, to turn *him* over for being a terrorist, but she somehow saw past all the bullshit.

"I'm clean too. My last lover was about two years ago," she muttered, seeming embarrassed.

Something told him Karen was the kind of woman who only slept with someone she trusted explicitly. She'd have to not only trust someone, but care for him. She'd need that emotional connection. A boyfriend or someone she'd gone on at least half a dozen dates with. With the kind of job she had and the little she'd opened up to him about herself, it made sense. The primitive caveman part of him was glad it had been so long for her, and he wasn't going to let her regret this.

Wordlessly he dropped his head to her breast and sucked her nipple into his mouth. Hard.

She gasped and arched into him, simultaneously wrapping her legs around his waist. His pants did nothing to hide his reaction from her. Not that he wanted to.

Rolling his hips against her, he shuddered, wishing there was nothing between them. But he needed to work her up more first, needed her panting even harder for him. One orgasm wasn't enough. Never before had he felt so fucking obsessed, but the need to give Karen pure pleasure was all-consuming. He didn't want her to forget him.

Karen felt as if all her nerve endings had been stimulated. She also felt as if she'd probably lost a little bit of her sanity. Sex wasn't a big deal to a lot of people, but for her it was. Always had been. She'd never bothered dating when she was in high school because she'd refused to end up another statistic stuck in that small town. Like her mother. She'd heard from the small-town grapevine that her mom had gotten pregnant with Clint, then married a loser because of it. Karen had sworn that would never happen to her.

In college she'd had a couple of boyfriends, but she'd cared more about keeping her scholarships than anything or anyone, so her relationships had been short-lived. After her last boyfriend couldn't handle her work schedule—and he'd been with another government agency and should have understood—she'd sworn off dating for a while.

She hadn't thought she'd been missing anything. Of course she'd never had a man as talented as Tucker teasing her body. Having all that raw male focus on her was intense. She'd already orgasmed once and it surprised her how quickly she had.

Maybe he was just that attuned to her. Now he seemed determined to give her another climax. Which was more than fine with her. She was desperate to touch him everywhere, loved sliding her fingers over all the hard muscles of his back and arms. She wanted to demand he strip off his pants but wasn't quite bold enough to do that just yet.

He moved his mouth to her other breast, gently biting her nipple between his teeth. Not painfully, but with enough pressure that she was very aware of her body.

Cool air rushed over her other nipple, the sensation making it tighten even harder now that he wasn't kissing it any longer. Her heart pounded an erratic beat in her chest, her breathing unsteady as she stroked her hands down his chest and ripped abdomen.

She tightened her legs around him as he continued his slow, maddening foreplay. Her inner walls clenched, needing to be filled by him. She'd never felt so needy before, but the hunger to have him inside her was making her crazy.

Reaching between them, she slid her hand down the cut ridges of his abdomen. He shuddered under her touch. When she dipped her hand under the waistband of his pants, skating lower and lower, his big body trembled, making a smile touch her lips.

Fisting his thick length, she wasn't surprised by his size or that he was commando. The man was big all over. She couldn't wait for him to push inside her. She stroked him once, loving the way he trembled under her touch. He was solid and hot and his reaction was all for her.

"Tucker," she rasped out, not sure what she wanted to say and unable to formulate much anyway.

His head lifted, his breathing erratic. The dark look in his eyes had another shot of lust punching through her. Oh yeah, he wanted her as much as she wanted him.

Thankfully she didn't have to say anything; he just leaned over to the bedside table and found a condom. She felt a little bad about using her friend's stash and bed, but not bad enough to stop what they were doing.

Nothing could do that, short of a freaking explosion in the house.

She yanked the condom from his hand, taking him off guard. "Strip," she demanded softly. As she tore the wrapper open, Tucker sat up and shimmied off his pants.

She sucked in a sharp breath at the sight of him. Feeling him and seeing him were two different beasts. The man was truly stunning. Thick and long, his cock jutted up against his lower abdomen. She wished it was brighter in here so she could see every inch of him.

Beautiful would never work as a description for Tucker. He was far too masculine, too . . . Her brain short-circuited as he bent forward again, crawling up her body. As he moved, she reached for him, stroking him again, once, twice, three times—

"Condom," he rasped out, plucking it from her other hand.

She'd wanted to put it on him, but he moved quickly, rolling it over his erection before he covered her body with his.

His mouth descended on hers, hungry and demanding. She wrapped herself around him as her lips met his. Digging her feet into his butt, she shuddered as his cock nudged her entrance. She couldn't ever remember being so turned on before, so wet.

Everything about Tucker had her questioning her sanity, but she knew without a doubt that she'd regret not doing this, not experiencing every second of pleasure with this incredible man.

She tugged his bottom lip between her teeth and arched into him, rubbing her breasts against his chest.

The friction had her shuddering, but she completely lost all thought when he pushed inside her.

Her inner walls clamped around him as he thrust fully into her. She sucked in a breath as he stretched her. He paused a moment, seeming to understand she needed to adjust. Pleasure spiraled through her when he began moving inside her. She dug her fingers into his back and rolled her hips against his, meeting him stroke for stroke as he started thrusting into her.

He tore his mouth from hers, nibbling a path along her jawline, using his teeth and tongue.

"Tucker." His name was pretty much all she was capable of saying at this point. She raked her fingers down his back, only stopping at his muscled ass.

Each time he thrust inside her, the muscles clenched, the action making her even wetter. The man's body was like a work of art, all perfect lines and striations. She could just imagine how he'd look under her as she rode him. Something she definitely wanted to try.

Just the thought made her tighten around him.

He groaned, burying his face against her neck. All his muscles were pulled tight and his breathing was hard, ragged. Raking his teeth against her sensitive skin, he nipped at her when he reached where her neck and shoulder met. "Touch yourself," he murmured, the order in his voice spiraling right through her, hitting all her nerve endings.

She reached between their bodies and touched her clit. She hadn't thought she'd be able to climax again, but it didn't take much stimulation until she was shuddering beneath him.

Pleasure poured through her when another orgasm hit, the combination of his strokes, talented mouth, hands, and her own touch too much. As soon as she let go, he did too.

"Fuck, Karen," he growled before crushing his mouth over hers again. His tongue danced against hers in the same way their bodies were joining, raw and primal.

She loved how he didn't seem to hold back at all as he continued slamming into her. As her orgasm ebbed, his did too, the rush of endorphins leaving her feeling sated and lethargic.

She wasn't sure how much time passed, but eventually he pulled out of her. Too tired to move, she watched as his butt flexed and clenched when he went to the bathroom to dispose of the condom.

He returned seconds later, moving with a surprisingly graceful quality. Like a skilled predator. But his expression was soft as he crawled onto the bed next to her and pulled her into his arms.

She curled into him, wrapping her arms around his waist as she buried her face against his chest. "You really are a furnace," she murmured into him. Despite the situation, she felt safe and cared for in his arms.

He let out an amused grunt, those talented, callused fingers stroking down her spine in a way she could definitely get used to. "No regrets?" The hint of worry in his voice surprised her.

Laughing, she shook her head and looked up at him. "No, just wondering if we have time to do that again before we have to go in."

His eyes heated with pure lust as they dropped to focus on her mouth. "We . . . should check in with Selene first." The words seemed to be torn from him.

Sighing, she glanced over at the clock on the nightstand. It was close to one in the morning. Yeah, according to Selene's timeline, Ortiz and Freeman would be here soon enough. Karen wanted to call first just to make sure the schedule hadn't changed. "You're right." Groaning, she buried her face against his chest. She hated that they had to leave, but she didn't regret a thing.

After a few long moments, she started to roll off him, but he pulled her close, his arms wrapping around her like a vise. He brushed his lips over hers. The kiss was gentle and almost chaste, but at the same time not. She could feel his erratic heartbeat, a match to her own.

Finally he pulled back, leaving her wanting more. "When this mess is figured out, I want . . . to take you out on a date." He laughed then, the sound harsh and abrupt. "I actually want more than a date, but I just . . . damn it, I'm no good at this—"

"I want more too. Dating and definitely more of *this*," she said, a grin tugging at her lips as she wiggled against him. Who would have guessed he was so sweet beneath that tough exterior?

"Yeah?" He seemed so hesitant it was hard to believe.

"Yeah." She dropped another kiss on his lips, lingering longer than she should, because she knew that in the next hour things were going to change.

She knew he was innocent, but that wouldn't matter if enough evidence piled up against him. But she was on his side and planned to use all the resources at her disposal to prove it.

# Chapter 13

Blood choke: aka carotid restraint. A type of strangulation applied from an opponent's back in which the attacker compresses one or both carotid arteries (not the airway), causing a lack of blood flow to the brain. Causes unconsciousness after ten seconds, death if longer.

Rayford rubbed his gritty eyes, but nothing could relieve the tension humming through him. He'd been at Hillenbrand's for most of the day, and then they'd called another meeting with all their associates.

Everyone was pleased about the four men taking the fall for today's bombings. Very soon they planned to link the same disgraced agents to the drone attack of the Nelson fund-raiser. But that was something that would have to happen organically.

Or at least *appear* to. The authorities now investigating the allegedly rogue DEA agents would soon find digital evidence tying the men to the theft of the drone. They would appear to have a trail of communications with someone from the military base with access to the drone. Rayford wasn't exactly sure who; Hillenbrand was keeping that information to himself. From there it would make sense to deduce that they'd either sold it or used it for their own purposes. It would look like one big conspiracy to attack their own country for money and fanaticism.

"I thought they'd never leave," Hillenbrand muttered as the last of the men exited the house.

Rayford grunted in agreement. "What was our inside man able to discover?" The DEA agent they were using had been doing some behind-the-scenes work for them using his company access. While their hacker was good, hacking in to the DEA might eventually trace back to them.

Something Rayford and Hillenbrand refused to risk. It would ruin the whole illusion of their scapegoats taking the fall.

"Things are still on track," Hillenbrand said, heading for his minibar. "You headed home?"

Rayford nodded. It had been an exhausting day and while his wife was understanding and not worried that he'd cheat, he wanted things solid in his marriage. He had to look as if he were doing business as usual to everyone. No one could suspect his actions, not even the woman he loved. He was pretty certain she'd lie to cover for him if necessary, but it was better if she never had to in the first place if approached by law enforcement.

"You sure? I'm calling one of my regulars over. I can have her bring a friend." Hillenbrand raised his glass to his mouth and took a big swig.

Rayford kept his annoyance in check. Hillenbrand knew how he felt about prostitutes and keeping his clean image. He gave a polite smile. "Why don't you have her bring one for Gary?" he asked, nodding to the hacker who'd fallen asleep on the Chesterfield about half an hour ago.

The man practically had an IV of Red Bull attached to him at all times, so it was a surprise he ever slept. At least he'd showered earlier and cleaned up so he didn't look or smell as if he were homeless anymore. Hillenbrand had insisted he do so before the other men arrived. Rayford understood why. Looks mattered at this critical juncture and they needed to appear to have the most capable hacker on their side. So far he'd proven to be a huge asset.

Hillenbrand laughed, a real booming one, and shook his head. "It's hard to trust a man with no vices."

Rayford picked up his coat and scarf he'd draped over one of the chairs. "You'd prefer I do drugs or have a gambling problem?"

Shaking his head, Hillenbrand had started to respond when a *beep-beep-beep* rent through the room.

Rayford turned to find Gary popping up from his half-lounged position, his eyes going wide. He gave Rayford and Hillenbrand a glance before he snagged his laptop from where he'd set it directly next to him on a wood-and-glass table.

"What's happening?" Hillenbrand demanded, putting his drink down and striding over to the hacker.

Feeling chilled, Rayford slid his coat on and moved across the room as well.

"Got a hit on the final Karen Stafford's cell phone," Gary murmured, his fingers flying across the keyboard, his expression focused.

Rayford knew that Hillenbrand had gotten the name of the missing woman from his contact at the local PD. She wasn't considered missing anymore apparently, but they hadn't been able to track down who she was exactly or where she worked or lived. Gary had found eight Karen Staffords living in the Maryland and D.C. area and eliminated seven of them because of the pictures from their drivers' licenses. Once they'd matched up the Karen Stafford from the missing person picture Hillenbrand had obtained to a driver's license, it should have been easy to locate her.

Only it had been impossible because the address on her license was an empty townhome seemingly owned by an offshore company. It was very strange. Especially since she didn't seem to have any social media accounts.

Who the hell didn't have social media accounts these days? Rayford had some theories about who she might work for, but it didn't explain why she'd been listed as missing.

"Where is she?"

"Townhome in Maryland. Good area. Place is owned by . . ." More typing. "A woman named Carline Johnson." More typing, then, "Definitely not the same woman." A picture of a pretty black woman in her mid to late twenties popped up on the screen before Gary minimized it. "For all I know the cell phone is bogus and not the Stafford woman's at all, but this number is linked to the same address as her driver's license and the bill is in her name. It's been off until just now. Which is pretty fucking strange. People might turn off their phones, but she had to have taken the battery out for me not to be able to ping it." Gary stopped typing and looked over at Hillenbrand. "Unless the phone moves, this is the address it's at. I don't know if it's hers or not, or if she's even there, but it's a lead."

Rayford glanced at Hillenbrand, unsure of what they should do. He was so confident in some things, but where this woman was concerned, he wasn't sure what the right course of action was. She'd been seen with Pankov but had been listed as a missing person until a couple of hours ago. Their contact with the PD had no idea who she was or why she wasn't considered missing anymore. And their DEA guy had no idea who she was either. What if they went after her and she was still with Pankov? What if she worked for an agency and was helping Pankov and his men? Or what if she was nobody as far as their plans were concerned? There were too many unknown variables at this point, and that made Rayford's stomach twist.

Hillenbrand pulled out one of his burner cells and typed in a long message. A few seconds later the phone buzzed. Hillenbrand glanced at the screen, gave a feral smile, then nodded to himself before tucking the phone into his pants pocket. He looked at Gary. "Good work. Keep an eye on it. I'm going to walk Rayford out."

Gary nodded and returned to his computer as Rayford headed for the door with Hillenbrand.

"Are you sure you don't want me to stay?" Rayford asked.

"No. You need sleep and there's nothing more to do now. I've got a guy on it. I'll let you know what turns up. Keep your phone on you." The "phone" referring to his burner, the one he'd kept private from everyone else in his life.

Rayford nodded and opened the front door. A blast of cold winter air rolled over him, making him shiver despite his thick coat. "Let me know what happens."

"I will," Hillenband said before shutting the door.

Exhausted, Rayford glanced down the quiet street as he began making his way to his vehicle. He couldn't see anyone watching him, but that didn't mean anything. It didn't matter how tired he was, he'd make sure to drive around awhile before heading home. To see if he had a tail. They'd all been so careful and now that their operation was in the final critical stages, he had to be even more diligent.

Fear lived inside him that everything would come crashing down on their heads, that he'd lose everything he'd worked so hard for. But no risk, no gain, he reminded himself. And if he wanted his boss in the White House, he had to see this through.

Tucker folded his clothes into his duffel bag and zipped it shut before picking up Karen's dry clothes. She'd just talked to Selene and they'd be clearing out of here in ten minutes. Before they did Tucker wanted to do a clean of the place, meaning dispose of any evidence they'd been here, especially the food remnants and the condom.

He wasn't sure how the NSA operated on things like this, but he guessed they'd have someone on hand to do an efficient sweep and clean of the place. Including washing the sheets.

After dropping his bag by the front door, he took the stairs two at a time. Since the bathroom door was closed, he set Karen's clothes on the bed and headed back downstairs. Because if he stayed and waited for her, he had a feeling they might end up naked. Okay, probably not, since he knew a team was arriving soon, but damn, he wished they had more time together.

He kept replaying every sound she'd made, how she'd tasted, the sweet way her body had opened for him. He could still feel the way she'd dug her fingernails and feet into his back and ass, urging him on. The way she'd moaned his name as she climaxed . . . He shook his head as he reached the kitchen.

Nope, not gonna think about that right now. Wouldn't do for his dick to be on full alert when her people showed up.

It didn't take him long to locate a garbage bag. He replaced the one they'd used and wiped down most of the surfaces in the kitchen with Lysol wipes. After wiping down the small laundry room anywhere he might have touched, he started for the stairs. He wasn't exactly worried about leaving prints behind, but with everything going on, he wasn't taking chances.

Remembering he needed to replace the small garbage bag in the bathroom, he stopped and detoured to the kitchen.

Adrenaline flooded him as he reached the threshold of the entryway. A soft *snick*ing sound came from the back doorway. The heat wasn't running and Karen was quiet upstairs, so it was easy to discern. He knew what it was immediately.

Someone had sprung the lock on the kitchen door—which led to the backyard.

It could be the two men coming for him and Karen, but they'd said they'd text Karen when they arrived. It was too soon for them to be there anyway.

Withdrawing his weapon, he backtracked the way he'd come. Instead of heading up the stairs, he ducked into the living room right next to the stairs. Using the shadows to blend in, he flattened himself against one of the walls so that he had the perfect visual of the hallway. Because of the way the house was designed, there was no other way for someone to get upstairs without having to go past him.

The only way anyone was getting to Karen was if he was dead. That wasn't happening.

Soft footfalls filled the air, the faintest squeak of shoe on tile. The intruder was inside the kitchen now. Tucker hadn't heard the door open or close, so whoever was in was good. Or decent enough for B and E.

He heard another quiet footfall from the direction of

the kitchen, then movement upstairs. He bit back a curse, hating that he hadn't had enough time to warn Karen. But he could use this to his advantage. Whoever was in the house now would hear the same thing he was hearing and realize the person upstairs wasn't trying to be quiet.

The intruder would think no one had been alerted to his presence.

Tucker's grip on his SIG was steady as he heard more footfalls, a fraction quicker than the last time.

A man stepped from the shadows of the hallway, moving down it with a pistol in his hand and a black mask pulled over his face. The pistol had a suppressor. Oh yeah, this guy wasn't one of Karen's people. Unless the NSA had sent someone to kill both of them.

He'd find out soon enough.

The intruder wasn't making hand signals to anyone, and when he passed the entryway to the living room— barely glancing inside, fucking amateur—Tucker moved from his position.

It was a calculated risk, but he'd only heard one set of feet and the lack of hand signals was a huge indicator this guy was alone. Not to mention that the guy who'd come after them earlier had been alone also. Most operators like this were. People did hits alone, not in tandem.

The risk was there that he might be ambushed from behind, but he considered it worth it. Because no one was making it up those stairs. No one.

Without his shoes on, he was quiet as he swept out from his hiding spot and into the hallway.

The guy was still moving forward without a backward glance. It had been foolish not to check the living room, and now this guy was going to pay for it.

Tucker weighed his options as he approached the guy from behind. He could simply end him now, he could tell him to drop his weapon and risk the guy trying to attack him, or—

A door upstairs opened. "Tucker, I think my underwear is still in the dryer. Unless you're trying to keep it, pervert," Karen called out, muted laughter in her voice.

The man stiffened and started to turn. He'd realized his tactical error. Too late.

Tucker slammed his weapon across the back of the guy's head. Sometimes they went down for good, sometimes they didn't. Crying out, the man stumbled into the hallway wall, knocking a picture off it. His weapon tumbled to the floor as he made to turn toward Tucker.

He didn't give the guy a chance. Moving lightning quick, he attacked from behind, wrapping his left arm around the man's neck and his right arm up under his armpit. Instead of doing a blood choke, he squeezed the guy's airway.

The man gasped and clawed at Tucker's arms. Tucker used his taller height and lifted him off his feet. He ignored the man's blows.

"Tucker!" There was a sound of fast movement, as if Karen was headed downstairs.

"Stay up there!" he shouted to Karen.

Still choking the man, he half turned so that he had a better visual of the hallway in case there was a partner.

Gradually the man stopped kicking and the hands that had been ineffectually trying to strike Tucker stilled, then dropped completely.

He waited another ten full seconds before loosening his grip. The guy fell like a deadweight, but he was still breathing. Tucker hefted him back to the kitchen and dropped him facedown on the tile. He located an extension cord and used it to secure the man's arms behind his back, then pulled his legs back so that he was hog-tied.

This bastard wasn't going anywhere.

The kitchen door had been shut, but not locked, so Tucker flipped the lock before calling for Karen.

She definitely wasn't quiet as she hurried down the stairs and hallway. Her switchblade was out as she entered the kitchen, the sight making him smile.

"You can put it away," he murmured as he pulled the mask off the guy. Didn't recognize him.

Eyes wide, Karen closed the blade. "Is he dead?" she whispered.

"No, I didn't cut off his carotid, just his oxygen." Tucker wondered if later he'd regret not killing this guy, but they needed to know more about who they were up against. He grabbed a handful of the man's hair and lifted his head. "You know him?"

Crouching down, Karen got a good look at him and shook her head. "No."

Some of Tucker's tension eased, but not much. "I

haven't used any of my current burner phones to contact my parents or even my guys. And none of them are on."

"You think someone triangulated my cell?" Surprise was in her voice as she stood back up. "I guess it's possible. Crap, I left it on, thinking that since"—she looked down at the unconscious guy—"my people already knew where I was, it didn't matter. Hey, is that how you found me?" she suddenly demanded.

Snorting, he shook his head and started patting the man down for weapons, ID, and communications devices. "He's got to have transportation near here." After the man had killed them, he'd have wanted to make a quick getaway.

Once the NSA agents arrived they'd be able to track it down. Tucker pulled a knife and another pistol off the guy. Nothing else, though. The man might be an amateur, but he'd been smart enough to leave any identifiers behind. Not that it mattered once they ran his prints and face. This guy was screwed. Of course that was only if he was in one or more of the multiple databases the NSA used, but Tucker guessed he'd be in one. Either a military or criminal history because the guy had moved like an operator, albeit not a pro like him, but good enough.

"Are you going to answer me?" Karen asked as he stood.

"We found you by old-fashioned investigative work. It helped that we knew what you looked like and where you worked."

"You followed me home from work?"

"Yep," he said, fighting a grin when she scowled.

Her frown deepened as she followed him into the hall. "You're lucky I was even in the office this week."

Yeah, he had been lucky, in more ways than one. He felt damn lucky he'd even met this incredible woman. He picked up the fallen picture frame from the floor, surprised it hadn't broken until he realized it was a hard plastic type of material that only looked like glass. "Are you angry we followed you, or that you didn't see us?"

"Both," she said as he slid the retrieved pistol over to his bag with his foot.

The guy sent to kill them might have been wearing gloves, but Tucker still didn't want to contaminate any possible evidence the NSA might find on the weapon. Because there might be evidence on the bullets, the magazine, any of the interior someone might have missed while cleaning it.

"I'm always careful when I leave work," she continued.

"The four of us split up and followed you, so it's not as if you'd have been able to spot a tail like that," he said, stopping to pull her into his arms. He dropped a quick kiss on her mouth, which immediately smoothed out the frown. He was impressed that she wasn't freaking out from the attacker breaking into her friend's house, but he couldn't be surprised. She held up under pressure like a trained soldier. "I want to do a sweep around the house—"

A soft knock on the front door made them both still. Tucker moved into action, tucking Karen behind him.

"Raptor?" a male voice called out.

"It's Ortiz. That's a code word," she whispered. "It's me. I'm okay," she called out, loud enough for the man outside to hear. She went to move around him, but Tucker held on to her hip and kept her in place.

"Stay behind me," he ordered, using his battle-mode voice.

Normally his men fell right into line when he used it. Instead Karen sighed, as if she thought his precaution wasn't necessary. "Okay, but it's my guy."

The way she said "my guy" rankled Tucker, the force of his annoyance surprising the hell out of him. He knew she didn't mean anything by it, but he wanted to be her only guy. Frowning at the continuing possessive thoughts, he unlocked the front door, then moved backward so that he and Karen were on the opposite sides of it when it opened inward. The door was a momentary shield. He kept one hand on her hip and the other on his weapon. He didn't train it at the door, though it went against his instincts to keep it lowered.

These men were coming to help him and Karen; he couldn't draw on them. He still wondered if they were going to restrain him and take him into custody, but even if they did he had to go with it. He couldn't risk Karen getting caught in any scuffle.

"I'm armed and there's a bound man in the kitchen," Tucker said as the door slowly opened.

The two men moved into the entryway like trained operators, weapons up, definite vests on under their shirts, and wearing don't-fuck-with-me expressions. Tucker kept his body in front of Karen, unable to completely ignore his instinct to protect this woman. He knew one of the men, had seen him on an op before, but they weren't even acquaintances.

"Put your weapon on the floor and move away from her," the man with dark hair and clear Hispanic features said. The same guy from the Tasev op.

The other man shut the front door with his booted foot, his hands never wavering.

"It's fine, you two," Karen said, elbowing Tucker as she stepped out from behind him.

Since he didn't take orders from strangers well, Tucker holstered his weapon instead of putting it on the floor.

The two men relaxed a fraction. The untrained eye wouldn't have picked up on it, but Tucker noted it in their stances, however slight.

"Step over here," the first man said, his focus on Tucker but his order clearly directed at Karen.

Wearing the same clothes she'd been in the previous morning, she looked sexy in her fitted running pants and equally body-hugging long-sleeved top. Her jacket must still be upstairs. And he knew that she wasn't wearing panties, something he definitely shouldn't be thinking about with two trained men holding weapons on him.

"A guy broke in here," Karen said, doing what the

man ordered as she stepped away from Tucker. "One of you needs to check on him. He's still alive, conscious by now, and I'm betting Wesley will be able to find out who sent him."

"He's probably got a vehicle close to here too," Tucker said, not fighting it when the man who hadn't spoken yet moved over to him and took Tucker's weapon.

The guy moved like an operator, smooth and efficient.

"You're sure you're okay? You haven't been coerced or hurt?" The man Tucker guessed was Ortiz spoke again.

"I'm fine. Will you two please take your guns off him?" she demanded. "He's saved my life more than once."

"After he kidnapped you," the other man finally said, but holstered his weapon.

"I never said he kidnapped me."

Both men snorted, but Ortiz holstered his weapon too and jerked his chin toward the kitchen. "You come with me," he said to Tucker.

Though he hated to leave Karen, he did, not wanting to make the situation worse than it already was.

"I'm Ortiz," the man said as they entered the kitchen. "Officially," he added, since they'd run across each other at Tasev's place months ago.

Tucker nodded. "Tucker Pankov." Which he no doubt already knew.

"You know the guy?" Ortiz asked, motioning to the man on the floor who was groaning softly.

190 Katie Reus

"Nope."

Bending down, Ortiz glanced at the guy's face and shook his head. "Don't recognize him, but that doesn't mean anything." He pulled out a handheld device from one of the pockets in his cargo pants before tugging off the guy's gloves. Though the man half protested, making grunting sounds and clearly out of it, Ortiz pressed the man's forefinger to the screen and typed in some commands. "We'll know who he is soon enough."

Tucker didn't comment on the hardware but was impressed. He knew some small teams in the FBI had the handheld biometric scanners, but they were expensive and very rare, only used by special divisions that dealt with serial killers and other high-profile cases. Too expensive for the DEA's budget. Apparently not for the NSA.

"So, what now?" Tucker asked.

"You and Karen are coming with me. I've got a team to follow us and they can grab this guy." He motioned to the man on the floor. "But Burkhart doesn't want anyone else to have eyes on you just yet."

Tucker nodded, understanding. If word got out that the NSA had a man wanted for his alleged role in the Botanic Garden bombing in its custody, Burkhart would have everyone breathing down his neck. "Someone needs to do a clean of the house." He wouldn't need to explain.

Ortiz nodded in the direction of the front of the house. "Freeman will do a complete wipe-down and a check for this guy's vehicle."

The man was awake now but hadn't said anything. His face was turned away from them, but his breathing was slightly erratic. Oh yeah, the guy was nervous. He'd talk soon enough, though, Tucker had no doubt.

"Sounds good." Tucker wanted to stay and help but knew that was impossible. He wasn't running the show anymore and right now he wondered if he'd just thrown himself into that proverbial lion's den.

All he cared about was clearing his guys and hopefully a future with Karen.

# Chapter 14

HUMINT: human intelligence: the gathering of information from human sources. It is done both openly and covertly.

"Hey," Wesley, said, answering his phone on the first ring when he saw Selene's name. "I'm about to talk to Paula Jacobs, so make it quick." He was sitting in an armored SUV in her driveway about to knock on the woman's front door at this ungodly hour. The sun wouldn't be up for a few hours yet.

"Pankov and Karen are here. We've got him in a secure waiting room. You want me to send an interrogator in for him or wait for you?" she asked.

Normally Wesley didn't micromanage, but in this case he wanted to be the one talking to Pankov, especially since he didn't want any more people than necessary even knowing Pankov was at his facility. "Wait for me. Is that it?" She could have just texted him, so he was surprised she'd called.

"Not exactly. Uh . . ."

Wesley blinked at Selene's hesitation. A trained sniper

and agent, she rarely held back about anything. "Is Karen injured?" he asked, ice snaking through his veins.

"No, it's not that. We did a full clean of her friend's townhome." She paused, clearing her throat. "Freeman informed me that there was a used condom in the master bathroom. It wasn't that old."

It took a lot to surprise Wesley. "Pankov and Karen?"

"I'm guessing but I haven't asked. Should I put her in a waiting room too?" Meaning, did he think Karen was working some angle and had known Pankov longer than she'd let on?

He'd had a team watching Karen about six months before he recruited her and had done an intense background check. All his people had to be thoroughly vetted. It didn't mean people never turned once they were working with him—he knew that firsthand—but he was going to go with his gut. "No, just keep an eye on her. Don't let on that you know about them. If there is a 'them.'" For all Wesley knew, Pankov had forced her. That thought made him want to order his driver to back the hell up and get straight to the office. "I won't be long here."

"Okay."

Once they disconnected he slid his phone into his jacket pocket. "I'm heading in," he said to his driver.

His driver, who was also former military and part of Wesley's security team whenever he needed it, frowned in the rearview mirror. "We haven't done a thorough enough check of her yet. You shouldn't go in alone."

"I think I can handle it." Right now time wasn't on

their side, not with a missing drone out there and one of the Botanic Garden bombing suspects sitting back at his office. And his gut told him that approaching Paula Jacobs, a woman who'd just had a baby a few days ago, with his hulking security guy was just going to piss her off.

Especially since the DEA agent had been so accommodating. He'd contacted her using her private e-mail, wanting to set up a meeting later today, and she'd responded almost immediately, telling him he could meet her now—hours before sunrise.

After a quick knock on the door, the front porch light clicked on. The place was upper middle class, close to a bunch of schools, and from the various toys, bikes, and basketball hoops he'd seen at almost every house on her street, he knew it was a family-friendly neighborhood.

The door opened and a guy who looked as if he could bench-press two of Wesley stood there looking grim and annoyed. His mouth pulled into a thin line. "ID?"

Not exactly surprised Paula's husband had answered, Wesley pulled out his credentials and showed them to the man. He'd read the woman's file and knew her husband owned multiple auto body shops in the city. They'd met in college where he'd played football—which, given his size, wasn't exactly surprising.

Once the man was satisfied, he handed the ID back to Wesley and stepped aside so he could enter. "She's in the living room," he said, shutting and locking the door.

Wesley knew the man's name was Sean, but it was apparent he didn't plan to introduce himself. Following the giant, he found Paula sitting in a recliner breast-feeding her newborn. She had a blanket thrown over herself and the baby, but it was obvious what she was doing.

He felt like a schmuck interrupting them now, but there was no other option at this point. "Agent Jacobs, I'm sorry to disturb you guys at this hour and on your maternity leave, but I appreciate your meeting with me."

She gave him a tired smile. Her blond hair was pulled up into a messy bun on her head; she had no makeup on and was still stunningly attractive. "It's no problem, and you can call me Paula. I knew it would be impossible for me to get away with this little guy attached to me so often. And I also knew we'd be awake, so I figured it'd be easier for you to just come here. Why don't you sit?" She tilted her head at the nearby couch. "And, honey," she said to her husband, "will you get Director Burkhart something to drink?"

He shook his head as he sat. "I'm okay, but thanks. And call me Wesley."

It was clear her husband hadn't planned to get him anything anyway, as he sat on the edge of the recliner, his expression grim, just staring at Wesley.

Wesley hid a grin when his wife nudged him, clearly annoyed. "Listen, my son is almost done feeding, which means he'll be going to sleep again soon for about two hours. And we're both exhausted, so why don't you just ask whatever it is you need to ask?"

Appreciating her candor, Wesley did just that. "How well did you know Max Southers?"

Paula's expression turned pained at the mention of Max. "We worked in different divisions, but our paths crossed enough that we were friendly acquaintances. He's going to be sorely missed. I . . . I wish I could say I can't believe what's been happening on the news, but you and I both know how close our country comes to being attacked every day."

"Do you think there's a Shi'a connection to Max's murder?"

She shrugged and the baby made a grunting sound but didn't stop what he was doing. "I know what the news reports have been saying, but I don't know enough about what he works—worked—on to even make an educated guess. I deal more with pharmaceutical and big-business drug crimes, which, considering you're the director of the NSA and sitting in my house at two in the morning, you already know. Just tell me why you're here, please."

"Someone used your security code to revoke clearances for Tucker Pankov, Cole Erickson, Paxton Brooks, and Forest Kane."

Now her brow furrowed. "The agents from the news? The ones suspected of the bombing?"

He nodded, watching her carefully. People could feign surprise and some were just natural-born liars, but her expression seemed sincere. And he was very good at reading people. "The same."

"I'd never even heard of them until the news broadcast, which isn't strange considering how big the DEA is, but . . . are you certain? Why isn't my boss here, then? I thought maybe you needed to talk to me about one of my older cases or something."

This was where things got tricky. "It's likely one or more of your superiors will visit you soon. I didn't get the information from them." He wasn't going to say how he'd retrieved it, but she'd connect the dots.

"Are you trying to accuse my wife of something?" her husband growled, the question not surprising Wesley. "I think we need to call our attorney."

"I'm not accusing her of anything." He pinned the man with a stare. "I know she didn't revoke the clearances, because she was in labor when it happened. My team has checked and there's no way she"—Wesley looked back at her—"*you* had anything to do with it. If I'd wanted to make this official, I would have. But I don't want to bother with red tape right now. I just need answers without involving anyone but us. If you want to call your attorney and your superior and set up an official meeting, fine." He paused, waiting.

Paula lifted the gurgling baby from her chest and handed him to her husband as she pulled her breast-feeding cover over her shoulder. "Will you burp him and grab me a bottle of water?"

It was clear the man wanted to argue, but he nodded, shot Wesley a dark look, and strode from the room, cuddling the baby on his shoulder.

"Look, my husband's really overprotective right now."

"I don't blame him." In fact, he'd judge the guy if he wasn't protective of his wife.

Paula gave a half smile. "I know who you are and the kind of clearance you've got. And I appreciate you coming straight to me because I realize that if you thought I was involved with whatever, you'd have just hauled me in for questioning. But I still don't know who could have accessed my security code other than my superiors. I'm careful about my information. And even if the order was given by me, is it possible it was a glitch? If these guys did bomb—oh, shit. You said the order was given when I was in labor. That was before the bombing." She scrubbed a hand over her face, clearly exhausted. "Have they been under investigation or something?"

Wesley shrugged, unsure about a lot concerning the four agents at this point. "As far as I can tell, not officially. To me, it looks like someone wanted to kick the four men out of the DEA's system." And he wasn't going to tell Paula why, because she didn't need to know. "They did it before the bombing and wanted to cover their tracks. But they didn't want to throw you under the bus. It's easy enough to prove you had nothing to do with revoking their clearances. What I want to know is who above you could use your access code and who you think had a reason to want Max dead."

"You think Max . . . Wait, what are you trying to say?"

Wesley knew he was only giving her bits of information, but he couldn't afford to tell her too much. Not when he didn't know enough about her. "I have certain evidence that indicates the four men accused of the bombing might be innocent and that whoever is behind the bombing is also behind Max's death."

"You think it's someone in the DEA?" She frowned, her eyebrows pulling together as her husband walked back into the room. She took the bottle before asking her husband to give them privacy.

To Wesley's surprise the man left the room again, maybe because of the serious look Paula had given him. Because of the nature of his wife's job he had a midlevel security clearance, so he'd be able to hear certain things and he'd also understand when he needed to make himself scarce.

"I don't know," he said. "But a lot of things aren't adding up and I don't know who to trust over there. It's the real reason I came to you. You've got an insider's perspective and according to my analysts, you're unlikely to be corrupt."

Her eyebrows rose a fraction, but she didn't seem surprised by his analysis. She had a good job, and her husband did very well financially according to Wesley's reports. Money wouldn't be a motivator for her, and religious reasons were also out given the information he had on her.

"What do you want to know, then?"

"Gut instinct—who do you think benefits the most from Max's death?"

"I . . ." She shook her head and shifted against the recliner, wincing slightly.

He really hated that he'd come here on her maternity leave, but he had to push. "Someone came to your mind."

"Yeah, okay, but you're talking murder. And I'm not saying I don't think the people I work with are capable of killing someone. But killing in self-defense and flat-out murdering or hiring someone to kill one of the deputy directors is crossing a serious line." She gave a sharp shake of her head, but he could see in her eyes that she suspected someone. Or maybe not suspected, but believed them capable enough.

Wesley nodded, letting her get her thoughts together.

Suddenly she straightened. "Is this on the record?"

He shook his head. "This whole meeting is off the record."

She relaxed a fraction. "Fine, off the record, Raul Widom has a lot to gain with Max gone. Agent, good at getting the job done, but he's such a showboat, loves being the center of attention, getting his face in the news for a win whether he deserves it or not. And . . ." She grimaced, clear disgust on her face. "He's a sexist of the worst kind. Subtle, tries to hide it, but if I had to work with him, I'd quit. That says a lot because I love my job. Guy doesn't like women, the kind who thinks no matter her rank, the female should be the one getting the men in a meeting coffee. Probably why he's been divorced three times."

Very interesting. Widom, a man moving up the ranks quickly, was on Pankov's list. "Anyone else come to mind?"

"Yes, maybe. I don't think he'd have the stones to

kill Max and I don't know that he'd gain anything from it, but Daniel Vane and Max didn't get along. Personal shit. It's not like he'll be able to take Max's position or anything, though. Guy's just midlevel and that's probably all he'll ever be." She lifted her shoulders casually. "Still, he comes to mind as having a hard-on for Max."

"Does either of them have access to your security code?"

"I don't think so. Widom is technically ranked higher than me, but we're in different divisions and he doesn't have enough clearance—that I'm aware of—to have access to my information. But I wouldn't swear to it."

"Thank you." He pulled out a business card that simply had his name and his private number and handed it to her as he stood. "You ever need anything or remember something, call me. This conversation will remain confidential, so if someone hassles you about anything, call me."

Clear surprise flitted across her face. "Thanks. And thanks for the heads-up about my security breach. I'm going to change my code now. Unless you think I shouldn't?"

"Change it."

"I will. I hope you don't mind, but I'm not going to get up and walk you out." She winced again, her discomfort clear.

"No problem. I appreciate your time." Wesley made his way to the front door and found her husband waiting there.

The man nodded politely at him as he opened the door, his manner somewhat less hostile than before.

Once Wesley was back in the SUV, he texted Elliott and Selene, letting them know to focus on both Widom and Vane.

Karen's fingers clacked over her keyboard as she pulled up another of Raul Widom's bank accounts.

"You can grab some rest in Wesley's office," Selene said quietly from the computer station next to her. She was also working, but she had a headset on and was communicating with others while she clicked away.

Half smiling, Karen didn't glance over, afraid the worry in her eyes would show. Once they'd arrived, Tucker was escorted away and she wasn't allowed to see him. She knew where he was, though—in one of the typical holding rooms. She wished she could be with him. "I'm too wired to sleep, but thanks."

With a critical eye, she started going over Widom's incoming and outgoing money. There were so many angles to look at right now, trying to figure out who had the means and the motive to set up four DEA agents, kill the deputy director, and plant bombs at the Botanic Garden. It felt like looking for a needle in a stack of needles. But they'd solved more cases with less. "Did Wesley get more intel on this guy?" she continued, wanting to know why they were giving him a bigger focus now. Karen knew her boss had called Selene not long ago and was surprised he hadn't called to check on her. Maybe he was still pissed about how she'd run with Tucker.

"Yeah. Him and the Vane guy," Selene said.

"When will he be here?"

"Who? Oh, Wesley? Not long now." Selene started talking to someone else on her comm then, and Karen gave all her focus to her own task.

Normally she'd be multitasking, taking on a lot more responsibility than looking at one man's files, but it seemed pretty clear to her that Selene didn't want her doing too much. It was also clear that Selene was keeping an eye on her. Maybe they were worried she wasn't handling things well. But she couldn't be sure.

About fifteen minutes later Wesley showed up, looking a little tired, but put together in a dark business suit. His expression was unreadable as he approached her and Selene's computer center. Karen started to stand and greet him when she saw him, but he nodded at the two of them, his expression neutral. Surprised, she tried to bury the hurt that he didn't seem happier to see her.

"You two, my office." His tone was brisk.

Selene gave her one of those unreadable looks too as she fell in behind Karen.

Dread filled her stomach. Had something happened to Tucker? Had they found evidence against him? Or maybe she was in trouble for what she'd done. She thought Wesley would understand, but he seemed almost cold right now.

Once they were inside the office, Selene shut the door with an ominous-sounding click, then pressed a button on the big window facing the open computer center, frosting the glass over.

Tension twisted through her even harder until she turned and Wesley pulled her into a brief but warm hug. "We were worried about you," he murmured, stepping back, more warmth in his green eyes. "I'm glad you're okay."

She let out a shaky laugh, thankful he seemed more like himself now. "I'm glad too."

He motioned to the seats in front of his desk. She and Selene sat, but instead of moving around to the other side, he perched on the front of it. It wasn't a power play type of thing either. She knew him well enough to spot that he was on edge and was likely to start pacing.

Wesley crossed his arms over his chest, all the lines in his body tense. "Ortiz tells me that Pankov seemed pretty protective of you."

The statement took her off guard, but she nodded and cursed her fair coloring as she felt her cheeks heat up. "He was. He . . . I think he felt bad about everything." She didn't want to come out and say he'd kidnapped her even though her boss clearly already knew. She felt a sort of loyalty to Tucker now.

Taking her completely by surprise, Wesley pushed off his desk and crouched in front of her. He looked almost nervous, but that couldn't be right. The man never got flustered. She'd seen him get into a heated conversation with the president multiple times and not break a sweat. Clearing his throat, he glanced at Selene.

"Freeman cleaned your friend's place thoroughly, including laundry. *Everything*," Selene said meaningfully.

Karen nodded. "Yeah, I know." It was standard for something like that. No one could know they'd been there. So why were Selene and Wesley—"Oh my God," she muttered, understanding what their deal was. "He, uh, found the condom?" It was an educated guess.

Selene nodded and Wesley just cleared his throat again. Unable to stop her cheeks from turning stoplight red, she covered her face with her hands and groaned. Dropping them, she looked between both of them. "It was probably poor judgment." Not that she regretted it. Of course she wasn't going to admit that, however.

"Were you forced or coerced?" Wesley asked, his voice a deadly razor's edge. He still hadn't moved from his spot but was watching her intently.

Her eyebrows rose. "No, not at all."

"Sometimes in hostage situations captives feel—"

"Wesley! Okay, did Tucker and his guys take me yesterday morning?" At Wesley's dark expression, she decided not to answer her own question. "You know what, that's not important. I was never forced or coerced. If anything . . . I sort of made the move on him."

At Selene's snort, she glanced at the other woman. "What?"

Selene's lips twitched, as if she was fighting a smile. "I'm just surprised, that's all. You're very . . . picky."

Selene and Karen had shared drinks more than once and talked about Karen's dating hiatus. "I wouldn't throw stones if I were you." Not considering that Selene had not only hooked up with the man on her last field assignment, but married him.

Selene simply grinned and looked at Wesley, clearly waiting for him to continue.

Her boss still appeared unsure, but he stood and leaned on the desk again. Some of the tension had thankfully left his body. "I hope that this thing with him hasn't impaired your judgment." Though it came out as a statement, she knew he was asking.

Karen shook her head. "If I thought it did, I'd tell you. You know me; I can do the job. And I'd planned to tell you about what happened between us. I just wasn't sure how to broach the subject. He tried to let me go more than once. If his plan was to use me for some reason, whether as a bargaining chip or to get information from you, he could have done it. The evidence we're uncovering speaks for itself, something you know or you'd have handed him over to the feds by now. He's a good man, Wesley. I'd stake my job and reputation on it."

Surprise flared in her boss's eyes for a moment before he pushed up from his desk. "Selene's got a lot to fill you in on, but . . . Do you need to sleep or—"

"I'm fine, promise. You've known me to work for days without a break."

He gave a curt nod, her answer good enough for him. "I just spoke with Paula Jacobs of the DEA. She had some interesting things to say. Let Selene catch you up. You can work till two or so this afternoon, and then you can talk to the agency shrink—"

She snorted.

He gave her a dry look. "Either talk to her and *then* head home, or just head home. Your choice. You'll have an escort and someone will be staying with you until you return to work." Before she could even think about protesting, he continued. "That's not up for debate." There was a buzz on his intercom and he picked up without pause, motioning for them to leave.

Once they were outside his office door, the buzz of activity increased, even this early in the morning. This definitely wasn't a nine-to-five type of job. Karen crossed her arms over her chest as she looked up at Selene, who was taller. "What's going to happen to Tucker? And who's the man who tried to kill us?"

Sighing, Selene nodded toward their computer station. "So far we've figured that this guy was in the same Army unit as the four men who allegedly went after Pankov and his guys. And the one who came after you two in broad freaking daylight."

"Allegedly?"

Selene lifted her shoulders. "I'm leaning toward believing Pankov. Can't believe you freaking slept with him," she whispered, looking around to make sure no one overheard.

Karen blushed, unable to stop her reaction. "Can we talk about that later?"

"Oh, we're definitely going to." Selene gave a mischievous grin before her expression went into pure work mode. "So far the wannabe hit man hasn't said two words, not even to ask for a lawyer, but I want you to rip apart his life."

Karen's heart rate kicked up a notch. "Yeah?"

"Yep. Do your magic. We've got Red Bull and coffee in the kitchen if you need a jolt."

Hell yeah, Karen thought. The guy who'd broken into her friend's house might have been just a hired hitter and "doing his job," but to her it was very personal. She was going to find out who'd hired him and from there, they were going to destroy who'd set up Tucker and his men.

She couldn't deny that it was personal for her now too. She couldn't bury her feelings for Tucker, would be stupid to even try. She wanted his name cleared. Right now she just hoped he was doing okay.

# Chapter 15

OSINT: open-source intelligence. Refers to a comprehensive range of information available publicly (Internet, media, public data, etc.).

Tucker flicked a glance up at one of the security cameras in the matchbook-size, all-white room. The NSA agents hadn't restrained him when bringing him to what they'd called a waiting room. With an armed guard inside, two outside and two security cameras—which seemed like overkill—he wasn't going anywhere. Even if he did overpower his guards, which was a possibility given his training, he wouldn't escape this building. Too many of the doors and elevators had biometric scanners for entry or exit.

He might be good, but he wasn't that good.

They'd gone through so many layers of various security before arriving on one of the top floors. No one would tell him anything, other than he was just going to have to wait. But clearly Burkhart didn't think he was going to go on a rampage or he'd have been locked down tighter.

He tried to think of anything but Karen. But that was impossible. The guys who'd picked them up had seemed concerned about her, but he still worried she might be in trouble for helping him. He also hadn't liked how friendly Ortiz had seemed with Karen. Stupid, but there it was. She made him feel possessive and protective and that wasn't changing any time soon.

Tucker straightened when the armed guard standing next to the door tilted his head to the side. It was slight, but he knew the guy had an earpiece in and was listening to someone, probably wasn't even aware of the small movement he'd made. The man's back suddenly went ramrod straight, his posture perfect.

Yep, Burkhart was on his way.

Less than two minutes later Wesley Burkhart strode into the room wearing a suit and looking every bit as powerful as Tucker had seen in pictures. With dark hair graying a bit at the temples, he had sharp green eyes and was clearly fit under his black suit. He moved like a true military man as he dismissed the guard. Considering his job, his former military service was public knowledge, so Tucker would have known the guy had been in the Navy even if he hadn't known of his connection to Max. Both Max and Burkhart had been in together, been friends for over three decades.

His guard didn't even pause, just left the room, shutting the door behind him as Burkhart sat across from him. He had a thin manila file that he set on the table as he watched Tucker.

"Where are your teammates?" he asked, his gaze never wavering.

Tucker had expected the question, just not so soon. "That's not important now."

"You and your men kidnapped one of my best analysts, so I'd say it's very important."

He didn't respond, not wanting to flat-out admit he'd taken Karen. He would later if necessary. He'd committed a crime and would cop to it, but they had more important things to worry about.

Burkhart continued watching him with that laserlike focus. The guy was intimidating, but Tucker had been through too many training schools to count, including SERE (Survival, Evasion, Resistance, and Escape) school, to let it affect him. After Tucker's having been in war zones and undercover in some of the shittiest places on the planet, Burkhart would need to torture him if he wanted more out of him.

There was a sudden gleam in Burkhart's eyes, as if he'd read Tucker's damn mind. Tucker frowned, wondering what the man was thinking.

"Cameras off," Burkhart said suddenly. Then he nodded, as if talking to someone. "Stop recording audio. . . . Affirmative."

Tucker figured it was a bullshit way to make him feel as if it were just the two of them, that no one was listening or watching. He didn't buy it.

"You know what I find interesting? Karen had the opportunity to leave you. First at the coffee shop, then after you two were attacked. She didn't either time. And I know that you two were recently intimate."

Tucker felt his blood chill at the man's neutral tone, not liking where this conversation was going.

"Either you forced her, which I doubt, or she's been working with you long before yesterday. It makes me think she wasn't kidnapped at all. I have no video of her being taken or—"

"What the hell are you trying to say?" Tucker demanded, a simmer of rage beginning to surface. He didn't like the thinly veiled accusations Burkhart was making.

"I'm saying that unless you cooperate, I'm going to make Karen's life very difficult. She doesn't look like a victim. No, she looks like a woman who helped to aid and abet a fugitive from the law. A fugitive accused of being a terrorist, of treason. She's going to end up in a hole—"

Tucker slammed his fist on the hard metal table. It was bolted to the floor and didn't move, but the sound echoed throughout the room. He couldn't know if Burkhart was bluffing him or not. His gut told him this was complete bullshit, but if he was wrong and it wasn't—he couldn't afford to let Karen suffer because of him. "My men and I took Karen and you know it. I didn't force her, but I clearly coerced her. Anything she did while with me was under duress. She's innocent of any wrongdoing. So why don't you tell me what the hell you're playing at?" His fingers curled against his palm.

"Tell me where your men are and she won't be locked up." The man's voice was icy, unforgiving.

If the man was acting he was damn good at it. From everything Tucker knew about Burkhart, he couldn't believe the guy would do that to one of his own. But he couldn't take the chance. The bastard might as well have dangled him over a cliff and given him a choice. He didn't want to betray his men, but the four of them had dragged Karen into this. He couldn't let her pay for their decisions. If she'd been different from what he'd expected after they took her, he might have actually considered hanging her out to dry, but he couldn't do that to Karen. Not only did he care for her way more than he'd expected, but she was a patriot just like him. She loved her country and wanted to help the people in it. He wouldn't let her hang for him. "Fine."

Burkhart blinked once, surprise flickering in his gaze and vanishing so quickly Tucker might have imagined it. "What?"

"Let me contact my guys. I'll get them to come in." He couldn't force them, but if he laid out the details, they'd turn themselves in. They wouldn't want her in trouble any more than he did.

"People don't often surprise me, Mr. Pankov." His mouth curved up, though it didn't exactly look like a smile. It was more a predator-like grin.

"You were baiting me." He didn't bother phrasing it as a question and was glad his gut instinct had been right about the man.

"Yes . . . Turn audio and video back on," Burkhart ordered.

"You're an asshole." Nonetheless, relief flooded Tucker that Burkhart wasn't going to hold Karen responsible for anything.

Burkhart grunted. "I've been called worse. Now, there's a lot we need to discuss. The men who came after your team, then you and Karen, are all from the same Army platoon. They've been out a decade and done contract work for various companies since, but that's the original link." He opened his folder and slid a piece of paper over.

It had pictures of six men, along with their names and standard info like DOB listed underneath them. Tucker recognized three of them; one from his house, one who attacked him and Karen at the intersection, and the guy who was still alive. He pointed to the picture of the man who'd broken into his home. "This is the guy who came after me originally. What's up with him?" he asked, pointing to the last picture. "He talked yet?"

Burkhart shook his head. "Letting him stew while we gather more intel."

Tucker nodded, understanding. It was pointless to go at someone unless you had an idea of what you were looking for. "Why are you helping me?" he asked even though he suspected. Sure, Burkhart owed Tucker from the Tasev op, but Burkhart wasn't a man to do anything he didn't absolutely want to. He wouldn't be where he was otherwise.

"Kill audio and visual," Burkhart said. A moment later he continued, his jaw set tight. "Max would have expected me to, the evidence screams *setup* to me, and . . . the Leopard contacted me. He confirmed that you four have no ties to any Shi'a organization, especially not the one you're purported to be involved with. His particular group is scrambling, pissed that someone is trying to push these acts onto them."

A sharp sense of relief slid through him. "He's okay, then?" Tucker hadn't spoken to Ali Nazari recently; none of his guys had. Not since directly after Max's murder. Brooks had reached out to him at great risk. Now Nazari would have to contact them if he needed anything, and the risk was simply too great for his undercover op. Since Burkhart had been part of Max's extraction plan for Ali if he ever needed it, Tucker wasn't surprised his friend had reached out to Burkhart.

"Yes."

When it was clear Burkhart was going to request audio and visual to be turned back on again, Tucker flattened a palm on the cool metal table. "Wait. My parents?"

"They're fine as far as I know. The DEA has a wiretap for all their phones, but they're not at their house."

Tucker tried not to let his relief show as he nodded once. "Thank you." He knew where they'd gone and they should be fine until this storm passed. Even if the DEA located them, they'd just be brought in for bullshit questioning anyway. But he didn't want his family to have to deal with anything like that.

After Burkhart ordered the security cameras to be turned back on, he pulled out another file and slid it over. They had a hell of a lot to discuss and it was clear Burkhart planned to be hands-on with everything.

Karen glanced at the time on her computer screen, then inwardly cursed herself. She had to stop staring at the time while she worked. It was beyond pathetic. But she knew that Wesley was in talking with Tucker, and the not knowing anything was making her crazy.

They'd been in there over an hour. She wondered why Wesley hadn't pulled her in yet. She'd certainly expected him to.

Shaking those thoughts away, she focused on her screen at a soft dinging sound. Highlights lit up different lines on three different bank statements for three of the six men they were investigating. Even though the six men had all been in the same Army platoon years ago, since then they'd had a multitude of different jobs, mostly in contract work. Some appeared to be hired mercenaries—at least their pay scale would indicate that, though proving it would be difficult. They'd never all worked for the same company either. Two had worked for the same one at one time, but there wasn't any other overlap for the rest of them.

Or so she'd thought.

The same bank account had paid three of the men but while they'd been working for different contract companies. She pulled up the payee information and started digging into the company's profile.

When she discovered it was an umbrella for multiple companies, including one that had a couple of contracts with the U.S. government, she gritted her teeth and picked up her phone. Elliott was on the same floor, but he was currently holed up in an office. He liked to work in silence sometimes and Wesley let him. Though she could multitask, she needed his help while she ripped apart the financial aspects of these files.

He picked up on the first ring. "Yeah?"

"Can you find out anything and everything on a man named Thad Hillenbrand? Owns a corporation called H-Brand Security." She was familiar enough with the name. "I think it's a parent for a lot of other companies. So far I've linked three of the suspects as having worked for one of his companies."

"On it," he said before disconnecting.

There was no guarantee the owner was behind anything, but as she started peeling back more layers she realized that the six men were all linked not only through the Army, but through companies owned by Hillenbrand. A man who at first glance appeared to have a solid, reputable company. But she found some credit card purchases for what she knew was a thinly veiled front for an escort company. People of a certain tax bracket in D.C. knew exactly who to go to when they needed high-priced escorts, and the way the company operated was slick. The client wasn't paying for sex, supposedly. Still, not exactly a nail in his coffin. He certainly wouldn't be the first man to use prostitutes. Especially not in a place like D.C. Should have been smart enough not to use his credit card, though.

As she sifted through more information, she discovered one too many offshore accounts and a connection for all six men. The unlisted offshore accounts—which weren't as hidden as he thought they were—could just mean he was evading paying all his taxes, but . . . she didn't think so. It was as if the man had a small army right at his disposal. She couldn't believe it was a coincidence that the six men who'd come after Tucker, his guys, and her were all linked to H-Brand Security. She shot off her information to Elliott, Selene, and Wesley.

She started to get up, ready to go find Wesley in person, but something else kept scraping at her subconscious. She pulled up the file of the nine-man rifle squad the six men associated with H-Brand Security had been part of.

Armed with the three other men's names and other personal identifiers, she discovered that one had died in Afghanistan, one was married with three kids and teaching high school history in Florida, and the third was still in the Army.

She started running social media accounts and bank records on the teacher, then focused on the third guy. A man named Toby Austin. As she started scanning his information, she realized that he was stationed at the same base the missing drone had been stolen from.

A flood of adrenaline surged through her, making her hands shake in excitement and nerves. If these men were connected to the stolen drone, it meant that Hillenbrand had to be connected to everything: the drone, the setup of Tucker and his guys, Max's murder, the Botanic Garden bombing. The question of why still remained unanswered, but holy hell, this was an incredible lead. A thread they didn't have before. She was going to exploit every angle and find out just what kind of access Toby Austin had—her eyes widened as a recent news article popped up on her screen with Austin's name in it.

Her heart beat an erratic tattoo in her chest. She had to find Wesley *now*.

She shoved up from her seat, energy humming through her. Seemingly out of nowhere Elliott appeared at her workstation looking just as excited as she felt. He was tall, lanky, and often easily excitable, as she could tell he was now. His dark eyes glittered.

"All six guys definitely have ties to H-Brand," she said. "And I think I found something huge. What'd you find?"

Instead of answering, he grabbed her upper arm gently and tugged. "Come on. We need to see Wesley now."

Hurrying out of the central command center, they made their way down a maze of hallways until they reached a room with two armed guards standing outside.

"He's still talking to the suspect," one of the men said to her when they reached the door.

"Please interrupt him," she said before Elliott got cranky. "He'll want to hear what we have to say."

The man tapped his earpiece. "I've got Karen and Elliott out here to speak to you." A pause, and then he nodded at them and opened the door.

Inside she found Wesley sitting in a chair opposite Tucker. Her gaze automatically went to Tucker, but then she focused on Wesley. Her boss had his jacket hooked on the back of his chair and they had files spread out between them. She wasn't surprised by the flood of relief that spread through her to see Tucker again. It was as if she could finally breathe again, knowing he was okay. All that could wait, though.

Before she could speak, Elliott started talking at machine-gun-fire rate. "Karen found a link between the suspects. A man named Thad Hillenbrand."

"Owns H-Brand Security, has government contracts overseas," Tucker said. Wesley nodded, as if he already knew this.

Karen raised her eyebrows, but Elliott continued. "She discovered that all six men work—or worked— for Hillenbrand. All under different company names, but he's the one paying their salaries. And I just found a link between him and a man named Daniel Vane. The DEA guy on your list."

Wesley stood, his expression intense, but he was definitely pleased with the news. Tucker, however, looked pissed. Vane was on his list as a suspect, so she understood his anger.

But this was the link they'd been looking for. Now that they'd found it, they could move forward with clearing Tucker's name and discovering why he and his guys had been set up.

"There's more," Karen continued, with that unmistakable hum she got when they were about to break open an investigation. "I ran the names of the three other men who were part of that same rifle platoon. One's dead, the other's a teacher, maybe involved, but from preliminary reports I don't think so. I ran the information of the third guy, a man named Toby Austin. He was stationed at the same base the drone was taken from." She sure as hell wouldn't need to explain which drone either. "As a mechanic, he had direct access to that drone."

"You said *was* stationed?" Tucker asked quickly.

"Yeah. '*Was*' because he's dead. I haven't had a chance to read any official reports, but I just pulled up a local news article that he supposedly committed suicide two nights ago."

"All this is connected—the drone, the setup of you DEA guys," Elliott said almost absently, just mirroring what everyone else in the room was thinking.

"Karen, run down the rest of the intel on the teacher. Eliminate him or we bring him in to be questioned. I'm going to contact the base and get every scrap of information on Austin. Elliott . . ." Wesley continued barking orders.

Karen was listening but shot Tucker a hopeful look. The half smile he gave her had butterflies erupting inside her. She knew they couldn't talk much now, but she wanted him to know that she was fighting her butt off to clear his name. She couldn't wait for all this to be over. Tucker was the type of man she could see having a real relationship with, and she wanted the chance to find out if this incendiary attraction between them could be more than just physical.

# Chapter 16

Situation report (SITREP): an intermittent report of the current high-risk situation.

Tucker glanced over at the sound of the conference room door opening. After Karen and her colleague had come to see Burkhart, he'd been put in another room to wait while they hunted down more leads.

That had been almost two hours ago. He'd been feeling useless just sitting here, the energy inside him building each second that passed with nowhere to go.

Seeing Karen step inside was a punch to his senses. Still wearing her running clothes, she'd pulled her hair up into a complicated twist thing and looked sexy as hell. She had a throwaway coffee cup in one hand and a small brown bag in another. All he wanted to do was kiss her senseless.

"I brought you some food and coffee," she said, a soft smile on her face as she rounded the table to his side.

He automatically stood and took the stuff from her, setting it on the table. Seeing her now, he could think of nothing but last night and being inside her, how he was definitely taking her on that date once this mess was over. "Thanks. Are there cameras in here?"

She shook her head and before she could audibly respond, he leaned down, slanting his mouth over hers, needing to taste her. Her fingers dug into his shoulders as she leaned into him, teasing her tongue against his as her hands slid higher and linked around the back of his neck.

When she let out a soft moan, he forced himself to step back, knowing it could hurt her reputation if someone found them in here making out. That was the last thing he ever wanted to do. Breathing hard, he stared down at her, unable to think straight for a moment. He found his voice first. "Can you stay for a few minutes?"

Her eyes grew heavy with desire. "Yeah. Come on, sit with me," she said, pulling him by the hand down into one of the cushy chairs.

Not caring about the food or coffee, he held both her hands in his, swiveling her chair so that they faced each other, wishing she was in his lap instead of her own chair. "You doing okay?"

Her cheeks flushed slightly as she nodded. "I think I should ask you that."

"I mean with Burkhart. You're not in trouble for anything, right?" Tucker knew what the man had told him, but he needed to hear it from her.

"No, of course not. He wants me to talk to the agency psychologist and head home early, but after what we just discovered, that's definitely not happening."

"Maybe you should go—"

She snorted. "Seriously, Tucker? You think I'm going to go home and get any rest knowing you and your team are still suspects? That other agencies are out there hunting for you?"

"I like it when you say my name," he murmured. To his delight, her cheeks went crimson.

She'd started to respond when the door opened. They both turned in their seats, their hands automatically pulling apart. He missed the feel of touching her immediately. Burkhart and Selene strode in, all business.

"Have you told him anything?" Burkhart asked Karen.

She shook her head. "Haven't had a chance."

Burkhart moved farther into the conference room, but didn't bother sitting, which told Tucker this was going to be quick. "I've got a team trying to locate Hillenbrand. He's not at his office in D.C. or at his home, but he's got a lot of places he could be. We've triangulated his cell to his main place of residence, but he's not on location. If you're willing, I want you to approach Vane at his house. We've got him under surveillance too and he's alone. This will all be off the books."

Tucker pushed up, eager to hear everything. Karen stood too. If they wanted him to go after Vane, in any capacity, he was in. "What do you want me to do?"

Burkhart didn't seem surprised by his acquiescence. "Break in, incapacitate him, make it look like you're on the run with nowhere to turn and you know—or at least suspect—that he's behind setting you up. We need more on Hillenbrand and we need that damn drone. We need to know who else he's working with and what their end game is. There are too many unknowns right now, and you're our best bet for getting that out of him. You'll be able to get him to talk faster than we will, especially if he thinks you're willing to kill him unless he talks."

Tucker *was* willing to kill the bastard, especially if he'd had a hand in Max's death.

As if Burkhart read his mind, his jaw tightened. "We need him alive. I can't protect you if you kill him."

Tucker might want to, but he wouldn't. "Understood. I want to bring Cole on this with me." His guys were at a D.C. safe house lying low. It wouldn't take Cole long to meet him. He knew his other men would balk at being left behind, but he needed at least some of them safe. It would be better to go after Vane with a partner. The two of them facing off with Vane would scare the shit out of the man. Right now they needed all the intimidation factor they had.

"Fine."

"I'll be part of the on-the-ground command center, monitoring everything," Karen added.

He glanced at her, and it took all his restraint not to cup her face or pull her into his arms. The woman was incredible. He loved that she believed in him and was so concerned about him. "Good," he said quietly, which earned him another soft blush from her.

He gritted his teeth, willing his body under control. Forget a simple date. When this mess was over he was taking Karen on a long vacation, somewhere warm where they'd be naked the entire time. Somewhere deep down, he knew she was it for him. He'd seen what his parents had, two seemingly mismatched people who worked in every way that mattered. His dad had told him he'd known his mother was it within a day of meeting her. Tucker had never truly understood that until now. Hell, he'd never thought about settling down or having anything solid, real in his life. He could see all that happening with Karen. Wanted it so badly he could damn near taste it.

But he had to keep his head in the game. He looked back at Burkhart. "If we leave soon we can catch him before he heads into work."

Burkhart's expression was hard and determined as he nodded. "That's the idea."

Rayford nearly jumped when he heard his wife's heels clicking across the kitchen tile. Taking a deep breath, he shut the refrigerator door and smiled as he turned to face her.

Impeccably dressed as always, Johanna smiled at him, her pale pink lipstick perfect against her ivory skin. Her black peacoat was draped over one arm, her black Gucci purse hooked over the other and she wore, of course, a black sweater and a black-and-white wool skirt. She didn't deviate much in her wardrobe colors and knew what worked well with her petite frame. He loved his wife, but he also loved what she did for his own career. She was smart and beautiful, so he could take her to any function. Not to mention that she had a job of her own, something that kept her driven and occupied her time. They had the perfect setup together.

"You're off to work early," she said, smiling.

"I could say the same to you." He held out an organic energy smoothie to her, which she took.

"Early showing. Very nice commission too." Her eyes glinted as they often did when she talked about money.

Though her parents were disappointed she'd gone into real estate after getting a law degree, no one could argue that Johanna Osborn wasn't good at her job. She'd had the connections going in thanks to her wealthy family, but that wouldn't have mattered long if she'd been a bad saleswoman. As it was, she made four or five times more than her husband annually. Some men might have a problem with that, but not Rayford. He was proud of her. Unfortunately she read people well and he could tell she was eyeing him curiously now.

"You'll make the sale," he said, confident in her abilities.

"I know," she murmured, brushing her mouth against his as she leaned into him.

For a moment he let his hands slide down to her waist and held her loosely. He was too tense to think about anything else and she wouldn't want to have sex this early anyway. Not after she'd already done her makeup and gotten dressed.

"What's wrong?" Her eyebrows pulled together as she stepped back.

Sighing, he played up his reaction. Since he couldn't hide his stress from her, he'd just give her a line about work. Which wasn't technically a lie anyway. "Just work stuff. You know how it is."

Her lips pulled into a thin line, but she nodded. "He's lucky to have you. Something he'd do well to remember."

Smiling at her biting tone, he shook his head. "It's not him, just the stress of everything, that's all."

She nodded but didn't look convinced. Her parents were huge supporters of Rayford's boss and he didn't doubt she'd ask them to say something if she thought he was being mistreated. He didn't want that to happen. Ever. He was his own man.

"You're going to be late," he continued, knowing talk of work would distract her.

She let out a short curse and glanced at her phone. "You're right—turn on the news, Rayford. Now." But she was already racing from the kitchen, her heels clicking quickly as he followed after her into the living room.

She flipped on the big flat-screen. They rarely watched anything other than the news, so it was already on CNN. His gut twisted as he listened to a reporter animatedly yet somberly deliver an account of another drone strike.

One that he'd had no knowledge of.

The International Spy Museum, while not part of the

national landmarks they'd discussed striking, was still symbolic and had been on their list of places to destroy eventually. Hillenbrand had gone behind their backs. He must have been planning it even last night when Rayford had seen him.

"This is terrifying," Johanna whispered, her eyes riveted to the screen.

Anger punched through him, but he nodded, not needing to feign his own alarm. He didn't think Hillenbrand would target him. No, the man needed Rayford, but he didn't like this turn of events. He should have been kept in the loop. With trembling hands, he pulled his cell phone from his pocket, not surprised when it started ringing. One of the staffers.

He answered on the first ring. "Get Daphne to start on the press release," he snapped out, not bothering with a greeting. He and his team at work had way too much to deal with right now. As soon as he got into his car, he'd call Hillenbrand from one of his burners and ask him what the hell was going on.

He didn't care how powerful Hillenbrand was. He'd be shooting blanks without Rayford's help in their end game. Leaving him out of the loop on any of this was not going to be tolerated.

# Chapter 17

Black operations: covert operations that are not ascribed to the organization performing them.

Tucker glanced at Cole as they slipped into Vane's backyard. The sun had risen, but the middle-class neighborhood was quiet in the pre-work hours. Soon enough people would be getting up, getting ready and leaving their homes, but for now a blanket of snow and quiet had descended around them.

From the time Burkhart had requested that he go after Vane till now. The man and his team moved fast when motivated. Tucker had read over the impressive files the NSA had collected on Vane on the drive here and reviewed the layout of his home.

Standard three-bed/two-bath with more room than one man probably needed, but from the real estate records, Vane had gotten a good deal on it when it went up as a short sale. Couldn't blame the guy for jumping on that kind of deal.

But Tucker definitely blamed him for hanging him and his guys out to dry. He was going to bring this dirty piece of garbage down and make sure he paid for everything he'd done.

Cole reached up and touched his earpiece as they hunkered behind a thick tree trunk. Tucker knew his friend was muting it, so he did the same to his. Now no one on the other end of the comm could hear them.

"What is it?" he whispered.

"You really trust them?" Cole asked just as quietly, referring to Burkhart and the NSA. "We're moving on a DEA agent's house with no authority. If things go south, it's our asses on the line. They won't admit knowledge of being involved with us."

What they were doing was definitely off the books, but if it got them the answers they needed, Tucker didn't care. Right now wasn't about following the letter of the law. They'd already crossed that line when they took Karen. He frowned. "You worried it's a setup? Why bother when they could just arrest us now?"

Cole tugged on his black skullcap. "Just wanted to make sure you were really on board."

They hadn't had a chance to talk one-on-one since the NSA picked Cole up on the way here about ten minutes ago. "I trust Karen. She believes us and she's doing everything she can to help us."

Cole's eyebrows lifted, likely at Tucker's heated tone, but he didn't say anything, just turned his earpiece back on, giving them full audible capabilities.

Tucker did the same. From this point on, until they breached the house and incapacitated the target, they wouldn't be talking except when necessary.

"Moving in," he said quietly to the others on the other end of the line. Burkhart had put together a small but highly qualified team for this op. Tucker liked the way the guy operated too. As deputy director, he didn't have to wait for operational approval for the most part. He made decisions instantly and got things done.

"The front and sides are clear," Karen said. She was currently in the nondescript van the team was using as their command center. The sound of her voice kept him focused.

She had eyes on the front of the house and most of Vane's neighbors' homes, thanks to temporary, nearly invisible cameras a team had set up along the street before Tucker and Cole even arrived. As soon as this op was over, the cameras would come down.

"Affirmative," he murmured. "At the back door." There were multiple possible entry points, but they were going to use the back door. It was the best tactical point of entry for multiple reasons. The back door didn't empty into the kitchen or the master bedroom, two places Vane would likely be in the morning while getting ready. They could have gone through a window, but this should work well. And he liked the privacy fence in the back. That, combined with the overcast, dreary sky, gave them decent cover.

"Security is going to fail in three, two, go," Selene said.

Tucker nodded at Cole and began his magic on the lock. Opened it in less than ten seconds with a silent *snick*.

Weapon drawn, Tucker stepped into the small tiled

utility room, Cole behind him. A washer and dryer were stacked on each other with a laundry basket full of towels and socks on one shelf. Detergent and other similar items were on another shelf. Not much else in the tight space.

The room should open up into a hallway. Pausing at the closed interior door, Tucker listened. When he heard nothing, he motioned to Cole that he was opening it and would be making his way to the stairs while Cole should move to the kitchen. They'd already gone over the plan, but he wanted to reiterate anyway. Tucker would take the upstairs and Cole the downstairs. Nice and easy sweep. Of course they knew that Vane would have at least one weapon. He wasn't some clueless civilian. He might not have military training, but the DEA had trained him well and he'd been in the field for years and knew how to use a weapon.

Just because Tucker expected this to be simple didn't mean he was letting his guard down.

On silent feet they spilled into the hallway. Tucker went right, his rubber-soled boots quiet against the long carpet runner covering the wooden floor. As he reached the bottom of the stairs, he could hear water running upstairs.

Could be the faucet, but he was betting on the shower, given the time of day. Moving quickly, he hurried up the stairs, stopping at the top to survey his surroundings. Doing a quick sweep of the two extra bedrooms, one of which was an office, he moved on to the master bedroom.

The door was half-open, so he slipped inside without touching it. Water was still running from the bathroom. That door was shut, but steam and light streamed out from the crack at the bottom.

"Target in the bathroom," he murmured in a low voice, wanting Cole to know he had Vane.

"Affirmative," came Cole's reply. "Downstairs clear."

After a quick sweep of the room, Tucker found two pistols. One in Vane's nightstand drawer and the other in his closet. By the time he'd pulled them both out and handed them off to Cole, who remained in the hallway, the water shut off.

Perfect timing.

Pumped up on adrenaline, Tucker took a deep, steadying breath. He couldn't lose it with Vane. Not until they had the information they needed. Tucker had to remember that, but it was hard when he knew Vane could have had a role in sending hitters after him, his men, and Karen.

He moved to the walk-in closet and slipped inside. The door had been partially open just like the bedroom door, so he left it exactly as it was. From his position he had a perfect visual of the bathroom door.

Moments later the door opened and Vane stepped out wearing only a towel around his waist. He had a smaller one in his hands, using it to dry his blond hair as he hummed a nonsensical tune. In his forties, the man was in good shape. When Vane was by the bed, putting enough distance between himself and the bathroom door, Tucker made his move.

Without touching the closet door, he stepped out from his hiding spot, weapon drawn and aimed right at Vane. "Move and you're dead," he said as Vane's eyes went wide with fear.

No, not just fear.

Raw terror.

Vane swallowed hard, his gaze flicking over to his nightstand for just a moment.

"I took your weapons. Got that one and the one in your closet. Even if you have more, you'll never make it to them before I pump your gut full of bullets. And I'll make you suffer. There will be no easy death for you, you fucking traitor." Rage vibrated through him. Tucker was in full battle mode, taking on the type of persona he used when doing undercover work. Hard, unrelenting. Vane needed to believe Tucker was capable of anything, would kill him without pause.

"What do you want?" Vane asked, a slight tremble in his voice.

Tucker motioned with his weapon to the bedroom door. "Move."

"Can I put some clothes on?"

"No." Tucker needed Vane terrified. Keeping him half-dressed took away any illusion of control Vane might feel he had over the situation at this point.

Jaw clenched tight, Vane turned, his body tense as he did what Tucker ordered. He opened the door only to fly back as Cole landed a vicious punch to his face.

Vane cried out, his hands going to his nose as blood spurted everywhere.

That hadn't been in their original plan, but Tucker went with it. By nature, Cole was the least violent of all his guys, so it was a surprise he'd made a move like that. Not that Tucker blamed him for his reaction. Vane had betrayed all of them. Even if they hadn't been friends, they'd still been on the same side. Obviously not.

"Quit whining," Cole growled, grabbing Vane by the arm and hauling him up. "A broken nose never killed anyone."

The man started to struggle but then seemed to get himself under control. Likely because he knew it was pointless to take on both of them. In his mind, Vane would just be biding his time, waiting for a chance to escape or overtake them. Too bad for him that time would never come.

Cole twisted him around and slammed him against the bedroom door before slapping flex cuffs on his wrists and pulling them tight. "We're going to have a little talk and if we believe you, we let you live. If not, you know what will happen. No one will ever find your body." His voice was a menacing rasp.

"Why the hell are you two here? You're wanted for treason, you pieces of shit," Vane snarled as Cole shoved him out the door. "Thought you'd be in Canada by now."

"We're wanted because of you." Tucker remained behind them, keeping his own weapon out even as Cole put his in his holster.

"What?" The single word came out high-pitched, unsteady.

Cole shoved him as they entered the kitchen, definitely harder than necessary. The move surprised Tucker, but he didn't say anything. They needed to be a unified front.

"Sit," Tucker barked, motioning with his pistol to the kitchen table.

Cole turned one of the chairs around for Vane and stood next to it, his arms crossed over his chest as he glared at the man.

Trembling, Vane practically collapsed into the chair, as if his knees had gone out on him. Cole restrained his ankles to the legs of the chair with more flex cuffs. He released his wrists from behind his back and quickly restrained them to the arms. Tucker could see the rage in Vane's eyes, but it was mixed with resignation. He could fight back, sure, but he'd lose and get seriously roughed up in the process. Because Tucker and Cole didn't need weapons against this piece of garbage. Vane might be trained, but he wasn't anywhere near as lethal as Cole and Tucker. There were some things only military training and being embedded in a war zone in a foreign country could teach you. Experiences Vane didn't have. It was almost a disappointment he didn't fight back.

"The International Spy Museum was just hit by that missing drone. Minimal casualties," Karen said over their earpieces. "Push that angle too."

Tucker was glad Karen could only hear what was going on. He didn't want her to see what was about to happen. Plus, it wouldn't do to have any of this on video. Not if it was used later in a trial. Not that there was much chance of that happening, since this was off the books.

Cole's gaze snapped to Tucker. He opened his mouth to say something, but Tucker shook his head once.

Tucker holstered his weapon and made a show of placing his gloved hands on a bamboo knife block and slowly sliding it out from its position on one of the kitchen counters. He moved it over to the center island and first removed a Santoku knife. It was about seven inches and decently made. He knew that really good ones could go for a grand and upward.

Wordlessly he laid it on the island counter in plain view of Vane. The man's eyes tracked it the entire time. Next Tucker pulled out a paring knife. "I once saw a man remove another man's ears with one of these. Bloody and impressive." And true. It had been on an undercover job and the man on the receiving end of the handiwork had deserved it, so Tucker hadn't lost any sleep over it.

Next he slid out a nine-inch steel sharpener. Long, cylindrical, and in the right—or wrong—hands, it could be used as an effective, painful weapon.

Cole laughed, the sound pure evil and, if Tucker hadn't known him, a little terrifying. "I can think of a perfect place to shove that."

"What the hell do you guys want with me?" Vane asked, his voice and entire body shaking, clearly understanding Cole's intent. The man's reaction was pathetic.

Tucker knew that once upon a time the half-naked man in front of them had wanted to be part of their elite group. Max had denied him. Now it was clear why. He'd have failed the training. The truth was, pretty much everyone caved under torture, but this asshole wasn't even trying to fake being brave. He was letting his fear win. Pathetic.

Instead of answering, Tucker took the steel sharpener and held the dull edge against one finger while holding the handled end in his other hand. He didn't bother looking at Vane, just eyed the cutlery with interest. "Yesterday morning Cole and I kidnapped a woman." Now he met the dirty DEA agent's gaze.

It was full of fear and loathing. Vane didn't speak, though, just stared and shook. God, the shaking was going to make Tucker nauseated.

"She had no training against men like us and was still braver than you." The truth was in Tucker's eyes, he knew.

During his years of training he'd learned various interrogation techniques. Torture sometimes worked, but it was a fifty-fifty thing. The human brain reached a point where you'd confess to anything to make the pain stop. Forming a bond with the subject also worked well, but that took a *lot* of time in most cases. Time was the one thing they didn't have. Today Tucker was going to go with the truth. Lay everything out and give Vane his options. None were particularly good, but there were always lesser degrees of consequences. "You're fucking weak. You know it. I know it. It's why Max passed you up time and again and why you keep getting passed up for promotions."

Vane's jaw tightened, his dark eyes flaring with rage, but he didn't respond.

"Some things I could understand, like, say, taking a few kickbacks, looking the other way for a contact. That's no big deal." Complete bullshit, but the words would hopefully serve his purpose. Make Vane think that they were on the same basic, criminal level. "It's not like we get paid enough to deal with what we do on a continual basis. Especially for you. You've got two female bosses above you and I know that's gotta burn."

Vane's lips pulled into a thin line and Tucker saw agreement in his gaze. As if he simply couldn't hide how he felt.

Yeah, pathetic. This guy never would have lasted undercover. He'd have been dead within a week.

"But working with a man like Thad Hillenbrand against your own people?" At this point they only had a financial connection and he needed to push it.

Vane swallowed hard.

"Yeah, we know about you and Hillenbrand."

"Who?" he rasped out, feigning ignorance.

Tucker's lips pulled into a thin line. "Come on. Even if you're going to deny working with the guy, don't deny you know his name. Thad Hillenbrand of H-Brand Security?"

Vane shrugged, the action jerky. He flicked a glance at Cole, who was still standing next to him, arms crossed over his chest as he glared down. Cole was looking at the guy as if he wanted to slice his head off and was seriously thinking about doing it.

"I've heard the name," Vane said.

"And?" Tucker prodded, setting down the sharpener and picking up the paring knife.

Vane stiffened, his back going ramrod straight as his gaze landed on the blade. "And what? What the hell do you guys want from me?" Vane's voice rose now. If he started screaming they might have to gag him. Wouldn't do for the neighbors to hear.

"I'm going to give you one chance to be honest with us."

"But I really hope you're not," Cole growled, leaning down close to Vane as he spoke. "Each time you lie, I'm going to make you bleed. And I'm going to like it."

Tucker cleared his throat, drawing Vane's attention back to him. They needed him scared, but not too scared to talk. And off his game, which he clearly was.

"We know you've been working with him and we know he's behind the missing drone."

The truth flared in Vane's eyes for just an instant. Good. They were on the right track.

"We know he sent guys after me, Cole, Brooks, and Kane. And we know he had Max killed." Tucker had to bite back his rage at the thought of Max. Damn it, he hadn't even been able to contact Mary, to see how she was doing with all this. God, she probably thought they were all traitors. Tucker shelved that thought, reminding himself they'd be able to see her once they'd found Max's killer. "And we know you're working for him."

When Vane started to protest, Tucker moved lightning fast, covering the distance between them in seconds until he was crouching down in front of Vane. He slammed the knife down on the chair, right between the man's splayed thighs, through the edge of the towel and dangerously close to the guy's junk.

Vane jumped, shouting in alarm as he tried to scoot back. There was nowhere to go.

Tucker tamped down the rage boiling inside him. "This isn't going to be a case of good cop, bad cop. You will get no reprieve from us if you lie. So I'm going to remind you again. Do. Not. Lie." Tucker didn't move, remaining where he was, up in Vane's face. He could judge the dilation of his eyes better in this position anyway.

"So, where was I . . . ? Right, that fucker you work with tried to have us killed. That's something none of my boys take kindly to." He kept the edge in his voice, was barely restraining himself being so damn close to Vane, knowing he could have had a hand in Max's death or even sending the hitter after him and Karen. He had to completely block out thoughts of her or he was going to lose it.

"I didn't know he was going to kill Max," Vane whispered.

A complete and utter fucking lie. Tucker saw it in his face. For a moment he contemplated letting it go, but he couldn't. Instead he sighed. "What did I tell you?"

Tucker didn't have to move or even signal to Cole. Cole slammed his blade right through Vane's hand, between the metacarpals.

Vane's whole body jerked. He gasped, his eyes going wide, and opened his mouth to scream.

Tucker slammed his gloved hand over Vane's mouth, getting right up in his face as he made garbled moaning sounds and twisted against the restraining hand. "I told you not to lie. And you're lucky you're not dead. *Lucky*. Think about that, let *that* stew in that little brain of yours. Why aren't you dead yet, Daniel?" He used Vane's first name intentionally. "We need you for something. If you lie to us again, we'll kill you and find another way to get what we want. It'll take longer, but we'll deal with it because it's better than dealing with a sniveling liar I have to carve up for answers. Next time you lie to me, I'm taking off your balls." God, Tucker hated that Karen was hearing this part of him, hearing him sound like a complete monster over the comm. He hoped she understood that he was just putting on a show even as he got a certain kind of pleasure from inflicting pain on the man who'd taken his mentor from him.

As quickly as the thought entered his mind, he pushed it right back out again. He needed to keep his head in this thing. So many lives were depending on their handling this situation right. He felt as if he were walking a tightrope. If he pushed too hard, they'd break Vane. If he didn't push hard enough and Vane called their bluff, they'd lose him.

"Nod if you understand," Cole said quietly with just a hint of that feral quality in his voice.

Vane nodded, his eyes wide as he moaned what

sounded like "yes." His face had gone white and his lips were compressed as thick beads of sweat rolled down his cheeks and over his forehead. His body kept jerking involuntarily—from shock, Tucker knew. But Vane was still coherent. That was all that mattered.

Tucker removed his hand from Vane's mouth. "We're on the same page finally. I'm going to ask some questions and you're going to answer them. Do you know who Toby Austin is?"

Vane's eyes flickered with surprise—maybe that Tucker knew the name—but he nodded. "Yeah," he rasped out, his gaze flicking to where the knife was still embedded in his hand, blood trailing down the arm of the chair and onto the tile.

"Did you have anything to do with killing him?"

Vane shook his head once, as if trying to focus. He sucked in a ragged breath, clearly trying to force the words out. "He's dead?"

"Yep. Committed suicide. But you and I both know that's not true. In a situation like this, the man in charge cleans house near the end of an operation. I've seen it a dozen times and I'm guessing you have too. Are you expendable to Hillenbrand?" Tucker held up a hand. "Don't answer that. I don't want to have to slice you up for another lie." He glanced up at Cole, a silent signal for what he needed to do.

Cole grasped the handle of his blade and jerked it free, earning a shuddering moan from Vane. At least he wasn't screaming. But he was breathing harder, erratically, as if he was trying to control himself even as he shook almost uncontrollably. There was no control over that, though. Guy should just let the shakes come, but Tucker didn't care. Let him fight it. His face had gone even paler as he stared at a spot over Tucker's shoulder. Blood continued dripping onto the kitchen floor, landing with soft little splatters.

"When did you start working with Hillenbrand?"

Vane paused, swallowing hard. "He approached me six months ago."

"Why go after Max and the four of us?" Tucker kept his voice completely neutral as he asked the question. If he let the leash on his anger slip, he might do something he'd regret. Something he couldn't take back.

Vane swallowed hard. "He needed someone . . . to take the fall for his plan." The words came out in a rush, as if he was forcing himself to speak. He took another deep breath, seeming to gather himself finally even though he was still shaking. "That's you guys. And he needed someone important like Max to die."

No doubt Vane had suggested them up on a platter to Hillenbrand. Tucker kept his anger at bay and didn't acknowledge that he knew it would have been Vane's idea. "Why?"

His eyes shifted away, as if he was thinking of a lie.

Tucker grabbed his chin and yanked his face back to him. He'd get an answer. *"Why?"*

"Politics. *Power.* Hillenbrand's got some guy working with him. Name is Osborn, works for Clarence Cochran." When Tucker's grip tightened, Vane tried to shake his head, failed. "I swear it. They want to start a war in Iran. If the Shi'as waged war on American soil, in D.C. no less, killing the deputy director . . ." He trailed off, swallowing again. "They want their candidate in the White House and they want him to start a war they can win. That's what Hillenbrand spouts anyway. I know he's more in it for the money. I don't think he believes anyone will actually be a winner in that war. But the contracts he'll rake in will be worth billions. And anyone with stock in the company will bank too. Osborn will make sure that Hillenbrand gets the necessary contracts if Cochran is elected. It's a win-win for them."

Tucker dropped his hand. He didn't need to ask why Hillenbrand would want to spark something like that. Money was definitely the motivation. The man already had a lot of government contracts, but if they went to war with Iran, that would mean more contractors were sent overseas. Which meant a shitload of money for Hillenbrand. Especially since it wouldn't be a short war. They never were. A decade minimum, especially with a country like Iran. They were close to having nukes now, if they didn't already. "Cochran's involved?" Tucker wasn't sure he could swallow that. The guy might be a bit extreme but this was crossing a serious line.

"I don't know for sure, but his top aide, Rayford Osborn, is definitely involved," Vane added, face shiny with perspiration.

Tucker had no doubt Karen and everyone else on the other end of the comm were currently running the names Vane was dropping. "Was or is Hillenbrand going to tie us to the drone theft?"

He nodded, his breath sawing in and out. "Yeah. I don't know how or when, but that's part of his plan too."

"Why'd he hit the International Spy Museum this morning?"

Vane stared at him, blinking once. "Hit it?"

"With the drone."

He blinked again and shook his head vehemently. "No way. No way he would do something like that without telling me."

Cole snorted and grabbed the back of Vane's chair. Wordlessly he dragged him across the floor, not being gentle about it. Tucker stayed close, stopping in the living room with them. Since he had the same type of system, he turned on the flat-screen mounted on the wall. The national news would have it by this time, but he scrolled to a local news channel.

After five minutes of letting Vane watch, he switched off the TV and sat on the coffee table, facing him. Cole stood behind Vane, arms crossed over his chest, looking like a menace. Even if Vane couldn't see him, he felt his presence, was aware of the barely leashed tiger at his back.

"I would ask you what Hillenbrand's next target is, but it appears you're not in the loop."

Vane wet his lips with his tongue. "Can I get some water?"

"No," Cole said before Tucker could respond.

"So, what was supposed to be the next target?" Tucker asked.

He wet his lips again, shifted nervously in the chair, his movement limited. The bleeding had slowed a little, but not by much. "The museum was on our list of targets, but it wasn't supposed to happen until later. And I don't know the exact dates or times of anything. I swear it!" His voice rose when Cole shifted slightly behind him. "He told us all that he would call meetings the night before or day of any attack. He likes being in control, the one pulling the strings. Everyone shows up when he calls."

Tucker wanted to know who "everyone" was, but held off. He figured Burkhart would be able to get all those names out of Vane later. "Was there a meeting last night?"

"Yes, but the drone hit was never mentioned."

"Where's he keeping the drone?" They'd done something to the tracking system when they took it. Something incredibly sophisticated to disable it.

Vane snorted. "I have no idea. I don't even think Osborn knows."

Tucker hoped Karen was already running info on Osborn. If the aide to a potential presidential candidate was involved, there was no telling how far this thing went. "Where do your meetings take place?"

He paused, but sighed as he answered, "One of his places. I tried to run the information on the owner from work once and it's not under his name."

"Give me the address."

Vane shook his head, his breathing erratic once again. "No. You still need me and I'm not fucking stupid. I'm not giving you everything now. I need some assurances that you're not going to kill me."

"Fair enough. . . ." He'd let Burkhart get that out of him. Finding that out wasn't part of Tucker's role in this. "Why'd you pick me and my guys to set up?" Tucker figured he knew the answer but wanted to hear it. Everything to this point was pretty damn condemning, but he wanted Vane to completely hang himself with his confession. It would be a pleasure to watch his face later when they played back all they'd recorded.

His jaw hardened, that barely concealed hatred shining through in his eyes. "Because fuck you all, that's why." His eyes were glassy now, his face gray. Maybe the blood loss was making him ballsy, because the statement took Tucker off guard.

Cole moved behind Vane, as if to strike him, but Tucker held up a hand. "How'd you do it? Getting our security clearances revoked would take some serious skill. And we know you laid some other groundwork to get it publicized that we're terrorists. What we can't figure out is how you did it." More lies, but he wanted a complete confession.

Despite being restrained to a chair with a broken nose and bleeding hand, Vane looked positively smug. "That was Max's problem. He always underestimated me. I got your security clearance revoked. *Me.* No one else. Watched that bitch type her code in and that wasn't easy," he growled, clearly talking about Paula

Jacobs. At least they knew how he'd gotten the other agent's code now.

He snarled, continuing, as some of the color returned to his cheeks, though Tucker guessed it was just Vane's rage. "And I laid a perfect trail to offshore bank accounts that led to you four morons!" His eyes had gone wild as he apparently dropped some of his need for self-preservation. "Not too obvious, but unless the forensics team on you guys are complete fucking morons, they'll find it. You four always thought you were better than me. Now your lives are destroyed. Because of me!"

Tucker hauled back and slammed his fist into Vane's nose again. He screamed, twisting and instinctively trying to move his hands to hold his nose.

Ignoring him, Tucker stood and walked out. He'd heard enough. "You get all that?" he murmured once he'd left the room.

"Every word," Karen said. Her voice was neutral and he hated that he didn't know what she was thinking. He worried she was disgusted by him now. Or worse, afraid of him. He wasn't sorry for the way he'd gotten Vane to talk, but he was sorry she'd had to hear him. "A four-person team is about to enter the residence through the front door."

"Affirmative." Before he'd finished the word, the front door swung open.

Burkhart, Selene, Ortiz, and Freeman strode in. Vane was going to be beyond pissed when he learned that everything he'd said had been recorded. Would it legally stand up in court? It didn't matter at this point. Vane was screwed and would be facing serious jail time one way or another.

The fact that Burkhart was here would show Vane how deep a hole he was going to be thrown into. Burkhart would act as a lifeline of sorts. He was the only one able to actually negotiate with Vane as far as a lesser sentence went. How much Vane cooperated from this point forward would go a long way in how things went down for him. If he helped them capture Hillenbrand along with whoever else was working with them, Burkhart would "help" him get a plea deal.

"The van's out front. They'll pick you up," Burkhart said, dismissing Tucker and Cole.

Tucker exited with Cole right next to him. He glanced around the still-quiet neighborhood, glad to note there was no activity. A nondescript oversize van waited at the curb, the engine so quiet he wouldn't have been sure it was even running if not for the exhaust. When they reached the back doors, one of them opened up. An armed man in black fatigues motioned for them to enter. As soon as they were inside, it started moving. Though it was small, there was enough room for the five of them to fit comfortably enough. There were six giant computer screens covering the walls, three on each side.

Karen and Elliott sat at two computer consoles. Seeing her was a relief to Tucker's senses. The agent thankfully took a seat next to Elliott, leaving three seats open. Tucker took the seat next to Karen, not surprised when Cole sat on the other side of him.

But he ignored his friend for now, swiveling the small chair to face her.

She shot a glance at Elliott and the other guy before turning back to him. "I'm glad you're okay," she murmured. Her expression and tone were soft.

The statement took him off guard. "That was a piece of cake," he said just as quietly. He'd never thought about his size one way or another before, but right now he hated how big he was. He wanted to reassure her that he wasn't a dangerous monster, but wasn't sure how to do that with an audience.

She looked as if she wanted to say more, those gorgeous lips of hers opening but snapping shut just as quickly.

What he wouldn't give to be alone with her right now, to tell her that everything he'd done had been an act. In his periphery he could see that the other two men weren't paying attention and he didn't care if Cole was, so he covertly took Karen's hand, stroking her palm with his thumb.

She swallowed hard as she watched him but curled her fingers around his. He knew only seconds had ticked by, but it felt as if it were an eternity as he stared into her green eyes. He could seriously drown in that gaze. The woman had become an addiction, one he wasn't giving up.

When they hit a bump in the road, she seemed to gather herself and quickly pulled her hand back. She turned to her computer. "We're headed to . . . an undisclosed location. The others will be behind us pretty soon if Vane cooperates."

Tucker wanted to ask questions but knew it was pointless. If she'd been able to tell him where they were going, she would have. The last thing he wanted to do was put Karen in an awkward position, so he simply nodded and leaned back in his chair.

Vane's coerced confession alone might not be enough to clear him and his guys, but now that they had so much info on him, all his dirty deeds were going to come to light very soon. For the first time in days Tucker experienced a serious relief that they were about to get cleared.

# Chapter 18

Soup sandwich: military in origin. Used to reference a screwed-up situation or an unsatisfactory performance.

"Talk," Cole murmured.

Tucker glanced around the undisclosed location, which turned out to be a spacious warehouse in the heart of D.C. The security on the outside was no joke, though. Cameras, armed guards, and at least one sniper positioned on a nearby rooftop. There were a dozen men and women quietly milling about the place, some working on computers, others laying out weapons and tactical gear on tables. It was odd to be on the fringe of this. He and Cole were so used to being in the fray on any op. He hated feeling useless.

They'd been relegated to sitting at a table by themselves while everyone waited for Burkhart to get there. "About what?" Tucker asked.

Cole had straddled his chair and was resting his chin on his hands as he watched Tucker. "Don't be an asshole. While we wait to find out if we're out of this fucking soup sandwich, you'd better tell me what's going on with you and Red."

"What do you want me to say?" Tucker tried to keep his gaze off Karen, but he kept straying back to where she sat with Elliott, apparently deep in conversation as the two of them worked on something on her laptop. He wanted to be over there with her, just to be close to her.

"You and Karen. How did it even happen?"

He shrugged, but turned to face his friend even though he didn't know what to say. Wasn't sure how much he wanted to share with Cole, with *anyone*, about his relationship with Karen. "We're . . ." What the hell were they?

"Fucking?" Cole asked, no malice in his voice. But the word pissed Tucker off. It must have shown in his eyes, because Cole raised his hands, palms up. "Shit, man. Sorry. You're not giving me anything here."

"She trusted us when we gave her no reason to. When that hitter came after us, she could have stayed and waited for her people, but she left with me, found us a safe place to hunker down. She went to bat for us with her boss. I respect the hell out of her. And I like her. A lot." Though that seemed like such a pathetic description of his feelings for her. What he felt for her was way more intense than just *like*. It was why, despite the trust issues he'd always had in the past with other women, those just didn't *exist* with her. If anything, he didn't deserve her damn trust after the way he'd kidnapped her. "I think . . ." Oh hell, he felt like a first-class

moron admitting it, but . . . "She might be it for me."
Instead of experiencing terror, he felt a rightness settling in his chest.

Cole blinked once in pure surprise. "Damn." He
shot another look at Karen, this time more speculative.
"Well, if the way she's been shooting glances at you is
any indication, she likes you too. And she is smoking
hot." That was definite male appreciation in his voice.

Tucker automatically looked over at her and found
her watching him. She wasn't sitting anymore, but
standing at the end of one of the tables. She tilted her
chin in the direction of one of the offices, then started
walking in that direction with purpose.

Wordlessly he stood and followed her. He didn't
know what she wanted, but any excuse to get a few
minutes alone with her was more than fine with him.
Behind him he heard Cole chuckling, but he ignored
his friend.

Instead of heading to one of the office doors, Karen
ducked down one of the only hallways. He hadn't seen
much of the warehouse, but he guessed it led to one of
the exits. When he stepped into the dimly lit hallway,
he saw an exit door at the far end of the hall, but there
were half a dozen doors along the hallway itself. She
disappeared through one of them.

After a glance behind him to make sure no one was
following, he hurried after her. When he reached the
open doorway, Karen grabbed his shirt and tugged him
in with her. Taking him completely by surprise, she
yanked him down, her mouth searching out his.

He crushed his lips over hers, feeling hungry and needy and a little obsessed. He'd needed to hold her, touch her, know that she wasn't afraid of him or revolted by what he'd done. It seemed like a miracle she wanted him as much as he did her.

He flicked his tongue over hers, tasting her sweetness, wanting more of it. Once again he was struck by how desperate he was to have this woman. Not wanting anyone to see them, he used his foot to shut the door to what he vaguely registered as a supply closet behind them.

As he did, she abruptly pulled back, breathing hard. She spread her palms over his chest, stroking him. "They'll be here in twenty minutes," she rasped out. "I just wanted a few minutes alone with you. I was so worried about you when you were in Vane's house. I've never really worried about anyone on an op before. I mean, I have, but not the way I was for you." The fear in her voice was real.

And surprising. That had been one of the easiest ops he'd been on. Ever. He'd been careful on it, but he wasn't sure that it even qualified as an op. More like a little B and E. He cupped her cheek, warmth and hunger for the woman in front of him spreading through him like wildfire. No one had ever worried about him like this. His guys watched one another's backs on missions, but no one outside the team ever worried about them. And the truth was, his guys weren't concerned in the sense that Karen had been. They were all highly trained and did their jobs, end of story. He stroked his thumb over her cheek. "I'm sorry you had to hear everything I said and did to him."

"Screw him," she growled with surprising heat. "He made his choices."

The anger behind her words took him off guard. As she looked up at him with such fierceness, he was struck by how far he'd already fallen for her. Oh yeah, he was trusting his gut on this even if he got burned in the end. It was how he lived his life, how he'd survived so long under cover. His instinct was the one thing he'd never questioned. So he did the only thing he could.

He kissed her again, hot and hard, as he backed her up against the door. She deserved better than a quickie in a supply closet, but this was their circumstance and he embraced it.

She grabbed his shoulders and hoisted herself up against him. He grabbed her ass and held her tight as she wrapped her legs around him.

His erection was a heavy pulse between his legs. What they were doing was stupid, but he couldn't seem to stop himself. Didn't want to. They might not be able to do everything he wanted, but he could at least get her off. The sudden thought of that had his hips rolling against hers involuntarily, as if he had no control over himself.

He reached between their bodies, sliding his hand down the front of her running pants and thanking God for the elastic material. She jerked against him, possibly in surprise, but let out a soft moan when he dipped his fingers under her panties and cupped her mound. He loved that she was bare. When he slid a finger over her clit, he felt how wet she was and groaned.

Pulling back, he gently nipped at her jaw. "Sweetheart, you're going to kill me," he murmured. "We shouldn't be doing this." There was no conviction in his words, though. If she'd left her team he figured she could spare the time.

"Don't stop." Her voice was a whisper as she reached between their bodies, squeezing her legs tighter around him to hold herself in place as she went for the button of his cargo pants.

He couldn't believe what she was doing but didn't want to stop her. Torn, he stared down at her. "I don't have a condom."

"Pull out." She didn't even pause.

A dozen things went through his head at that moment, but he knew he wasn't going to fight this. He was willing to take on any risk because he needed her too badly. At this point he didn't think he could stop if someone held a gun to his head. "We'll be quiet," he said more for her benefit than his. He didn't work with these people and he knew without a doubt that this was out of character for Karen. Hell, her last lover had been years ago.

If she didn't care about the location, he didn't either. They were so far away from everyone he couldn't hear them anyway, so he knew that he and Karen had actual privacy. However temporarily.

Nodding, she started on his button and zipper again. As she worked it free, he reached behind his back and pulled at her shoelaces, tugging her sneakers free. Next he latched onto her running pants, shoving them and her panties down her legs as she shoved at his pants. They both hummed with a franticness he couldn't begin to contain.

He was practically vibrating with the need to be in her. He couldn't believe he was going to be inside her with no barrier. The thought alone was making him ache so hard he was afraid he'd embarrass himself.

Not bothering with his shoes or their shirts, he just let his pants fall to his ankles as he cupped her mound again. Everything about this moment felt desperate, as if he'd die if he didn't get inside her. His heart pounded an erratic tattoo against his chest, wild and out of control.

He'd never felt like this about anyone before.

She was so damn slick it made him shudder. "The thought of getting caught turn you on?" he murmured, dipping two fingers inside her. She was so tight, so wet.

Shuddering, she clenched around him, rolling her hips into his hold. "*You* turn me on. I can't believe we're doing this," she rasped out on a jagged breath when he pulled his fingers out of her.

He wanted to taste her, but he wanted to be inside her more. After their conversation from the night before, he knew they were both safe, so that wasn't even a worry. Moving his hips, he shifted slightly so that his cock was positioned at her entrance. Before he could push in, she impaled herself on him, burying her face against his neck on a moan as she did. Ever so lightly, she bit his neck. Not enough to leave a permanent indent, but it almost felt as though she was marking him.

Oh God. A kaleidoscope of colors flashed in front of him as her silky sheath tightened around him. He'd never fucked without a condom before. Never.

This wasn't just anyone, though. It was Karen. The kind of woman he couldn't have made up in his fantasies because she was so much better than anything his imagination could have conjured up.

He grabbed her ass, holding her tight against him for just a moment. It was hard to breathe or think straight when he was buried so deep in her. His balls pulled up tight, that familiar tingling sensation at the base of his spine an embarrassment. Stamina had never been an issue for him, at least not since he was sixteen, but the raw intensity of this situation was making everything in his brain short-circuit.

Forcing himself to take a deep breath, he kissed her, teasing her lips open, dancing his own tongue against hers. She shuddered, her inner walls clenching in a sort of rhythm even though he wasn't moving.

Her breathing was erratic and wild as they kissed, so he reached between their bodies and began stroking her clit. That set her off. She writhed against him, but he didn't move yet because he didn't trust himself.

He needed her to get off, felt frantic to feel her climaxing around him. He nipped her bottom lip between his teeth as he gently pinched her clit between his thumb and forefinger. When he rolled the tight bud, she jerked against him and buried her face against his neck again.

She shifted her head and bit his shirt, another soft moan escaping from her as she tried to remain quiet.

He knew she was close now. Her inner walls were tightening around him faster and faster, her breathing more and more erratic as she clutched on to his shoulders. Even through his clothes her nails dug into him, the bite more pleasure than pain.

He started thrusting, unable to stop himself from moving inside her. The pleasure was too much, the feel of her pure heaven.

"I'm coming," she whispered, the words sounding almost torn from her as she bit into his shoulder now. Her body shuddered under her orgasm, her soft little moans making him crazy.

He held their bodies away from the door with one arm, not wanting to make any noise by slamming against it. Using the strength in his legs, he held her up, clutching her ass as he continued thrusting, his own release not far behind hers.

He was so damn close, so close—he hated to pull out of her but knew he had to. Grabbing her hips, he withdrew, his dick immediately mourning the loss of her.

Taking him completely by surprise, she fisted his erection before he could, her gaze on his as she continued stroking him, hard and fast.

He wanted to touch her but didn't trust himself. What he wouldn't give to finish inside her with no barriers, but this was the next best thing. He slammed one palm against the door behind her head and held up his shirt with the other hand as she brought him to release.

Her gaze remained fixed on his, heated and intense as he came against his stomach. He refrained from crying out, but his body trembled as the pleasure punched through him in wave after wave. He'd never felt anything so intense.

He couldn't stop shaking for a few long moments from the onslaught of his climax. She was with him every second, her gaze still pinned to his.

For a moment he worried things might get awkward, but a satisfied grin spread across her face before she leaned up and brushed her lips over his.

"That was one of the hottest experiences of my life," she murmured, moving quickly to one of the metal cabinets.

"Mine too." He wished he could come up with something better, but his brain was still in sex mode. He stared at her bare ass, saw the marks from his fingers on her pale skin, and was glad he'd left them. He wanted her to feel him on her, in her, long after this. He wanted to imprint himself on her body so she thought about him the way he did about her.

She made a victorious sound as she pulled out a small packet of generic-brand wet wipes. After taking a couple for herself, she handed the pack to him.

They cleaned up and dressed in less than a minute, both moving with a necessary quickness. While he wanted to linger, to hold her the way she deserved, it wasn't possible. He knew she likely had stuff she needed to be doing, and Burkhart would be here very soon.

"Karen . . ." His hand was on the doorknob, but he couldn't force himself to open it, to face the reality of their situation until he told her how he felt. Even if he didn't exactly know himself, he knew that whatever this thing was, it was serious for him. "When this mess is over, I know I said I wanted to take you on a date, but . . ."

Her face went carefully neutral and she tugged at the bottom of her shirt almost nervously, watching him with a sudden wariness.

He realized he was messing this all up. "And I do," he rushed out. "But . . . I don't care if this is too soon, but I'm not going to be seeing anyone else except you. I don't even know how to say this, but, uh, I want to be exclusive with you. I've never *not* used a condom before." Something he needed her to know. God, he felt like a stupid teenager. He hadn't actually dated anyone in so long and she made him feel so off his game anyway.

The smile that spread across her face told him he must have said something right. "Good, because I don't share," she murmured in that sexy, sensual voice, and tugged him down for another quick kiss.

At the sound of footsteps coming down the hall, they both pulled back on a sigh. He hated that they had to head back into reality, but the sooner this op was over, the sooner they could start a future together.

# Chapter 19

Command center: central location for processing data, giving orders, and supervising a critical situation.

"You two, with me," Burkhart ordered, nodding once at Tucker and Cole as he passed where they were talking quietly at one of the tables.

Not needing to be told twice, they both jumped up and followed after him. Tucker noticed that Vane wasn't with them and wondered where he was. Maybe Burkhart hadn't wanted Vane to see this place. All Tucker knew was, they'd better not have let that bastard go.

Burkhart stopped at another table where a printout of a detailed schematic of one of the D.C. Metro stops had been rolled out. There was also a laptop open with a 3-D image of the same thing. Half a dozen men and women were all looking at handheld devices, likely with the same specs. Was Burkhart bringing them in on an op?

He tensed in anticipation at the thought and spared a glance at Cole, who he could tell was thinking the same thing. He resisted the urge to look over at Karen, who was busy typing away at a computer station with Elliott, Selene, and three others who he guessed were analysts. It was hard to believe that he'd just been inside Karen about five minutes ago. Something he did *not* need to be thinking about right now. It didn't help that her cheeks were still flushed. He was counting down the seconds until they could be alone again.

"Vane has set up a meeting with Thad Hillenbrand," Burkhart started, eyeing the quiet group of eight, which included Tucker and Cole. "Everyone's been debriefed." His gaze flicked to them for a moment. "I've been in contact with the heads of any agency—including the DEA, but only in a limited capacity—with a vested interest in you two and your teammates. And only the heads—we can't risk a leak if there are more dirty agents. They know you're not terrorists, but we're not informing the media or anyone without a top-level clearance yet. We want Hillenbrand in custody before that happens. Even so, I'm giving you the option of being part of the team to bring him down."

Tucker guessed he was doing it out of respect for Max. He didn't much care what the reason was; he was just grateful to be part of the operation. "What'd the DEA say?"

Burkhart shrugged. "They're pissed and want access to you two and Vane."

From his tone it was clear the DEA wasn't getting their way. Fine with Tucker. "Where's Vane?"

"Restrained and waiting in an SUV a couple blocks from here."

"You're sure he's not setting you up?" Tucker asked.

"We're not sure of anything, but we've got two trackers on him. Only one he knows about." Burkhart grinned at that. "All his financials are frozen at this point and he knows there's nowhere for him to run, so it'd be stupid to try. Even if he does, we've got him boxed in. The meeting goes down in an hour. Before then I want you two to listen to the audio between Vane and Hillenbrand."

Tucker started to nod, and then Karen strode up to their group. Her cheeks flushed only the slightest bit as she looked at him, but she swallowed hard and held out a tablet for Burkhart.

After a second of scanning, Burkhart grinned and nodded at her. "We'll add it to the warrant." His attention was on the agents now. "Vane gave us the address for where he's been meeting with Hillenbrand. It was buried deep, but Karen found a link between the address and H-Brand Security. We've got eyes all over the city looking for him, Rayford Osborn and a few other conspirators Vane gave us. There are ten of them total and it seems he has an administrative person from the local D.C. PD in his pocket. It was how he knew Karen's name from when she went missing. We're not moving on any of them, though. Not until we've got Hillenbrand locked down. He's the key to all this, and the only one who knows where the missing drone is according to Vane." Turning toward the table, Burkhart motioned for Tucker and Cole to move closer.

"You two are going to be dressed as homeless men

and you'll be outliers for the op. I'm sorry I can't give you more, but you'll be in the vicinity at least when we bring Hillenbrand down. You're going to be on opposite ends of the Metro stop." He pointed to two separate sections of the map.

Tucker understood why they couldn't be in the thick of everything, especially since their faces had been splashed all over the news. If they were dressed as homeless men, most people would avoid looking at their faces and give them a wide berth. It was smart as far as keeping them undercover went. He figured Burkhart was just trying to include them, probably out of a sense of loyalty to Max. "We don't mind being on the fringe. We just want our lives back."

"Thank you for including us," Cole added.

Burkhart grunted an acknowledgment and then motioned to the tables where the analysts were set up. They fell in step with him as he talked. "This is only one part of the op. Like I said, we've got teams out looking for Hillenbrand right now. We might not even need Vane's meeting with him, but just in case, I'd like you to listen to the audio."

Tucker nodded as he and Cole sat in front of two laptops at a table connected to Karen's. "What did you give Vane in return for his cooperation?"

"He's not getting the death penalty," Burkhart said, but he wasn't looking at them. "Is it ready to go?" he asked Karen.

Capital punishment had been abolished in D.C. and Maryland but Vane and his group of terrorists had committed enough crimes over state lines that they could be charged and convicted in multiple states. They'd also broken numerous federal laws. Not to mention the theft of a drone from a military base, which was a whole other beast. Tucker figured there was more to the negotiations than that, but didn't push because it wasn't his problem. As long as Vane went away for his crimes, Hillenbrand was caught, and Tucker and his men could return to their lives, that was what was important.

"Just put the earbuds in and press PLAY," Karen said to Tucker and Cole before returning to her own computer. Despite what they'd recently shared, she was in complete work mode now.

It was sexy.

Tucker and Cole both put in the earbuds and were silent, focused as they listened to the conversation between Vane and Hillenbrand.

Hearing the voice of the man—a stranger—who'd had a part in trying to destroy his life made Tucker's blood boil. Corrupt people like that made him sick. People who thought rules of the world didn't apply to them and tried to prey on anyone they could.

"You want to tell me why I was just attacked in my own home?" Vane snarled, his rage definitely real. That was good. It would sell it to Hillenbrand.

"By who?" Hillenbrand's voice was cautious.

"By someone you were supposed to have taken care of." A pause. "Pankov."

Hillenbrand sucked in a breath. "Don't say—"

"Yeah, yeah. What the fuck ever! My nose is broken and my hand is fucked up because of your incompetence. I've laid a lot of groundwork for our op. This shouldn't have happened. He never should have known about me."

"Where is he now?"

"Cooling in my garage."

"Did he say how he found out about you?"

"No. Our conversation wasn't long, but he mentioned a woman he'd taken. After that, things turned ugly."

"Was the woman with him?"

"He was alone."

A long pause followed, but Tucker could hear breathing, so he knew the two men were still connected. Finally Hillenbrand spoke. "I sent someone after the woman I think he took. My guy hasn't reported in. It's well past check-in time too."

"She wasn't with him. And we need to meet, but first I have to clean out my garage."

"Meet?"

"I retrieved burner phones and other identifiers off him. I can't risk running anything at work. Maybe your guy can." It was a very plausible reason even if it was a lie.

Another pause. "Fine." He rattled off a busy Metro stop.

Vane agreed, which was smart on his part. Burkhart had probably told him to agree to wherever Hillenbrand wanted to meet. It would make him seem less suspicious. And the place was public, which could be good and bad. It was always bad when innocent civilians could get caught in the cross fire.

Tucker had his gloved hands shoved into the pockets of the long, threadbare coat the NSA had given him as part of his cover. Underneath the coat he had on military-style fatigues, but as part of his cover, he had to appear down on his luck, if not completely homeless. At least the coat didn't smell like urine—which was more than he could say for Cole's disguise.

Stains covered the coat, though, and he smelled a bit like garbage, pungent and ripe, but he'd sadly smelled worse. In the Corps he'd been stuck behind enemy lines more than once and had forgotten about showering or bathing in those conditions.

His aviator hat with wool lining was dingy but kept his ears and half his face covered. He smelled bad enough that most people were purposely ignoring him and definitely not looking at his face, but the extra cover was perfect in case any agencies were scanning CCTVs for his face. Burkhart might have let the heads of various agencies know they were cleared, but the locals certainly didn't know it. It was a risk he was willing to take to be part of this op even if he and Cole were basically just lookouts. If they spotted Hillenbrand entering the subway, they'd let the team know.

Keeping his head angled down, he scanned the people coming and going. Everyone was rushing, huddled into their coats, and trying to stay warm. Some were looking at their cell phones as they headed down the stairs into the subway entrance, not paying attention to their surroundings at all.

Hillenbrand was thirty minutes late for the meet. And each minute that passed increased the likelihood that either he wasn't showing up or he'd sent someone else who'd spotted one of the NSA agents. Tucker didn't think the latter was likely.

The team of agents all had their earpieces perfectly hidden. According to Burkhart, everyone in the group had undercover training, so they were all used to blending in to their surroundings.

When two uniformed cops came into view around a corner, talking and drinking to-go cups of coffee, Tucker held up his hands to his mouth, pretending to cough. The last thing he needed to do was get stopped for loitering. "Two cops at my two o'clock. Heading into the station. I'll use my pass, enter, then loop back out in a couple minutes."

"Affirmative," Burkhart said. "Still no visual on the tango." His voice was tight, but if he was frustrated, he was keeping it in check.

Tucker moved casually, keeping his movements steady as he fell in stride with other commuters making their way down the stairs.

"You're clear," Karen said less than a minute later. "They've continued on. No other visual of local authorities in the direct vicinity."

"Affirmative, moving back to street view." He casually scanned the platform and waiting passengers as he turned to leave.

Vane was standing near one of the back walls with two agents flanking him. But Tucker wouldn't have known they were agents. One looked like a man in a business suit, talking rapid-fire into his cell phone, and the other was a woman wearing running gear much like the kind Karen had on. She had on earmuffs and hadn't looked at Vane once.

On his way up Tucker spotted a few of the other agents but only recognized them because he'd seen them in pre-op mode.

He remained in his undercover role as he shuffled up the stairs, not moving too quickly. He was tense, though, wanting this thing done. Unfortunately he knew that it didn't matter what the hell he wanted.

"He's not coming," Wesley murmured to the team of analysts in the command center.

Karen nodded in silent agreement but didn't move her gaze from her oversize screen. Almost an hour had passed now since the set meeting time between Vane and Hillenbrand. She and the other five analysts in the van were monitoring the surrounding area and keeping tabs on the agents on the ground.

For the last half hour it had been mostly silent other than the scheduled check-ins. Even though she and the others in the van had eyes on them via security cameras, everyone still audibly confirmed their position at intervals.

When she saw another uniformed police officer heading Tucker's way, she said, "Victor, a local headed your way."

The agents all had call signs for this op. Normally he'd be a *T* or *P* call sign, but they had others on the team who'd already been assigned those letters.

"Moving down the stairs now." His response was crisp.

She couldn't wait for this whole thing to be over. Normally when she was on an op, her head was completely in the game. For the first time ever she was truly worried about one of the agents. It was hard not to be concerned about Tucker even if she knew how trained and lethal he was. The truth was he was really just a glorified lookout, but he hadn't been publicly cleared, so her mind immediately went to worst-case scenarios. She had this fear that a local cop might recognize him or Cole and . . . anything could happen. But she shook all those useless thoughts away.

"Everyone pack it in," Wesley said suddenly. "We're getting out of here." Without waiting for a response, he exited the back of the van.

Karen couldn't know for sure, but she guessed he was headed down to the subway to get Vane himself. Wesley was going to grill the man now, find out if he'd set up their team and wasted a lot of valuable resources on this meet that never happened.

"What the hell is that?" Selene muttered, more to herself than anyone else.

Karen was still watching the multiple feeds on her own screen but glanced over at Selene.

The tall blonde's jaw was clenched tight as she stared at one of her own feeds. "Karen, pull up sector two, section four. There's a guy crouched behind a tree, but I can't zoom in enough to see what he's doing," she murmured.

That was where Cole was waiting, on the opposite side of the station from Tucker. Karen's fingers flew across the keyboard as she pulled up the feed Selene had indicated.

"Oh my God," Selene said just as the feed flashed on Karen's screen.

Karen's stomach dropped. A man had stepped out from behind a tree with a small RPG, a shoulder-launch missile with deadly capabilities. "Evacuate now!" she shouted at the same time Selene said something along similar lines into her own comm. "All teams move out now. There's a man with an RPG headed for the south entrance. Charlie, he's out of your line of sight," she snapped out to Cole, using his call name. "Move west about twenty yards and take him out."

She saw Cole and the others on various screens moving into action even as raw fear detonated inside her. The team was moving out, with two of the agents grabbing Vane and running for the exit. She could hear them over the comm shouting at people to run. Where the hell was Tucker? She couldn't see him on the screen.

Cole cleared the pillars that had been blocking his line of sight, his weapon raised.

It was too late.

Karen jumped to her feet out of instinct as he took aim at the man. The rocket fired, a whoosh of smoke emitting from it—

All their screens went to static as a rumble shook the ground. Their van was across the street, so without the visual she couldn't see a thing.

"Tucker!" she shouted, not caring about using his call sign.

No one responded, not even Wesley.

"All the comms are down," Selene said, her expression tight but her voice calm. "You armed?"

Karen nodded even as ice flooded her veins. The entire crew of analysts were always armed for on-the-ground ops like this.

"Come on," Selene snapped to Karen, then barked out orders to the rest of the team in the van.

Under normal circumstances Karen would be the one giving orders to the team, would know what to do. But right now all she knew was that she needed to get to Tucker.

# Chapter 20

Oscar-Mike: from the phonetic alphabet meaning "on the move." Often used by Marines.

There was a ringing in Tucker's ears as he looked at the bits of sky visible through the busted concrete above him. Blocks had fallen everywhere, covering most of the stairs leading down to the subway.

His elbows were sore from when he'd fallen back on the stairs, but he was physically fine. Tucker knew how damn lucky he was that he'd been on the stairs when the strike happened. It was a miracle he hadn't been hit by any falling debris. The reality would sink in later, he knew. He just hoped his luck held out now.

Withdrawing his weapon, he spoke quietly. "Command center?" Dead silence. "Command?" he shouted, not able to stop himself. A sharp punch of fear for Karen slid through his veins. Calling on all his training, he shelved what-if thoughts. Without knowing the extent of the damage, he had to do his damn job and focus. He couldn't completely shelve thoughts of Karen, though. She was right there at the forefront of his brain.

The sound of groaning down below kicked him into gear. Sirens wailed in the distance, but he ignored all distractions as he made his way to the bottom of the stairs. Karen had said there'd been a man with an RPG near Cole's location, but that didn't mean there weren't more explosives down below. He had to be careful.

To his right he could see legs visible from underneath a pile of rubble. From the dress pants, a man. He'd seen loss of life on so many different scales when he'd been in war zones or during his undercover stints, which were sometimes like war zones. Men, women . . . children. Killing innocent civilians for whatever stupid cause was always so fucking pointless. Anger tightened his gut, but he moved it out of his mind and started to scale a pile of concrete. More blue sky filtered through from the huge chunk of ceiling that had been ripped away.

He had to holster his weapon as he reached the top of the eight-foot pile so he could use both hands to climb over. Once he cleared it and saw what had been the platform, his gut tightened again. Bodies were littered everywhere. Some moving, some not. He could still hear a few shouts for help but didn't have a visual on the voices. Probably people buried under rubble. He couldn't think about them right now. He had to find the rest of the team, stop another attack that might be coming. Damn it, he hoped Cole was okay. He'd been on the fringes just like Tucker. His only saving grace.

Carefully he climbed down the other side of the pile,

his feet slipping at the bottom. He quickly righted himself and started moving around the west side of the platform, since it was the least damaged. He withdrew the cell Burkhart had given him because his comm wasn't working. He called Cole, who answered immediately. Relief flooded him. If he'd lost Cole . . . no, he couldn't even go there.

"Where are you?" Cole demanded.

Damn, it was good to hear his voice. "Inside the station. I was in the stairwell when it happened. I'm fine. You okay?" he asked quietly as he continued picking his way around to the other side of the platform. He'd seen three agents on this side. When he saw a man in a suit sitting against a pillar, pressing a hand to his bleeding head, he held the phone away from his mouth for a moment. "Help is on the way," he murmured.

The guy nodded, clearly out of it. Tucker hated that he couldn't help everyone, but he had priorities now. Finding the missing agents and Vane was critical.

"Yeah, the shooter's dead. Burkhart's racing toward me right now. Hold on." A second later Burkhart came on the line.

"Who's down there with you?"

"I haven't spotted anyone yet. Is the command center okay?" He had to know that Karen was unharmed.

"Yes. The attack was only on the subway."

The relief that surged through Tucker was short-lived as a sharp *pop, pop, pop* rent the air. Plaster and tile exploded a few feet from his head.

On instinct, he dove over a small pile of jagged

bricks, his jacket snagging on something sharp as he landed on another pile of debris. He dropped the cell phone as he withdrew his weapon.

"Victor." Someone snapped out his call sign as if from a distance.

Without moving from his position, he belly-crawled the few feet to where the phone had skidded and held it up to his ear. "I'm here."

"What's going on?" Burkhart demanded.

"Someone shot at me. I don't have a visual on the shooter yet."

"The agents guarding Vane haven't checked in and they're not answering their cells. Operate under the assumption that it's Vane. I'm heading back to the command center now to see if we can track him. Keep this line open."

"I will. Putting it in my coat pocket now. Going to try for a visual."

"Affirmative."

Tucker slipped his phone into his pocket and crawled down a few more feet, using the rubble as cover. Easing out from position, weapon drawn, he quickly swept the area.

There were fallen bodies and destruction everywhere, but no Vane. If he was Vane and he'd had an opportunity to grab a weapon, he'd go for the escape. It would make sense in this kind of chaos.

Instead of doing a full sweep and searching the rest of the place, Tucker went with his gut and backtracked the way he'd come. Once he reached the top of the first pile he'd climbed, he kept his weapon in his hand. Adrenaline pumping, he peered over the top.

Clear.

Moving faster this time, he scrambled down the other side. As his feet hit the bottom, he could hear Burkhart's voice.

With his free hand, he fished the phone out. "Yeah?"

"Got a ping on one of Vane's trackers. It's flickering in and out. He's moving, though. On foot, given his speed. Once you exit, move south. We'll guide you."

"On it." As he cleared the top of the stairs and out onto street level, he felt his heart jump into his throat. Karen was racing down the sidewalk toward him. Her eyes widened, as if she was startled to see him ascending the subway entrance. Sirens wailed louder now, so he holstered his weapon, not needing to draw attention to himself. The cops and EMTs would be here in less than thirty seconds if he had to guess.

"What are you doing?" he demanded as she reached him, pulling her back down into the first few steps of the stairwell.

"I had to know you were okay." Her eyes were wide as she scanned him, looking for injuries.

"Grab him before he gets in a vehicle," Burkhart ordered.

"I've got to grab Vane," Tucker said to her, moving back to the sidewalk.

She fell in step with him and he could tell by the set of her jaw she planned to go with him. He couldn't waste any time convincing her to go back to the van. "Karen's with me."

Burkhart cursed, but continued giving orders. "We can't get anyone else on the comm and Cole's too far away. You're the closest agent I have in the field now."

"Understood." There was no way Tucker was going to lose Vane, no way this bastard was escaping. Part of Tucker wanted to tell Karen to head back to the command center, to try to convince her she'd be safer there, but for all he knew there were more armed men with RPGs at the Metro stop. He'd rather she be with him where he could protect her personally.

Burkhart ordered him to turn left at the next street. Three cop cars whizzed past, sirens blaring. As they waited for an ambulance to fly by, Burkhart cursed. "He's moving faster now. Too fast to be on foot."

"I'm giving you to Karen." Tucker handed the phone to her as they started running across the street. "I'm stealing a car and I need you to direct me with his instructions," he said to her as they reached the other side. He couldn't break into a vehicle and hold his phone at the same time.

She snagged the cell phone without missing a beat, her strides steady as she moved at a fast clip. As she talked to Burkhart, he motioned to an older-model minivan parked along a curb. There wasn't anyone on the street now, not with everything happening blocks over. It would be complete chaos there.

He made quick work of the lock, then hot-wired the

van. All in less than sixty seconds. Karen held the phone away from her ear as he pulled away from the curb.

"Keep heading east, it looks like he's headed for the highway," she said before putting it on speaker.

"I can't leave here right now, not until I find my people." Burkhart's voice was tense and Tucker knew this had to be hard on him. Because there was no way all his agents had survived that blast. An RPG wouldn't have killed everyone, but the fallout from the debris had been bad, at least from Tucker's visual. There'd be upward of twenty to thirty deaths, minimum. "Elliott thinks from Vane's trajectory that he's headed for a private airport about ten minutes from where you are. I've got a team headed in that general direction just in case. They're farther out than you—Make a right at the next light," he said abruptly.

When he didn't use a street name Tucker realized they were tracking his cell too. Of course. He was so focused on stopping Vane he wasn't thinking.

"I'm sending Selene after you too, but she's . . . Hold on." Burkhart barked out orders to someone in the background; then he cursed again, this time savagely. "Another team just picked up Hillenbrand at a townhome he owns. Not in his name, but one of his corporations'."

Tucker glanced at Karen, saw the relief on her face. "He alone?"

"No, had some guys with him. Looks like he was planning a trip out of the country. It's a fucking shit storm here. I'm giving the order to move on everyone we've had under surveillance now. Rayford Osborn and all the other names Vane gave us. I'm giving you to Elliott now. He'll be patched in to me at all times. Bring me Vane." The words were an order before he handed them off to Elliott.

"Hey, guys. You're only a couple blocks behind him. He's making his way east, so if we lose the tracker, keep going to the airport."

"Have you guys heard from Ortiz?" Karen asked abruptly.

Tucker shot a glance at her, saw how pale she was. Those were her people in that blast too. Reaching out, he grasped her hand. She took it, linking her fingers between his and holding tight.

"Not yet. The local PD and a couple other agencies have already sent rescue parties in. They've found survivors and our guys are strong." Elliott's voice cracked before he cleared his throat. "Focus on Vane. I'll keep you updated as soon as I find out anything on this end."

"Thanks, Elliott." Karen's voice was soft, but Tucker heard the pain there, wished he could take it away.

As they drove, some of Tucker's adrenaline ebbed. Not completely, but he felt more in control now. Elliott directed them until they hit the highway, just as he'd predicted.

"Why'd you leave the command center?" Tucker asked Karen during a lull in Elliott's directions.

"We lost communication with all of you, audio and visual, and I didn't think really. Selene headed for the other entrance where the shooter was and I . . . I had to know you were okay. We'd lost a visual of you on the cameras even before the blast. Honestly I didn't really have a plan. I thought I'd lost you. . . ." She blinked rapidly, looked out the window.

His throat tightened and he grasped her hand again. She'd raced headfirst into danger because she'd been worried about him. He didn't know what he'd done to deserve her, but he wasn't letting go. He started to respond when Elliott spoke, his voice excited. "He's getting off at the next exit. We're already in contact with the airport security. You two will be granted access with no hassle. Security has been instructed to stay back and give you room to work. We don't want to spook him or risk him getting suspicious that we're onto him."

And if the security got involved it could turn into a giant cluster fuck. It'd be a hell of a lot easier for Tucker to bring him down solo. Nice and neat. And there was no time for him to wait for the backup team. Not when Vane was headed to the airport. Seconds would matter at this point. "Do we know how he's planning to leave?" Obviously he was going private, but he'd have to use a company.

"Not yet. If he's going to attempt to leave the country, it'll be under an alias. We haven't found one yet, but we're scouring the charter companies."

Getting through airport security was as easy as Elliott had predicted, though the guards at the gate had eyed the minivan and Tucker and Karen with surprise.

Probably because he was dressed like a homeless guy and she looked as though she should be out running a marathon. Not exactly federal agent dress code.

"He's probably going to hire a private charter to upstate New York," Elliott said after they'd cleared security. "Get as close to Canada as he can, then head over in a car."

Tucker figured the same thing. It would make sense.

"Or at least I'm guessing," Elliott continued. "Head to hangar D-Eight. He just entered it and . . . huh, it's a helicopter charter flight service. One sec. . . ." The sound of typing filled the air as Elliott likely hacked into their system. "According to their schedule they've got one of their helos already on a tour and one scheduled to leave in half an hour. Guy named Theo Smith made the reservation last minute from . . ." More typing. "A cell phone registered to one of our agents." Elliott cursed but quickly regained his composure. "Must have used it and then left it behind because it's still pinging from the blast site. Gotta be Vane. Shit, looks like another call was made to Osborn. Give me a sec." Elliott would be telling Burkhart that Osborn had likely been alerted before Burkhart had ordered all his teams to move in.

Hopefully they'd brought him down first. He wouldn't get far anyway.

"We're almost there," Karen said as Tucker continued driving.

It was a cold, sunny day with high-priced planes and a few helicopters parked on the tarmac and countless more in hangars. A new shot of adrenaline surged through him. They were closing in on Vane. Tucker was going to leave Karen behind when he brought him down. He couldn't risk her getting caught in the cross fire. He didn't think she'd balk about staying in the vehicle. Soon he and his guys would have their lives completely back.

"Any news on Hillenbrand?" Tucker asked, wanting as many details as he could get.

"He's in a secure holding cell now, but Burkhart hasn't been able to break away to talk to him yet."

Because he was helping the ground crew pull out bodies. Something Elliott didn't have to say out loud, but both Tucker and Karen knew it.

"What about the others?" Karen asked.

"Osborn hasn't been found, but we've got a team at his house, his work, and his wife's real estate agency. She's convinced we have the wrong man." He snorted. "You're close to the hangar now."

"What's the best place to park and remain hidden?" he asked, knowing Elliott had the schematics of the entire airport.

"Hangar next door should be fine. It's a storage unit for helicopters, owned by the same charter company. But the backup team is only . . . twelve minutes behind you."

"I'm not waiting." No way in hell was he giving Vane even twelve extra minutes. Anything could happen in that time. He glanced at Karen. "And I need you to stay here." The van had dark tinting on the windows and would give her good cover. "If you see anything out of the ordinary, just leave." He didn't know enough about the airport layout to have her hide somewhere and he'd rather her be in control of a vehicle with a clear mode of escape.

He was glad when she nodded. "You be safe."

Nodding, he didn't say anything else while he parked next to another vehicle in a makeshift parking area where Elliott had directed them. Now it was time to take Vane down.

Karen tried not to stare at the timer she'd activated on the phone. It wasn't as though the team would show up in exactly twelve minutes, but the analyst in her needed to see the countdown. Tucker was more than capable, but she wouldn't apologize for being concerned about him. Only a minute and a half had ticked by. She hated just sitting here while Tucker was out there hunting Vane down and placing himself in danger.

Turning in her seat, she glanced in the side mirrors of the minivan. Tucker had parked in a small parking area next to the neighboring hangar, beside a silver Jeep. They'd turned the minivan off so the engine wouldn't make any noise while she waited. So far she hadn't seen anyone entering or leaving the hangar, but even if they did, it wasn't the one Tucker was infiltrating. She hated not having him or that hangar in her line of vision. And she hated that he'd gone in alone.

Vane was only a small cog in all this. Now that Hillenbrand had been taken into custody, they'd bring down everyone in this organization of insanity. Or at least that was the hope. But Karen knew that bringing down Vane meant a lot to Tucker because of the man's personal betrayal. Even if Hillenbrand had approached Vane, the DEA agent had to have been the one to suggest which people to use as pawns. And he was the reason Max Southers was dead.

Tucker would never forget that. Neither would Wesley for that matter. Karen knew it didn't matter what Wesley had said about negotiating with Vane; in the end, her boss would make sure he paid dearly for his crimes.

"Have you heard anything else?" Karen asked Elliott, who was quiet except for rampant clicking on his keyboard. She knew he was handling about half a dozen things right now and could hear other analysts in the background, but she couldn't help worrying about their people. Guilt threaded through her that she wasn't there to help, but she had to know Tucker was okay and the price of that decision was sitting here waiting in an agony of suspense.

"Not yet. I'm sorry. But Wesley hasn't checked in yet."

"Thanks." She certainly couldn't bother her boss about that now, not when he was being pulled in twenty different directions himself. She could only imagine the destruction inside the subway. The exterior hadn't been as bad as she'd thought, but that might not matter if enough structural damage had been done inside.

"The tracker is out," Elliott said abruptly.

"What?"

"Vane's tracker flickered off and never came back online."

Which could mean nothing. Or it could mean that he'd found it. What if he was aware that they were onto him? He'd be ready for Tucker. Or he could be leaving for another escape route. And what if he had more men with him? The intel they had didn't seem to suggest that, but it was possible. He'd called Osborn, so he'd at least reached out to someone.

Ten minutes until the backup team arrived. Which felt like an eternity.

She tensed when she saw a black Lexus nearing the parking area. Even though the windows were darkly tinted, she ducked lower in her seat and watched the vehicle slow, then park five car lengths down from her.

A man exited a moment later, then glanced around, his gaze flicking over the van she was in, but he clearly didn't see her as he continued scanning the surrounding area. Dressed in a long gray peacoat, black slacks, and dress shoes, he had an overnight bag in one hand. He looked her way again and she leaned forward this time, knowing the tinted windows covered her.

Her heart jumped into her throat as recognition slammed into her. "Rayford Osborn just showed up," she whispered to Elliott even though Osborn couldn't possibly hear her.

"You're sure?"

"Yeah. It's him. He's headed for the rear of the storage hangar." Probably parked here and was doing the same thing Tucker had done: heading for the neighboring hangar. "He's got to be working with Vane." It couldn't be a coincidence that both men had shown up here at the same time.

"Hang tight. I've got to alert Wesley." He clicked off before she could respond.

Silencing the cell phone, she tucked it in her jacket pocket and slid from the vehicle. She didn't care what Tucker had said about waiting. He had no idea that Osborn was here. For all she knew, the man could take Tucker off guard, ambush him.

She withdrew her weapon and checked the chamber out of habit. While she might not be as trained as Selene, she still had a lot of weapons training. All part of the job. Gripping it tight in her hand, she scanned the parking area once more and then raced after Osborn, who'd disappeared around the back of the hangar. She was going to stop him before he got to Tucker. Her sneakers were quiet against the pavement as she ran, but her heart was beating triple time.

As she neared the corner of the hangar, she slowed her pace and steadied her breathing. Another glance behind her showed the parking area still quiet. Good.

She risked a peek around the back of the building— and found herself staring down the barrel of a gun.

# Chapter 21

Bird: military slang for helicopter.

T ucker glanced into an office as he made his way down a hallway in the hangar he'd just broken into. Though breaking in was a weak description. A child could have gotten in here undetected. He'd come in through a side door, easily avoiding two of the video cameras outside. He could break in here at any time and steal a helicopter if he wanted. Pathetic.

The office had a desk with paperwork scattered all over it and a laptop in the middle, sitting on top of some of the papers. A space heater was in the corner. Not surprising, since so far Tucker couldn't feel a difference from the iciness outside and in here. There was an echo of voices in the distance, so he slowed his pace as he neared the end of the hallway.

It opened up into a huge hangar with multiple helos inside, along with a couple of ATVs and crates storing who knew what. A quick visual scan of the place showed the hangar doors rolled up and a royal blue helicopter waiting outside in the bright sunlight.

It was smart of Vane to hire a helicopter tour company instead of chartering a plane. Tucker figured he'd wait until they were in the air, then pull a gun on the pilot and tell him where to go. Or maybe he'd pull a weapon before they'd taken off. Either way it would give him a quick escape, and if Vane killed the pilot after landing somewhere, it would cover his trail for a while. Probably give him long enough to escape the country.

Too bad for Vane that wasn't going to happen.

Tucker stepped out into the hangar, his rubber-soled boots silent as he made his way around the inside perimeter of the place. The voices were coming from near the hangar door. Male voices, but he wasn't certain how many there were.

Tucker shrugged out of his dingy coat and shoved it behind a crate. Underneath the homeless getup, he had on black fatigues.

Less than sixty seconds later he'd made his way almost to the front of the building. He hunkered down behind a bird he wasn't even sure worked, using it as a cover.

". . . just waiting on my friend. He'll be here in a couple minutes." That was Vane.

Friend? Tucker moved down the length of the helicopter, stopping at the rear to peer around it. With a visual of Vane confirmed, another shot of adrenaline surged through him. He was talking to a man who was clearly the pilot.

"No problem, I'm not in a rush today."

"We appreciate you fitting us in so last-minute."

The man wearing a leather bomber jacket and jeans shrugged and crossed his arms over his chest. "It's off-season right now. Not many people want to go up when it's this cold."

Tucker scanned the hangar again before stepping out from his hiding place, weapon drawn. He'd find out who Vane was waiting for, but he was going to incapacitate him now.

"Hands in the air, now!" he shouted as he strode toward them.

The pilot's arms dropped, his face going hard and his stance defensive. But he put his hands in the air at the same time Vane did. Vane's wounded hand had been professionally bandaged by someone at the NSA before the subway meet, but he'd still be in pain for a while.

"It's over, you piece of shit," Tucker growled at him.

Vane's nose was bandaged and there were faint black smudges under both his eyes. They'd only continue to look worse in the next week. The dirty DEA agent's jaw tightened, but he didn't respond.

"On the floor, hands still up." Tucker motioned with his pistol to Vane. "You know the drill. After you're on your knees, lie on your belly."

"Who the hell are you and what do you want?" the pilot asked, hands still in the air.

"Federal agent, and this man is under arrest. Just keep your hands up and all this will be over in roughly ten minutes. I've got a team on the way."

"He's lying," Vane said, even as he got to his knees.

"His name's Tucker Pankov and he's wanted for treason."

The pilot looked at him hard then, recognition flaring in his eyes. Tucker pointed his weapon at him too. "On your knees, then belly." He hadn't planned to cuff the pilot too, but it seemed as if he had no choice. Tucker didn't need some guy trying to be a hero. "In ten minutes you'll be thanking me for saving your life."

Vane was on his stomach now, groaning as he moved.

Keeping his weapon in one hand, Tucker reached into his back pocket and pulled out two zip ties. He tossed one in front of Vane's face. "Behind your back, slip them on."

Vane did as he said, albeit awkwardly and cursing under his breath as he moved. Weapon still trained on the pilot, who'd moved to his belly, Tucker stepped up to Vane and placed his boot on the guy's back. Moving quickly, he bent down and finished tightening the zip tie before doing a pat-down of Vane. He found a SIG tucked into the back of his pants. Had to have been taken from one of the agents.

Tucker slipped it into his own holster. "If you killed one of Burkhart's guys, you'll never see the inside of a prison cell," he murmured low enough for Vane to hear, his intent clear. He wanted him pissing-his-pants terrified. And it was likely true. Burkhart didn't seem like the kind of guy to let the death of one of his people go. He'd be covert about it, but he'd see Vane dead and in the ground.

Next he moved to the pilot and zip-tied his wrists.

"Sorry about this," he murmured. Then, as an after-thought, he continued. "After this is over, get better security."

The man didn't respond, but his body language made it clear he was angry. At least he wasn't spouting off hollow threats. Tucker searched the pilot too, found a cell phone and pocketknife, took both.

"What's the security code to your phone?" he asked, scanning the interior of the hangar again. It seemed oddly quiet. "Where is everyone?" he asked again before the guy could answer his first question.

The man paused, but answered a moment later. "Assistant's on lunch break and my partner's got another charter up right now. One of the romantic tours with champagne and chocolate, so it's longer than normal. Look, if you need me to take you somewhere I'll do it right now. We can leave before my people get back and no one has to be the wiser. There's no reason for anyone to get hurt."

Tucker's eyebrows rose. It was hard not to be impressed by the man's nobility. "No one's going to get hurt. What's your security code?"

Sighing, the man said, "Six, two, eight, one."

Tucker put some distance between himself and the two men as he swiped it in. He'd started to call Elliott when movement from the open hangar door snagged his attention. His weapon was up in an instant, all the breath whooshing from his lungs. Rayford Osborn had a gun to Karen's temple and was using her as a shield.

No, no, *no*.

A flood of ice invaded Tucker's entire body, making it impossible for him to breathe. Everything else around him funneled out as Osborn shoved Karen forward. Bastard was still careful to keep her in front of him. She had a bag in her hand too, likely Osborn's.

"Drop your weapon," Osborn shouted, his voice trembling as much as his damn hand.

Oh hell, that wasn't good at all. If Osborn didn't have any experience with firearms, he could accidentally kill Karen.

"Osborn?" Vane shouted from behind Tucker. "I'm tied up over here!"

Without turning around, Tucker knew that Vane wouldn't have a good visual of them. He was on his stomach and there was a helo blocking him off.

Tucker remained steady, his stance strong as he kept his gaze pinned on Osborn's. He didn't let himself meet Karen's eyes. Didn't want to see the fear there. If he looked directly at her he could get distracted, and that couldn't happen.

Not with her life in the balance.

"It's over, Osborn. There's a team arriving at the airport now. You'll never get out of here, but you haven't done anything you can't take back. Hillenbrand sucked you into this, we all know it."

His brown eyes looked wild, but he didn't take another step forward. He also didn't move his pistol away from Karen's head.

Tucker couldn't help it—he flicked a glance at Karen. Her emerald green eyes flashed with anger, not fear.

Okay, anger was good. He wished he could convey to her that he was going to get her out of this no matter what it took.

"Where's the pilot?" Osborn demanded.

"Right behind that bird." Tucker motioned with his chin but didn't drop his weapon.

"All right, all right," Osborn murmured, seemingly to himself. "I can still do this."

"Can I put the bag down?" Karen asked quietly. "It's heavy."

"What . . . ? Fine," he snapped.

Moving slowly, Karen let her arm stretch out before she let the bag drop. It landed with a heavy thud, the sound echoing in the hangar. It was smart that she'd asked him; otherwise Osborn might have freaked at the sound and shot her. When she brought her hand back to her side, Tucker watched as she carefully slid it into her jacket pocket. He didn't focus on the movement, though, not wanting to draw attention to her. He was terrified for her, but he had an idea what she was doing.

Osborn shoved her forward. "Come on, this is almost over. You'll go back to your life soon."

"Osborn, listen to me, you haven't done anything that can't be undone," he said, repeating what he'd said before, trying to drive the point home. A lie, but Tucker was willing to sell his soul to save Karen. He'd do or say anything. "It's clear you were sucked into this. If you testify against Hillenbrand—"

"Shut the fuck up! And put down your gun. I'm not telling you again!"

Vane was shouting in the background, demanding to be set free, but Tucker tuned him out. Tuned everything out but Osborn and Karen. Soon the backup team would be here and everything could go to hell if Osborn got spooked.

Tucker had to bring him down before that. He looked at Karen again, saw the determination in her gaze, knew she was planning something. Did she have a weapon tucked in her jacket? Had to be her brother's knife. He knew she kept it on her. If Osborn took the weapon off her and she made a move, he'd have one shot to bring the guy down.

One chance.

"I'm putting it down now," he said, his gaze still on the woman who'd come to mean so much to him. Blood rushed in his ears as he bent down, slowly moving his weapon to the floor.

Osborn pointed his pistol at him now. "You should have just left us alone! We're doing this country a favor," he snarled, his face a mask of mottled rage.

Karen's hand pulled free of her pocket, her brother's knife in her hand. Tucker ignored the continued ranting of Osborn and forced his heart rate to slow, to remain steady. He gave the subtlest of nods to Karen, hoping she understood.

"I'm putting it down now," Tucker said quietly. He raised his free hand out to his side, using it as a visual distraction.

Osborn's head turned in that direction. In one fluid movement, Karen slammed the blade behind her into

Osborn's thigh. She threw herself to the floor as Osborn screamed out in pain.

A shot fired, pinging off the floor mere feet from Tucker. He didn't flinch as he aimed and fired at Osborn.

*Pop. Pop. Pop.* He hit Osborn center mass.

Osborn's eyes widened, his weapon falling from his fingers as he fell to his knees, then half rolled onto his side with a quiet groan.

Tucker ran to him, kicked the weapon away. The pistol skittered across the floor. He checked the guy's pulse. Thready, fading fast. Out of his periphery he saw Karen picking the pistol up and tucking it into the guy's bag, out of reach. He wanted to go to her, pull her into his arms, but he had to make sure the threat was over first.

Osborn was gasping for breath as Tucker patted him down, looking for more weapons. He found none. For the first time since this whole shit storm had started, a true sense of relief slid through him. Maybe he should press on the guy's wound, try to stanch the bleeding, but that wasn't going to happen any time this century. The fucker had held a gun to Karen's head. Trying to stop the bleeding would be pointless anyway. He'd be dead in minutes.

Tucker stood, still holding his own weapon as he did another visual sweep. "Was he alone?"

She nodded, eyes wide and a little bit shaky, but she was alive. "Yeah."

They moved toward each other at the same time. He

holstered his weapon as he crossed the few feet to her and crushed her to his chest. She was alive. He repeated that to himself even as he kept his eyes open, scanning the area. He hugged her tighter, was glad when she returned the hard embrace. "Did he hurt you?" he rasped out, his voice shaky.

She shook her head against his chest and didn't loosen her grip around him. "No. It's finally over." Her voice shook the tiniest bit, but fearless woman that she was, she was keeping it together commendably well.

Better than any civilian.

Out of instinct, he looked over his shoulder just to check on the two men. Vane was still on his stomach, cursing and squirming, but he wasn't going anywhere.

It was truly over. As they stood there embracing, the backup team arrived. No lights or sirens announced their presence, but when Selene jumped from one of the vehicles, relief damn near overwhelmed him.

He knew that the mountain of paperwork, interviews, and debriefings they'd have to go through would be a giant pain in the ass and very lengthy in the near future, but soon he'd have Karen all to himself. He was counting down the seconds.

# Chapter 22

Blown: discovery of an agent's true identity or a clandestine activity's true purpose.

*Two days later*

"I never doubted you boys for a moment," Mary Southers said, her voice surprisingly strong as she clasped Tucker's hands tightly in hers. Her husband's funeral had been this morning and she was holding up better than anyone else it seemed. A slight woman, she had short dark hair and everything about her was soft and feminine.

Tucker's throat tightened as he looked down at her. They were in her kitchen, along with a few other women who attended Mary's church. They were getting food ready and talking quietly, but he tuned them out. The majority of the people were in the living room or sitting room, but some were on the back porch despite the cold. It had been a very long day.

He tightened his grip on hers. "I can't tell you how much that means to me to hear. We wanted to contact you right after . . ." God, he couldn't even say it and felt weak for it. "But we didn't want you inadvertently pulled into that mess."

Pale and tired-looking with slightly puffy eyes from crying, she let the ghost of a smile touch her lips. "You could have called, but I understand. And you're all heroes now, especially you and Cole."

*Heroes* was a stretch, but at least they weren't painted as terrorist villains anymore. Of course they'd never be able to do undercover work again, but he and his men had been cleared of all wrongdoing. They were still debriefing various heads of agencies, all with the support of the DEA and NSA. He knew there would be more to come in the next couple of weeks. Some of it would go public, but most of it never would. His agency was pissed and embarrassed about their mole since Vane had caused so much damage. They were cracking down everywhere and tightening security.

He cleared his throat, feeling awkward. "I know everyone is saying this, but if you need anything let us know. We're all here for you and the boys." Her two sons, both still in college, were in the living room and holding up better than Tucker had expected. They both had friends with them, though, and that always made a difference.

She patted his hand and smiled. "I know that. And I'll let you know."

When one of her church friends came over asking about where to place a casserole in the dining room, Tucker made his way out of the kitchen. He didn't see any of his guys or Karen in the living room or sitting room, so he headed out back.

Sure enough, the four of them along with Burkhart and some DEA guys were all standing near one of the outdoor heaters, talking and drinking beers.

As he approached the group, Cole threw his arm around Karen's shoulders. "If you ever get tired of him—"

"Don't even finish that thought," he muttered, taking Cole's beer from his hand.

Cole grumbled good-naturedly and left, likely to go grab another beer. Tucker immediately moved in next to Karen and wrapped his arm around her.

She tucked right into him, sliding her arm around his waist. He loved the way she smelled, all fresh and citrusy. "How's Mrs. Southers?" she murmured.

"She's a rock."

Kane and Brooks nodded, their expressions somber.

Burkhart nodded in agreement too, the pain in his eyes clear. "She'll weather this just like she does everything. She's a warrior." He raised his beer bottle a fraction as if in toast to her, and it was clear today was hard on the man.

From Tucker's interaction with him, he knew Burkhart rarely showed emotion, but he would have known Mary as long as he had Max, since they'd been in the Navy together so many years ago. Max had had a good life and been a truly good man. His loss would be felt for a long time to come.

"So, what are you boys going to do now? Stay with the DEA?" Burkhart asked.

Tucker glanced at Kane and Brooks as Cole returned, beer in hand. They hadn't officially made any decisions, but they'd been talking the past two days about making changes. Maybe nothing would come of it, but maybe it would. He was leaning toward a job in private security, maybe personal security or something as an instructor. The four of them had even bounced around the idea of starting their own company. But that was way in the future.

Tucker shrugged. "No idea yet."

Burkhart's expression turned speculative, but he nodded. "Keep me in mind if you're looking to move on."

Tucker nodded once but didn't respond. Now wasn't the time.

"I'm going to head out," Cole said.

Tucker was thankful his friend had said it first. They'd been at the Southerses' house most of the day, since the morning funeral, and it was time to head home.

After they said good-bye to everyone, Tucker was thankful to finally be alone with Karen in his truck, headed to Maryland. There was no one else he wanted to be with.

"You want to go somewhere else, grab a beer?" she asked, reaching across the console for his hand.

It was instinct to hold her hand now, to reach for her whenever she was near. "No, I just want to tune out the rest of the world for the night."

"I don't blame you. I'm sorry you lost such a good

friend." Karen seemed to intrinsically know that Max had been more friend than boss. Hell, more father figure than boss, even though he had a father he loved.

He squeezed her hand. So much had happened in the past two days he was still trying to process it all. Hillenbrand had a string of lawyers backing him, but the man was never going to be set free. His bail had been revoked and he'd remain in prison until his trial. If it even made it that far. There was so much evidence against him, Tucker didn't think it would.

The stolen drone had been found in one of Hillenbrand's warehouses. So far two of the men who'd been with him during his attempt to flee the country had admitted that the RPG attack in the subway had been ordered by Hillenbrand and for two reasons. Hillenbrand had wanted Vane—a loose end for him—dead. He'd also suspected that Vane was setting him up and had wanted another distraction for his escape. And he hadn't wanted to risk using his stolen drone with all the agencies on such high alert. He'd been planning to save it for later.

"How's Ortiz?" he asked, wanting to know about the agent, who was also a good friend of Karen's. They'd been to visit him and Freeman yesterday afternoon. Ortiz had suffered from a broken leg and concussion and Freeman had a broken arm and clavicle. Both men had seemed to be doing well, but he knew Karen was still worried.

"Good, he texted me today letting me know they'd be releasing him and Freeman both soon. It's gonna suck for a while and they'll be on desk duty even after they're healed, at least for a couple weeks, but they're alive." Her voice was tinged with unmistakable sadness.

"I'm sorry about your agents." Two of her guys had died in the attack. They'd been to both their funerals before going to the hospital yesterday.

Three funerals in two days was too much for anyone.

"Thanks." She let out a ragged sigh, squeezed his hand.

After driving in silence for a while, he said, "After we have breakfast tomorrow I've got to head back to my place, see what a mess my people and the FBI made." He didn't like the thought of leaving her, but he hadn't even been home since everything happened, so he had no clue what it looked like after the DEA and whoever else had gone through it. He and his team had been publicly exonerated—very publicly, with the media running feeds about them almost twenty-four/seven—and they'd been dealing with answering questions from too many people to count. Especially since they'd all killed someone. He'd taken more than one life in the line of duty, and killing Rayford Osborn had been a big deal. The media were going crazy over it, but he and his guys were all declining interviews. Turned out that Osborn's boss, presidential candidate Clarence Cochran, had no idea what his right-hand man had been up to, but it didn't matter. His political career was probably over. Anyone linked, even inadvertently, to this mess was screwed.

"I'll help if you want." Karen sounded almost tentative.

"I know you're crazy with work right now," he said as they came to a stoplight. He knew she'd have no problem coming with him, but he didn't want to affect her job.

"Well . . . I talked to Wesley and he's giving me the week off. I have so much vacation time built up over the last few years it's a little sad. I figured it'd be a good time for us to get some downtime together."

"I'd love for you to help." He cleared his throat, glad he had to keep his eyes on the road. "I, uh, was thinking of heading down to Georgia to see my parents in a couple days. Once I'd straightened everything out at my place." He wanted her to come with him.

"That's great. I bet it's been so hard on them. Plus, it'll give you time away from the media storm here. They're like vultures."

"I want you to come with me," he blurted out when it was clear she hadn't realized that was what he meant. He shot her a quick glance at another stop.

Her eyes widened. "To see your parents?"

"Hell yeah. Unless you don't want—"

"Yes, you silly man. I've never met parents before, though." She bit her bottom lip then, his brave, brilliant analyst suddenly looking unsure of herself.

That thought alone made him want to laugh. "They'll love you. Maybe not as much as I do, but close."

She blinked once, twice. *"What?"*

Aw hell. He'd wanted to tell her in a better setting

than this, with candles and romantic shit. After glancing in the rearview mirror, he steered into the right lane, then pulled into a gas station.

She was silent as he parked. He left the engine running so the heat would stay on, keeping her warm.

Feeling more awkward and unsure than he ever had, he turned to her. He'd rather be in a war zone dodging bullets than face her rejection. Their hands were still linked, so he squeezed hers gently. "I don't expect you to say anything back, but yeah, I fucking love you." He inwardly cringed at his choice of words but forced himself to continue. "Since I was in the Corps I've had to make split-second decisions, often life-and-death ones, on an almost constant basis. I trust my gut instinct in any situation and I love you. I've never been in love before, but I know what I feel for you is it. I also know it's too soon for any sane person to—"

"I love you too." A wide grin spread across her beautiful face as she said the words. "I've gone over this in my head a million times it seems, trying to tell myself I'm crazy to even contemplate it. The analyst in me says it's too soon, but . . . I love you."

He leaned forward, tangling his fingers through her hair as he crushed his mouth over hers. He definitely hadn't planned to spill his guts to her at a gas station, but he didn't care where they were, just that they were together. And that she felt the same way.

God, she loved him too.

Relief like nothing he'd ever known pummeled

through him, battering his insides. This wonderful woman actually loved him. It was way too soon for future talk, but deep down he knew that his future was with Karen. Now that he'd found her, he didn't plan on letting her go.

# Epilogue

*Six months later*

Karen let her head fall back against the cushioned cabana bed. Tucker had pulled all the curtains closed and no one was on the beach right now anyway, but she still made herself stay quiet. The salty tinge in the air rolled over her, the sound of the nearby waves soft and steady. But all her focus was on the very sexy man who had his face buried between her legs.

"You like that?" he murmured, his tongue flicking lazily against her clit.

"Yes," she whispered. She loved it, something he very well knew. He just liked to tease her. They were at his parents' beach house in north Florida and had decided to take an early-morning walk. On the way back up to their home, Tucker had pulled them into the private cabana on their property. But it was right on the border of the public beach area.

"Louder."

"Damn you, Tucker Pankov," she whispered again.

Chuckling in that maddening way of his, he nipped at her inner thigh. "You get a pass for saying my whole name." Then he returned to what he was doing, teasing her with that far-too-talented tongue until she was writhing against him and moaning his name. Screw being quiet.

She slid her fingers through his hair, holding his head to her because she couldn't bear to let go of him. Her orgasm was sharp and intense, as it always was when they had sex in a semi-public area. Ever since that storage closet, she and Tucker had found interesting places to make love. Only six months had passed since they were together, but it felt like a lifetime. It was as if she'd known him forever and now she couldn't imagine her life without him.

Before him she'd have never taken a mini-vacation, but having him in her life had made her realize there was more to life than work.

He lifted his head as her climax ebbed, the grin on his face pure wicked as he crawled up her naked body. She leaned up to kiss him, her lips meeting his as he settled his hips between her legs.

They were so attuned to each other now it stunned her. She'd never felt like that with anyone before. Arching her hips into his, she savored the way he thrust into her, his thick length filling and stretching her.

She clutched tightly to his shoulders as she dug her heels into his ass. Each time he slid into her, she felt the way those tight muscles clenched under her feet.

It didn't take long until she was coming again, him right behind her. He had way more control than she did, because he managed to quiet his moans against her neck as he came inside her. He nuzzled her neck, kissing and nipping her sensitive skin just the way she liked, just enough to make her absolutely crazy.

The ripples of her second orgasm pulsed through her, not as intense as the first one, but just as wonderful. After what seemed like forever, he pulled out of her and rolled onto his back next to her. His breathing was as erratic as hers and she knew if she looked over at him, she'd see a satisfied, probably smug expression on his face. But she was too tired to even move her head.

"I think I'm just gonna stay here for a bit," she murmured.

"Nope. My mom's making breakfast. If we don't return soon, she'll come look for us."

The thought of his mom's cooking was enough to make her get up, but truly, the thought of his slightly terrifying but wonderful mother finding them on her cabana completely naked was what did it. She bolted upright and Tucker just laughed.

"Can't believe you're scared of her," he said as he sat up behind her, reaching for his swim trunks.

Karen fastened her bikini top into place before tugging her tank top over her head. "Not scared, just have a healthy respect for her. And don't even pretend you're not freaking terrified. I've seen the way you and your dad are around her."

Tucker just snorted, as if Karen were crazy. But she

knew the truth. His mom had some sort of mojo thing she did with her gaze. As though she could just will you into doing what she wanted. It was fascinating.

Once they were presentable, though Karen knew her cheeks would be flushed, they exited the cabana and headed up the long wooden dock to his parents' vacation home. The place was incredible and she understood why they spent their summers here.

They rinsed their shoes and feet of sand before Tucker opened the sliding glass door into the kitchen.

The smell of fresh coffee and whatever his mom was cooking—biscuits and gravy—made Karen's mouth water.

"I'll get you coffee," Tucker murmured before kissing her on top of the head.

"Everything smells good," Karen said, heading for the table where Tucker's dad sat. Vitaly Pankov was a big man, just like his son. He didn't talk much, but he was friendly and welcoming.

Vitaly nodded once and looked up from his iPad, where he was reading the news. "Everything my Darla cooks is good." He had a slight accent and it warmed Karen's heart the way his gaze flicked over to his wife, filled with such obvious love.

"Don't try to get on my good side." There was a hint of annoyance in the petite woman's voice that told her something must have happened this morning between the two of them.

Karen had spent enough time with them over the past six months—with them coming up to visit her and

Tucker in their new place in Maryland—to realize that Darla Grace did not hide her emotions well. The former beauty queen had impeccable poise for the most part, but man, she had a temper.

"How was your walk?" she asked, glancing over her shoulder to look at Karen, a warm smile on her face.

"Wonderful. I told Tucker we're going to have to get here more often. Thank you guys again for inviting me." It was so weird to interact with such a loving family, but she could definitely get used to this.

As Tucker sat next to her, placing a steaming cup of coffee in front of her, Darla made a tsking sound as she turned back to the stove. "You don't have to thank us. What you can do is start planning on grandbabies for us."

Karen was glad she hadn't taken a sip of her coffee, because she started choking on air. Grandkids? What? She and Tucker hadn't even talked about marriage yet and yes, she was old-fashioned like that. She didn't want kids without a ring and all that jazz.

"Just ignore her, it's a thing Southern women do," Tucker murmured, with his father just grunting in agreement.

Though she wasn't sure if the agreement was to the grandkids part or the Southern women part.

"Just think, you two will have a wonderful story to tell your kids about how you met."

Tucker, the traitor, didn't respond, just picked up an orange from the bowl in the center of the table and started peeling it while studiously ignoring her gaze.

Feeling awkward and as though she should respond, Karen cleared her throat. "That's true, though I think I'll leave out the part about him kidnapping me." Not that she was even thinking about kids.

Now Tucker started choking. His father raised one eyebrow, which might as well have been a shouted response from anyone else.

"My son *kidnapped* you?" Darla demanded, drawing Karen's attention to her. She'd turned away from the stove now to face them, one hand on her hip and the other was holding a spatula like a weapon.

"Um . . ." Frowning, Karen racked her brain, but couldn't remember their exact past conversations about everything. They'd come to see his parents directly after everything had happened six months ago and explained what they could without giving away any national secrets. Karen had just assumed Tucker had told his parents how they'd met. "Yes." She practically squeaked out the answer.

"Cole and the guys helped," Tucker muttered, sounding a little like a petulant twelve-year-old.

Darla's expression went nuclear, but she didn't say anything. Just turned back to the stove. The silence was deafening and Karen wanted to kick her own butt.

"I thought you told them," she whispered.

"Tell my parents that I kidnapped a defenseless woman?" He asked the question as if she were insane.

Okay, damage control time. "They were really nice kidnappers and it was because—"

Tucker shook his head sharply, cutting her off. "You're just going to make it worse, sweetheart."

"She's not angry at you anyway. She's upset with me." There was the slightest trace of a Russian accent in his voice as Vitaly stood. He was smiling, though, as he made his way to his wife. He murmured something too low for them to hear as he set his hands on Darla's shoulders and nuzzled her neck.

Tucker grabbed Karen's hand and mouthed, *Come on* before practically dragging her from the kitchen. Once they'd made it upstairs, Karen said, "I'm sorry. I really thought they knew."

He just grinned and shook his head, pulling her into the guest bedroom they were sharing. It was decorated in a beach theme with royal blue and turquoise as the main colors. "Don't worry about it. Trust me—she's not really mad at me. My dad probably 'forgot' one of their little anniversaries again. He does it on purpose because he likes to make up with her."

Karen frowned. "Anniversaries as in plural?"

Tucker nodded. "Oh yeah. She's a freak about that kind of stuff. An anniversary of their first kiss, first date, first other stuff I don't want to know about. She likes to celebrate *everything*."

"You want me to start keeping track of all our firsts?" Karen asked teasingly. "Like the first time we had sex in a cabana?"

"Dear God, no."

Laughing, she shook her head. "Good, I can't keep track of that kind of stuff anyway. Will I have time for a quick shower before breakfast?" She had shopping plans with his mom and she still felt sandy and gritty.

Almost distractedly he nodded as he made his way to one of the dressers. "Yeah. I'll grab your coffee for you."

"You are definitely a keeper," she said, shutting the bathroom door behind her.

Less than two minutes later she wasn't surprised to hear the door open. He'd either gotten her coffee or planned to join her. Maybe both.

"The coffee's on the counter. I put it in an insulated mug so it'll stay warm."

That little act was one of the reasons she kept falling harder and harder for him. She hadn't realized there were degrees of love, but for her, it turned out there were. After all that insanity so many months ago, she'd fallen hard, but it was the small day-to-day things he did that showed how much he cared that had her completely addicted to the sexy man. "I love you."

"Me or the coffee?" he asked, pulling the shower curtain back and stepping inside.

She grinned as she rinsed the shampoo out of her hair, drinking in the sight of him. "Both."

"At least you're honest." He placed his big hands on her hips as he moved flush against her. His thick length was hard against her abdomen.

Feeling her body heat up with a seemingly unquenchable need for him, she slid her hands up his chest. The sight and feel of his naked body never failed to get her turned on.

He was looking at her strangely, kind of intently as

he slid one hand into her wet hair, cupping the back of her head. He opened that wicked mouth of his and had started to say something when the water turned cold, making her yelp and try to scramble out of it.

Tucker just laughed and moved them so that he was under the stream, blocking her body while the water returned to normal. The random changes in the temperature made her crazy, but it was apparently something that happened because of the piping. Whatever it was, it certainly woke her up better than coffee.

She wondered about that look he'd just given her, but he kissed her as the water went from cold to hot—and so did her body. Then she didn't think about anything else other than his kisses for a long time.

"I'm seriously thinking about quitting my job and becoming a beach bum," Karen murmured, leaning into Tucker as they strode up to the front door of his parents' place. After the seafood dinner they'd just had, she was ready to jump him and then get some sleep.

"You'd be bored in a month." He opened the door for her but wrapped an arm around her waist from behind and pulled her close.

She heard the door shut behind them as he leaned down to nuzzle her neck. A shiver went through her body, her nipples automatically tightening in response to his kisses, but she nudged him with her elbow. "Your parents are here," she whispered, knowing he was likely to want to get physical right up against the front door. She and Tucker had gone out to dinner and his parents had declined to go with them, so she knew they would still be up.

His grip on her tightened for a moment, and then just as quickly he let go, coming to stand next to her. When he looked down at her, that same intense look he'd given her in the shower this morning was on his face. He linked his fingers with hers and silently tugged her down the hallway toward the kitchen.

She was surprised they weren't making a beeline for the stairs but didn't question him as they continued to the French doors that led to the back porch.

When he opened them, she stared in surprise. White twinkle lights had been strung up across the lattice covering most of the deck and hot tub area. At least a dozen no-flame candles were placed around one of the mosaic-tiled tables, and in the middle was a silver tray with a bottle of champagne and two flutes on it.

Blinking, she turned to Tucker just as he went down on one knee.

She nearly jolted at the sight and her eyes grew wet as it finally registered what was happening. His parents must have set all this up while she and Tucker were out.

When he took her left hand and slid a diamond ring onto her ring finger, she still couldn't find her voice. Her heart beat out of control with so much joy, but her throat had seized as she tried to fight back happy tears.

"Will you make me the happiest man on this planet and marry me?"

She'd never seen him looking so serious. Or nervous.

As if there was ever any doubt what her answer would be. "Yes." She wanted to shout it, but all she could manage to get out through her emotion-clogged throat was that one word. The only one that mattered.

Relief and a healthy dose of lust covered his face as he stood, crushing his mouth to hers. He moved them until the backs of her knees collided with one of the cushioned lounge chairs.

Then he was on top of her, his kisses more frantic, but she pushed against his chest, taking a moment to admire the way the diamond sparkled under all the twinkle lights and moonlight before she met his gaze. "Your parents—"

"Are gone for the next few hours." Again with the knee-weakening, wicked grin that made her glad she was already flat on her back.

She wrapped her legs tighter around his hips. "I want to try some of that champagne."

He rolled his hips against her, his need evident. "After." The word was a hungry growl.

She grinned, her body already primed for him. "Definitely after." Before he could move, she closed the short distance between their mouths, taking his bottom lip between her teeth and tugging on it playfully. She loved Tucker so much it was scary and wonderful at the same time. She couldn't wait to spend the rest of her life with the man who'd completely stolen her heart.

## ACKNOWLEDGMENTS

I owe a big thanks to my wonderful editor, Danielle Perez! Thank you for pushing me to make this book shine. To the entire team at New American Library—Christina Brower, Jessica Brock, Ashley Polikoff, and Katie Anderson—thank you for all the behind-the-scenes work you do. For my fabulous agent, Jill Marsal, thank you for being in my corner. Kari Walker, as always, thank you a million times over for all your insight when reading the first draft of *Edge Of Danger*. For my husband and son, I'm forever grateful that you put up with my crazy writer's hours. And I owe another thanks to my husband for answering all my random research questions. Any mistakes are my own, or I intentionally took creative license. For Sarah, thank you for all that you do. You keep me sane. As always, thank you, thank you, *thank you* to my Deadly Ops readers! I'm thrilled to bring you another book in this world and I hope you enjoy this latest installment. Last but never least, I'm incredibly grateful to God for so many blessings.

Don't miss the next novel in the breathless
Deadly Ops series by Katie Reus

# A COVERT
# AFFAIR

Coming soon from Headline Eternal.

Amelia Rios took the tulip-shaped champagne glass from her date, Iker Mercado, with a smile. At forty-five, he was seventeen years older than her and definitely the oldest man she'd ever been on a date with. Not that she dated much, not with her schedule. But Mercado was interesting, charming, handsome and didn't have a reputation as a manwhore. If he had, she would have declined his invitation. In her experience, playboy types tended to have little respect for her gender. *No, thank you.*

If anything, the man had practically lived like a saint for the last twenty-five years. She knew from gossip that his wife had died at nineteen during childbirth. He'd only been twenty, yet had raised his daughter and never taken another wife or really even dated. If gossip was to be believed, of course. In this case, she did.

"You look beautiful tonight," he murmured, his gaze raking over her appreciatively. But not in a creepy way. Everything about him was so polished, from his tailored tuxedo to his genuine smile. When he looked at people or talked to them, he was always engaged and none of it seemed forced.

"You look pretty good yourself." She smiled, pasting

on the brightest one she could muster. She rarely came to events such as the auction Mercado was putting on. She always felt like an impostor at things like this. While no one could say she didn't look the part, with her sleek black dress, new manicure and pedicure, and thanks to a friend, an intricate hairstyle that looked as if she'd paid a fortune to have it done, she still felt like a fraud. It was her own insecurities, something she was well aware of. Didn't change the fact that she felt like a big fake standing around with so many women of Miami's high society, all of whom were decked out in glittering, blinding jewelry. Part of her wondered why Mercado had even asked her to this thing. He'd pursued her decently enough too, asking her out three times before she'd agreed. She was pretty—she knew that—but so many of the women were wealthy and elegant with the right pedigree. She was none of those things.

"So, how do you think it's going? Or is it too soon to tell?" she continued, taking advantage of it just being the two of them. Considering he was the one putting on the silent auction for charity and was a well-respected man, they'd barely had more than a minute of alone time tonight. Oddly, she wasn't that disappointed. The man was perfect on paper and incredibly nice, but she didn't feel much of a spark.

"Well, I believe." He stepped a fraction closer, letting his hand settle on one of her hips in a loose but somehow still possessive gesture. It didn't make her uncomfortable, but it was surprising. "Though I now see that asking you to this for our first date was a mistake."

Shock rippled through her at his words. Did he not think she was the right kind of woman to bring to this? "Was it?" Her words came out icier than she'd intended.

He blinked in surprise, a small frown pulling at his mouth. "We've had no private time. I'd like to take you out again soon, just the two of us. Maybe I'll cook for you."

Oh, God, she felt like an idiot. She wanted to crush all of her insecurities, but sometimes they just flared to the surface with no warning. The clenching in her gut dissipated when it registered he hadn't been insulting her. "I—"

"Iker!" A female voice cut off the rest of what Amelia had been about to say.

Which was maybe a good thing. She wasn't certain she wanted to go on another date with him anyway. If the spark wasn't there, she doubted it would magically appear during another date. Deep down she wondered if she'd ever feel that "thing" with anyone. She had once, but that was so long ago. Over a decade. And she was pretty certain she'd just built up the combustible attraction in her mind. No one could have been that sexy, that intense, that—

She realized that Mercado was introducing her to someone. Naomi Baronet. A beautiful woman with bright red hair swept up into a simple twist. She was likely in her forties. Her features were sharp, defined, and elegant. Amelia smiled and shook the hand the woman was offering. Thank God she didn't have to do the air-kiss thing so many people had been doing tonight. "It's a pleasure to meet you."

"You as well, Miss Rios." Her eyes glinted with something that made Amelia feel uneasy. The woman watched her like she was a bug under a microscope.

But she kept her smile in place. "Please call me Amelia."

"And you must call me Naomi. I've been wanting to meet you for a while now." Her smile was easy, her teeth a brilliant white, but there was no warmth in her eyes.

"You have?" She couldn't imagine why. Amelia had never even heard of this woman.

Naomi nodded, her eyes narrowing just a fraction as Iker slid his arm around Amelia's waist, holding her loosely, but still close. It felt as if he was being protective. "Yes, I know you've been working in tandem with Maria and all those . . . unfortunate women." Disdain laced the last two words, even as she tried to mask it. "I know Maria's father disapproves of all the time she spends at that center, but she's such a giving woman. I don't know how she does it."

*Unfortunate women? "That" center?* This woman was like a cartoon character. Amelia forced herself to keep her voice even. Sometimes her temper got away from her, and tonight was not the time for that. "She does a great service to our community. And those 'unfortunate' women are basically young girls who had nothing growing up and simply want a better life for themselves. And they're not afraid to work hard for it." Ice coated her voice even as she tried to order herself to keep that facade in place. But people like Naomi, who wore entitlement around themselves like a silk wrap, annoyed her.

The woman blinked in surprise, but before she could respond, Iker's grip on Amelia tightened. "Naomi, I see someone I need to speak to, but save me a dance." As he steered Amelia away, she inwardly cringed.

"Ah, sorry if I was—"

"Don't apologize," he said through a smile. "She is . . . an unlikable individual. And if you see me dancing with her later, I beg you to come rescue me." The light humor in his voice eased the tightness in her chest.

"You're not friends with her?"

"No. I've done business with her brother, but that's the extent of our relationship. She's here because she wants to show off her jewelry and be seen. She doesn't care about our community." It was clear he did care.

Amelia wondered what was wrong with herself. Why she didn't feel more of a spark for him. The setting tonight was perfectly romantic. Afro-Cuban jazz played in the background, the band he'd hired nothing less than spectacular. The music—along with the servers walking around wearing fedoras and the birds-of-paradise centerpieces—gave the auction a vintage, glamorous Old Havana feel.

"There's something I need to tell you," he continued, pulling her closer to the dance floor, expertly maneuvering through the throng of people. "I had you checked out before asking you on a date."

Gathering her thoughts, she took a sip of her champagne before responding. "You mean, like, investigated?"

He nodded. "Yes. I don't date much, and I'm careful when I do."

Whoa, he must be wealthier than she'd realized, something that made her incredibly uncomfortable. "Okay." She wasn't even certain how to respond.

He rubbed a hand over the back of his neck, seemingly uncomfortable as well, which was at odds with the polished man. "I wanted to be up front with you. I should probably apologize, but I'm not sorry. I've gotten burned in the past by women who wanted only one thing from me."

A ghost of a smile touched her lips. It was refreshing that he was being so honest, but also a little unnerving. "I Googled you," she admitted. Definitely not the same thing as having her investigated though.

He smiled, the charming man perfectly back in place. His hair was a honey brown with just a few faint hints of gray peeking through. "And?"

"And you seem pretty decent."

He laughed at that. "You do wonders for my ego."

Shrugging, she took another sip of her champagne. "So what did you find out about me that I probably wouldn't have shared on a first date?" She couldn't help but wonder what he'd discovered in his investigation. Probably that she'd changed her last name. Maybe he'd figured out why, maybe not. She wasn't going to offer up the information, not until they got to know each other better. It was too hard to talk about.

"You're the owner of two successful restaurants, something I already knew anyway."

"How do you know they're successful?"

Now he shrugged, all casual innocence. "About a year ago I looked into buying commercial property near La Cocina de Amelia. I checked out the surrounding businesses to see how profitable they were."

Smart. "Did you buy the property?"

A brief nod. "I did. I wish I'd gone into one of your restaurants back then, though. Maybe we would have met sooner." His eyes darkened at that, undeniable heat simmering there.

She felt her cheeks warm up just a bit at the boldness in his gaze. She still wasn't sure she felt anything for him and loathed herself for it. Loathed that after a decade she still had lingering feelings for a man she knew she'd never see again. It was her own fault, but it didn't lessen the emotions one iota. Glancing away, she nearly dropped her glass when she spotted Nathan freaking Ortiz moving around the edge of the dance floor, headed her way.

Nathan. Ortiz.

Had she lost her ever-loving mind? She gave herself a hard mental shake and looked away. When she found her gaze drawn directly back to the man again, she realized that, no, she hadn't lost her mind.

Taller than her—but who wasn't?—muscular, yet lean, he filled out his tuxedo with absolute perfection. He had the sleek lines of a graceful predator. Though he wasn't looking at her, there was no doubt in her mind that he'd seen her and was making his way over. He was moving with far too much purpose. What was he doing here? Was he living in Miami again? The last she knew, he'd joined the Marine Corps, but that had been twelve years ago. She guessed he could be on social media, but she only had accounts for her business, not herself, so she didn't know. She'd been tempted a time or two to look him up, but had never followed through.

Just watching him move was like watching— Gah, she couldn't even think of a good analogy, but a low-grade heat started building inside her, her nipples tightening almost painfully in awareness. The man was even sexier than she remembered, but there was nothing boyish about him anymore. He'd been eighteen the last time she'd seen him, so he'd be almost thirty now. He had a bit of scruff on his face, not a full-on beard, but oh sweet Lord, he was gorgeous. She absolutely hated that her body just seemed to flare to life at the mere sight of him. Like a switch flipping, she didn't even feel like herself right now. She wanted to crawl out of her skin to escape this surreal sensation of watching the man whom she'd never gotten over make his way toward her and her date.

Amelia tore her gaze from Nathan as he disappeared behind a cluster of people and focused on Iker, who was still smiling at her. Guilt suffused her, but thank God he couldn't read her mind. She wanted to ask him to dance, to drag him out onto the gleaming wood floor and get away from Nathan. If that made her a coward, she didn't care. When Iker plucked a new champagne glass for her from one of the passing servers, she didn't protest.

"I'd like you to meet an associate of mine," Iker murmured, slipping his arm around her waist in the same way he'd done around Naomi, only this time his grip was tighter, less casual. Definitely a male-territorial thing, if she had to guess.

When she turned in his arm, looking up to meet his associate, she shouldn't have been surprised to see Nathan. But the shock of seeing him up close was a punch to her senses. Blood rushed to her face, and she inwardly cursed her reaction.

"Amelia, this is Miguel Ortiz."

*Miguel?* Nathan's eyes were the same dark espresso she remembered. She didn't know what to make of the name Miguel, but didn't comment on that. If he was using another name, she figured he didn't want to admit they knew each other. So she didn't acknowledge that she knew him and instead smiled politely as she held out a hand.

He took it, shook her hand almost stiffly, formally. It was weird touching him again after so long. Just feeling his skin against her brought up far too many memories. Ones that should stay buried. The man had always been so talented with his fingers and mouth. So, *so* talented. Something she shouldn't be thinking about.

"A pleasure to meet you." His words were raspy, but it was clear he didn't plan to acknowledge her either. Okay, so he was definitely using an alias.

She'd be lying if she said she wasn't curious why. No matter what, she certainly wasn't going to call him out in front of anyone else. She swallowed hard, forcing her throat to work. "You too." Two words—she was a freaking rock star. She swallowed again, this time subtly. "Are you in antiquities too?" she asked, looking between the two men, thankful that she seemed to have herself under control.

Nathan looked at Iker, something dark in his gaze. "Something like that."

She wasn't sure what passed between them, but Iker seemed annoyed. He was still all charm, but something had shifted.

"Would it offend you if I asked your date for a dance?" Nathan asked, his gaze perfectly placid and polite. But there was something in his eyes she couldn't get a handle on.

"I don't speak for Amelia." Iker's voice was butter smooth.

Now Nathan turned that laserlike focus on her again. "Will you dance with me?"

A soft Cuban beat filled the air as the lights dimmed a fraction. "Ah . . ." She glanced at Iker. She didn't want to be rude, and they'd both already danced with other people earlier in the evening. Still, it felt as if it might be impolite to say yes, but she really wanted to talk to Nathan—or Miguel—and ask why he was using another name and why he was in Miami. For a brief moment she wondered if he was in some sort of criminal business, but almost immediately she discarded that idea. The Nathan she'd known had seen the world in black and white. He'd been so damn honorable about everything. Since she wasn't going to find out by guessing, she let her curiosity win. "Do you mind?"

Iker's expression was soft as he shook his head. "No, but save the next one for me." Surprising her, he kissed her forehead in a sweet gesture.

Before she could react or think, Nathan took her hand and she found herself in his arms. She was glad she'd worn heels, so she was better matched for him, heightwise. He was right at six feet tall, the same as Iker. But Nathan's presence was somehow bigger, more intense. Of course that was probably just to her, not the entire room.

As one of his big hands landed on her hip, more of those stupid memories pushed up, including the one of her at his school's prom. It had been so damn cliché, but they'd lost their virginity to each other after the prom. It was a sweet memory, one she'd always cherished. Despite the surreal quality of the situation, she wanted to lean into him, to soak up all of him. It had been so long since she'd seen him, since she'd ended things with him in the worst way possible, and it was difficult to believe he was here.

"The beard's new," she murmured as they swayed with what could have been a practiced rhythm. It seemed that years of separation didn't affect that. Their movements might as well have been choreographed.

To her surprise, a hint of a smile played across those full lips. "How long have you been with Iker Mercado?"

"I don't answer your questions, *Miguel*, until you tell me why you're calling yourself—"

The grip on her hip tightened, a clear indication for silence, before he gently spun her in time with the steady beat. She was incredibly grateful for the simple three-step dance pattern. Unlike some of the complicated dances from earlier in the evening, this one she could do without thinking. Which was good because way too many questions invaded her mind. He was obviously being secretive for a reason and she wanted to know why. Her mind circled back to the criminal angle, but she couldn't make that work in her head. It didn't fit. Still, twelve years had passed. People changed.

They were silent as they danced, and though she figured she should probably wonder or care if Iker was watching them, she had eyes only for Nathan. But as she looked into his dark eyes it was a reminder of all she'd lost. Pain she thought she'd locked up bubbled to the surface, clawing at her insides. If she thought too hard or long about everything that had gone down between them, she'd slip into a funk and not be able to get out of it for a day or so. She couldn't do that now.

Still moving in time with the music, she looked at his chest instead of at his face. It made it easier to breathe.

"Are you going to say anything to him?" Nathan finally murmured.

She figured she understood what he meant. Would she tell Iker that his name was Nathan? She didn't even have to think about it. "No, but you *will* give me answers."

"Not here," he said simply. Since he hadn't said no, she understood he meant to tell her later. Which just piqued her curiosity even more. "You look beautiful," he continued, his grip possessive.

Slight irritation popped inside her at the way he held her. "Thank you. You look good too."

His lips quirked up almost playfully. "Just good?"

Seeing him almost smile did something strange to her insides. She should be pushing him for more answers, but found herself giving him a half smile. "Would 'handsome' make your ego feel better? Or maybe . . . 'pretty.'" She snickered at the dark look he gave her. When they'd been together he'd gotten grief from plenty of the boys in her neighborhood for being a "pretty boy." Until he'd kicked the ass of more than one of them.

"Are you and Mercado serious?" Nathan's gaze grew even darker, all traces of amusement fading.

She shouldn't tell him a damn thing. He wasn't even using his real name. Still, she couldn't seem to stop the truth from coming out. "It's our first date."

Though it was marginal, his grip on her relaxed. "Good." There was a wealth of meaning in that one word.

"When do you plan on answering my questions?" Because she had plenty.

"Meet up with me after the auction." He wasn't even bothering to ask her, just ordering.

It pissed her off. Despite her curiosity, she pursed her lips and met his gaze dead-on. "If I'd ever had a mother who cared about me, I'm sure she would have told me not to meet up with strangers. And you, *Miguel*, are a stranger." A stranger who'd seen every inch of her naked.

His jaw tightened in annoyance. "I'll answer your questions. I swear."

There was no real way she was just walking away after missing him and wondering about him for twelve damn years. She couldn't even pretend not to be rabidly curious. "Can you remember my phone number if I tell it to you?"

He nodded, so she quickly rattled off her number. It was slight but she felt him relax a fraction. As the song ended, she stepped away from him, surprised at the feeling of loss as his arms fell from her. She quickly turned, making her way back to her date.

Iker was talking to two men, but frowned over her head, likely at Nathan, as she made her way to him. She pasted on a smile for Iker when he met her gaze though, hoping it looked real.

Unfortunately, all her thoughts were on the man she'd left on the dance floor and the answers she'd soon be getting from him.

DEADLY OPS BY KATIE REUS: NO HOLDS BARRED.

Heart-stopping thrills.

Jaw-dropping action.

Addictive mystery.

Edge-of-your-seat suspense.

And a romance to blow you away.

Available from

headline
ETERNAL

# KATIE REUS'S MOON SHIFTER BOOKS...

Sexy alphas. Fierce heroines.

Wild and dangerous action.

This mesmerising series has got it all.

Available from

headline
ETERNAL